The Swirling Red Mist:

A Tale of Murder

The Swirling Red Mist:
A Tale of Murder

Geree McDermott

Published by

South Pacific Publishers

Pichilemu, Chile

ISBN: 978-956-398-184-1

Author: Geree McDermott

Assistant to Geree McDermott: Katterina Cuesta Lepe

Cover Designer: Fantasia Frog Designs

Cover Model: Nancy Gomez Vargas

Cover Photographer: Claudia Perez Gallardo

TABLE OF CONTENTS

CHAPTER 1

"OH, MY GOD, you're sitting next to the Unabomber, are you crazy?"

Bonnie glanced at the man at the end of the bench dressed in black sweat clothes, then looked up at Riki's second floor dorm window. "Ha, ha, you are so funny."

Riki gazed down at the bench where Bonnie and the man sat. "He even has the right sunglasses and hoodie." Riki switched her phone to her other ear. "But okay, so he's not the real Unabomber, but he could be the Unabomber's twin."

"Whatever. When are you coming down?" She lifted her hair off her neck. "Come on. It is so hot out here I'm melting. Let's go to the Student Union."

"Okay, I'll be down in a flash. Ciao." Riki waved and turned away.

She dropped her phone into her purse and twisted her long auburn hair into a bun on top of her head. She was about to turn off her radio when the KSSX disc jockey said, "To the students at San Diego State University on their last day of finals, chill! Do not let the heat get to you. Own your exams."

"I intend to do just that." She turned off the radio, rushed downstairs and out the front door.

She headed across the sidewalk to the bench where Bonnie studied a textbook while the man in black studied her. As she neared, she slowed because he continued to stare at her. Then he bolted off the bench, ran down the path, and disappeared around the corner.

Riki stared after him before she walked the rest of the way to Bonnie. "Oh, my God, it's sweltering out here."

"Thank God you finally came down." Bonnie closed her textbook. "I cannot believe it is so hot today, and it is my last and hardest final, too. I am sure to fail."

"So, who was the guy in black?"

"No clue, just some loser."

"He looks like the Unabomber, don't you think?"

"You mean, because of the hoodie and dark glasses? Yeah, he looks like the Unabomber, I guess." Bonnie stuffed her textbook into her backpack.

"Wasn't it strange how he ran away when I came over?"

"What do you mean?"

"It was like I scared him or something."

They started down the path toward the footbridge.

"Hmm, I hadn't noticed." Bonnie dragged her fingers through her long blond hair. "Well, maybe he was late for a final or something."

"Yeah, that was probably it, but he must be roasting in those hot clothes. Why would anyone wear sweats on a scorching day like this?"

"Don't know and don't care. He must be a freak, right?"

"Yeah, it was weird, that's all." Riki shrugged. "But, you're right, who cares?"

"Not I, I'm just glad I'm wearing shorts and a tank top, like you."

"Of course, what else would we wear today?"

"My thoughts exactly, and it is going to get even hotter, too." Bonnie exchanged her reading glasses for sunglasses. "My final is at 11:00, when's yours?"

"Mine's at the same time. I hope I don't flub the exam because of the heat."

"This is not a good day to take a final."

"Why don't we chill with chocolate shakes to stimulate our brain cells?"

"That works for me." Bonnie adjusted her backpack. "Are you ready for your test?"

"Yeah, I feel good about it. I mean, how hard can it be? It's in art history and should be a breeze if the heat doesn't fry my brain by then."

"Lucky you, mine's statistics and it is so hard I could fail without too much trouble, but I need this class to graduate." Bonnie bit her lip. "My parents would kill me if I don't graduate and I wouldn't be too happy about it, either."

Riki patted Bonnie's arm. "Relax, you always say you won't pass, and then you get the highest grade in the class."

"Yeah, right, I wish."

"Isn't it great these will be our last tests? After graduation, no more school, tests, teachers, or classes. We'll be free and on our own."

"It will be so fantabulous."

"I am so excited! We'll be college graduates and on Monday, we'll be business-women living and working in Solana Beach. How very cool is that?"

"It is the coolest ever!"

Their smiles faded because in the middle of the footbridge stood the Unabomber-look-alike, again.

Bonnie glanced at Riki. "Well, obviously he isn't late for anything."

They watched him turn and jog away, again.

Riki stared after him. "I don't know what it is, but there is something strange about that guy."

"You mean other than his clothes and that he runs away every time he sees you?"

"Yeah, it is almost as if he's waiting for me or something. But there is something else weird about him." She rubbed her chin. "What is it?"

"Are you sure he's a guy?"

"That might be it." Riki scratched her head. "I can't tell. What do you think?"

"It could go either way, but he runs like a girl."

They went into Aztec Student Union, got their shakes, and headed for their usual table where their friend Crystal sat looking at her phone.

Riki set her shake on the table. "Hi, Crystal, how's everything?"

"Hey, you guys! Sit for a while."

"Are you finished with your finals, Crystal?" Bonnie held the cold shake cup against her forehead.

"In my dreams, I have one in two hours and another at 4:00. What about you guys?"

"My last one is at 11:00."

"Mine, too. Oh, God, I am sure to fail it."

Riki rolled her eyes.

"But, how nice you have only one final left, I wish I had only one left."

"When's your graduation?" Bonnie sipped her shake.

"It's on Saturday at 1:00. When's yours?"

Bonnie groaned. "Mine's on Saturday too, but at 8:00 in the morning. And, of course, they want us there at 7:15."

"Ouch! Why did they make it so early?"

"I don't know, how asinine can they be? Don't they know we're all going to frat parties Friday night?"

"That is so inconsiderate of them." Crystal glanced at her phone. "Riki, when is your ceremony?"

"It's not until Sunday at 9 a.m. which is way too early for me because I am moving into my apartment this weekend. I'll be lucky if I make it to my own graduation."

"Oh, that's toxic." Crystal put her phone on the table. "I hope you make it. It's important."

"Well, I'm thinking that I may not bother with the ceremony. I mean, it's not like I have a family to watch me graduate or anything, so it doesn't matter if I walk or not."

"It matters." Bonnie took Riki's hand in hers. "I'll be there."

"No, you don't have to go. I know that you do not want to get up early twice in a row any more than I do. Really, no worries, I don't mind."

Bonnie still held Riki's hand. "I'm so sorry about your mom and dad."

"I know. Thanks." She stood. "Well, my final is across campus so I think I'll walk over there now."

"I'll chill here a little longer."

"Okay, good luck, I'll see you later."

"Hey wait, what are you doing after your final?"

"I'm taking some stuff up to the apartment. I have everything loaded in the jeep, so I can leave right after the test. Want to go with me?"

"No, thanks, I have things to do here first."

"I can wait for you."

"No, that's okay. I could be a long time. I'll meet you there."

"Okay, see ya."

"Good luck. Oh, and beware of the Unabomber's twin brother."

****

The intense heat dragged her down as she walked past Aztec Green and Manchester Hall. Although she looked for the man in black, she did not see him. At East Commons, she went in to use the restroom.

On the way out, almost to the exit, she stopped. He stood outside the door. Suddenly he turned and rushed to the ATM and pushed buttons.

Riki slipped out a different exit and tried to hurry, but the heat slowed her. Finally, she arrived at the Fine Arts Building and went through the door without a backward glance, but when the door closed, she peered through the window. He stood outside the building and stared at her.

She rushed to the classroom where students waited in the hall for the professor. She felt as if she would throw up and moved toward the restroom, but right then a weird guy from class pushed through the group and charged up to her breathless.

"Hi, Riki, I wasn't sure I would make it. I overslept and ran all the way from Maya Hall." He paused. "Hey, are you okay? You are all red and sweaty. You look stressed." He inched closer. "Are you worried about the test?"

"Um, no, I'm hot from walking across campus." She looked at the floor. He wore black sneakers like the man who had followed her.

She looked up. "Weren't you wearing sweats earlier this morning?"

"You can't be serious, no way."

"Oh, I thought I saw you jogging earlier."

"No, I just got out of bed ten minutes ago."

Riki inched backwards. "Oh, right."

"Well," he said, "I ran here from the dorm, but I wasn't jogging and I'm not wearing sweats, obviously."

"I get it. Excuse me. I need to talk to Sue and Della over there. Good luck on the test."

"Yeah, good luck to you, too. Maybe we can get together this summer sometime. Can I call you?"

Riki ignored him and joined the women. "That creepy guy over there is annoying me again, as usual."

Della put her phone in her purse. "I know, he is so toxic, isn't he?"

"Yeah, I don't trust him, last semester he kept begging for my phone number and when I wouldn't give it to him, my phone vanished. I think he stole it."

The three women stared at him. He noticed, blushed, fumbled his backpack, and dropped it. Books and papers spilled onto the floor and they turned their backs on him.

****

Riki whizzed through the exam and was the first to finish. As she gathered her things, she looked at the creep one last time. He concentrated so hard, his tongue poked out the corner of his mouth like a total dweeb. She suppressed a gag as she turned in her exam.

Now oblivious to the heat, she bounced across campus to the bookstore and went straight to the Blick Art counter. "Hi, Ross, how are you?"

"Hello, Riki, I'm good, how about you?"

"Fine, in fact, I'm great. I took my last final! I am graduating on Sunday! Isn't that fabulous?"

"Congratulations, Riki. I will miss you."

She leaned on the counter. "This may be the last time I see you."

"You have to come back and visit."

"Sorry, but once I'm out of here, this place is history."

"I hear you."

"I need to order art supplies, but I have a problem."

"How can I help?"

"I'm opening an art studio gallery in Solana Beach and I want to order large easels and canvases, but I don't have a way of getting them up there. My jeep isn't large enough to hold them."

"Not a problem. I can have Roger deliver everything to your new address tomorrow. And because you are such a talented and valued customer it will be free of charge."

"Wow, thanks. That would be super. In that case, I need four large easels and forty stretched canvases in premium pre-primed canvas."

"Okay, canvases in what size?"

"Let's see, twenty canvases 4' x 6' and twenty 5'x 8'." She chose a spectrum of acrylic paints. "And, I need ten large tubes of each of these and four white palettes."

"What about brushes?"

"Yes, I need new brushes." She chose thirty in a variety of bristles and sizes and added spray bottles, combs, and palette knives. "This should suffice for now."

"I can tell you are about to unleash great creativity."

"I hope you're right, I can't wait to get started."

"Need anything else?"

"No, I think that's it."

"All I need now is your address."

"The address is 501 South Cedros Avenue in Solana Beach. I'll be there from around 10:00 until 6:30."

"Okay, I will try to get the truck up to you sometime around one or two, if that's okay."

"That's more than okay, it's perfect. Thanks, again."

CHAPTER 2

RIKI PARKED IN the alley behind her building, went in, and opened the windows on the ground floor. Fresh ocean air soon replaced the stuffiness. She danced around the rooms before she ran upstairs.

In the apartment, she opened the east window and looked down on busy South Cedros Avenue. Next, she moved into the kitchen, opened the west window, and looked across the deep trench concealing train tracks that led to the depot a couple of blocks north. On the other side of the trench, stretched Old Pacific Coast Highway 101 where beach themed stores beckoned her. And, a block further west, although she couldn't see it, was Fletcher's Cove and the beach.

She skipped downstairs, held the door open with a brick, and began to carry boxes upstairs. As she carried a box of linens, the blast of a loud air horn startled her and she dropped the box. She looked around, took a breath, picked up the box, and carried it upstairs followed by ten more trips for ten more boxes.

In the living room, she surveyed the array of boxes scattered about the floor and opened one containing pottery. She took out a colorful Mexican vase and turned it over in her hands. It reminded her of the day she bought it in Tijuana from a sidewalk vendor when she and friends from her Ethnic Art class had gone to explore the local art. Later that day, they had gone to a cantina where they ate enchiladas, drank margaritas, and danced to reggaeton. It was a fun excursion. She centered the vase on a shelf. Next, she removed the lopsided bowl she made in ceramics class and placed it next to the Mexican vase, but the vase made the bowl look even worse so she pushed the bowl into a corner. When she found the voodoo doll she made in Folk Art class with the name 'Doug' pinned to its chest, she had to laugh and stuffed it into the lopsided bowl. She continued to unpack and enjoy memories, some good, some wistful, and some laughable.

She hung her favorite paintings and placed an old couch draped with a vivid purple sheet in front of the large living room window. In the kitchen, her meager collection of dishes, glasses, and mugs filled one cupboard and funky blue and green towels added a splash of ocean color.

She straightened the clock on the wall and centered a bowl of apples on the little kitchen table, and walked from room to room making small adjustments. When the apartment felt like she lived there, she sighed. Everything was perfect, except for the empty kitchen cupboards. She grabbed her purse and started downstairs, but stopped half way when she saw the backdoor standing wide open.

"Oops," she said, "I meant to close it hours ago. Oh well, no harm done." She continued down the stairs, kicked the brick out of the way, locked the door, and drove to the supermarket.

Thirty minutes later, she parked outside her backdoor again and stared. The backdoor stood ajar held open with the same brick she had used. She was afraid to go inside or even get out of the jeep. Instead, she called 911.

"What is your emergency?" the dispatcher said.

"I came home and found my backdoor wide open and I am positive I locked it when I left. I am afraid someone could still be inside. I don't want to go in alone. Is it possible for an officer go in with me?"

"Not a problem. I will send a patrol to help you. Please give me your name and address."

"My name is Erika Hollis and I'm behind my building on South Cedros Avenue in Solana Beach. The address is 501. I'm sitting in a green jeep."

"I have a patrol unit close to your location. The deputies should be there within fifteen minutes."

"Okay, thanks. I'll be waiting." She locked the doors and idled the engine. She tapped her fingernails on the steering wheel, adjusted the rearview mirror, and palmed the gear shifter. She fluffed her hair into a wild tangle. The minutes dragged.

Finally, a Sheriff's vehicle pulled up beside her. The deputy said, "Are you the party who called dispatch about a possible break in?"

She nodded and lowered her window. "Ah, yes. I called 911." She turned off the engine and met two deputies at the gaping door.

"I'm Deputy Traxler." He was older with sparse hair and a flabby stomach.

"And, I'm Deputy Norman." He was younger with better hair and a flat stomach. "I'm Erika Hollis."

Deputy Norman said, "Why do you believe someone broke in?"

"I locked the door before I left to buy groceries, but when I came back, it was wide open like this."

"Are you the owner of this building?" Deputy Traxler asked.

"No, I am renting and I am in the process of moving in."

Deputy Traxler peered into the dim interior. "Tell us what happened."

"I had to carry a lot of boxes upstairs, so I left the door propped open. Well, I am embarrassed to admit it, but I forgot to close it. I didn't realize it was still open until I finished unpacking and was leaving to buy groceries."

"How much time had elapsed?"

"Oh, around four hours, I guess."

Deputy Norman said, "Does anyone else have a key to your place?"

"As far as I know, only Kathy the landlord and I have keys. Kathy assured me she changed the locks when the last tenant moved out, so no one else should have a key."

He examined the lock. "I see no signs of forced entry, so it is unlikely someone broke in after you left. I think he came inside when the door was open."

She unclasped her hands and crossed her arms. "He was inside with me."

"You're fortunate. It might have been much worse."

Riki shuddered. "I know."

"I'll go in. You wait here with Deputy Traxler."

"Okay."

He looked around the alley. "Are you opening a new business here?"

"Yes, I'm opening an art gallery. I'm an artist and plan to work and live here."

"Do you have any idea who may have wanted to break into your place?"

"No, I don't, but today on campus, a strange guy dressed like the Unabomber followed me from my dorm to the building where I took my final exam."

"Where are you a student?"

"San Diego State, I graduate on Sunday."

"Congratulations."

"Thanks."

Deputy Norman came to the door. "It is all clear. It doesn't appear vandalized, but you need to check to see if there is anything missing, okay?"

"Yes, of course."

She toured downstairs and everything looked the same, but not in the apartment. She stopped in front of the shelves. "He moved things around, but he didn't take anything. That's weird." The bathroom looked as she left it, but something was wrong in the bedroom. "Oh, my God, look what he did! That is so gross." She pointed at the imprint of a body on her bed. "Why would he do that?"

"He may have a sexual fixation and fantasized about you while he was on your bed."

"How sick is that?" Riki held her hand over her mouth. Deputy Norman took her by the arm and led her into the living room. She sank onto the couch. "Do you think he may have, um, masturbated on my bed?"

"That would be my guess."

"Am I in danger?"

"It's hard to tell, but you need to be very careful. We'll take the bedspread to check for semen stains and we'll dust for fingerprints on the door. Has anyone other than yourself been in here?"

"No, I'm the only one."

"Is there someone you can call to stay with you?"

"My friend is moving in two shops down and said she'd be there later. She could be there now."

"Let's see if she's there. I don't think you should be alone."

The deputies escorted her the short distance to the bookstore and Deputy Traxler pounded on the door. Bonnie opened it a minute later.

"Oh, my God, what's happened now?"

"I'll tell you about it later." Riki turned to the deputies and took their hands. "Thank you so much for your help. I'll be okay."

"You're welcome, Ms. Hollis. We'll keep an eye on your place, and if you need anything, call us."

"Sure thing, Deputy Norman, and thanks again."

Bonnie pulled her inside and closed the door. "What the hell is going on?"

"My stalker was in my building, with me."

"What? You're not kidding, are you? Tell me what happened."

"Okay, but I need to sit."

Bonnie put her arm around her. "Let's go to the reading corner." They made their way through the bookstore to a cozy corner where they sat on overstuffed chairs. "So," Bonnie said, "did you see the stalker? What did he do?"

"Nothing, I mean, I didn't actually see him, but I know he was there."

"Oh, my God, what happened?"

"I was so stupid." Riki put her head in her hands. "I forgot to close the backdoor when I carried in the last box. I just started unpacking boxes and hours later, when I left to go to the store I found I had forgotten to close the door. He snuck in while I was upstairs and was in the building at the same time I was."

"Oh, Riki, how could you forget to close the door?"

She rubbed her forehead. "I just forgot. That's all."

"But, you are the most cautious woman I know."

"Yeah, I can't believe it myself."

"So," Bonnie said, "how do you know he was downstairs when you were upstairs?"

"When I was at the store he took off, but he did something weird. He left the backdoor propped open with a brick. When I got back and saw someone had been in the building, I called 911. I didn't know if he was still inside or not." Riki paused, took a deep breath, and let it out. "Am I in a horror movie, or what?"

"I know what you mean, this is terrifying."

"Fortunately, I didn't close the windows downstairs when I left. Otherwise, I might have found him."

"Or, he may have found you." Bonnie stared at her. "He could have raped you, or worse."

"Yeah, I thought of that." She wrapped her arms around herself.

"Why do you think he made it so obvious?"

"Who knows? Maybe he wanted me to know he had been inside with me, and then he left. How strange is that?"

"Yeah, it is his way of intimidating you."

"Well it weirded me out big time, so if that was his motive it worked."

"What happened when the cops showed up?"

"They made sure no one was hiding in the building. He didn't burglarize the place, but he touched my things as if he was just looking around, but the creepiest thing he did was lie on my bed."

"Wicked, how do you know?"

"We saw the imprint of his body on the bedspread." She covered her eyes.

"That is super creepy."

"What is even creepier is the deputies took the bedspread to check for semen stains."

"Yuck." Bonnie tucked her hair behind her ears. "Do you have any idea who it could be?"

"No, I don't have a clue."

"Any terrible break ups?"

"I can't remember any old boyfriends who were interested enough in me to do this."

"Oh, yeah, you're right."

"Hey, be nice."

"I am being nice. I'm agreeing with you, aren't I?"

"Well, yeah."

"But, it is true, there isn't anyone in your past who could be so obsessed with you to stalk you and break into your home."

"So, who can it be?"

"Well, it could be a casual acquaintance, or a guy in one of your classes. Someone you met at a party?"

Riki rubbed her chin. "The only one who stands out is a creepy guy in my Art History class, but it couldn't be him because he was still taking the exam when I left and couldn't have followed me."

"Well, maybe it's like in that old song and you're this guy's imaginary girlfriend."

Riki stared at her. "You cannot be serious."

"Yeah, you're right. I don't think guys have imaginary girlfriends, do they?"

"Well, at least not normal guys. But this man is not normal. He's menacing and a total freak. I bet he has never had a real girlfriend."

"So, maybe you are his imaginary girlfriend."

"The deputy said he might have a sexual fixation on me because he laid on my bed and may have, well, played with himself while he fantasized about me."

"Gross, that is so toxic. Are you spending the night here?"

"No, I'd rather sleep in my dorm room tonight."

"I understand." Bonnie checked her phone. "I'd go with you, but I have so much work left to do in the shop, I'm staying here tonight."

"That's okay, but I think I'll leave to go back to the dorm now."

"I'll walk you to your jeep. Are all the windows closed?"

"Yeah, the deputies took care of that."

"Let's check your door before you leave, okay?"

"Yeah, that's a good idea." They walked down the alley to Riki's and pulled on the door handle. "It's locked."

"Good. Let's take a look at your jeep, too."

"But, he was in the building. He didn't touch the jeep."

"The stalker may have come back and left something on it or in it. My sister's friend had a man leave weird notes and gifts on the windshield of her car at night and the next morning, she'd find them. Then, he started leaving things on the driver's seat which meant he had a key to her car."

"Oh, my God, what did she do?"

"She kept the notes and gifts and recorded everything he did in a journal. When she found things inside her car, she freaked and called the cops."

"Did they catch the guy?"

"Oh yeah, he's locked up now."

"How did they find out who he was?"

"She set up a surveillance camera on her car. A couple days later, she found a stuffed animal on the driver's seat and gave the video to the police. It showed a guy from her office opening her car with his own key and put something inside."

"So, she knew the guy who was stalking her?"

"Yeah, victims often know their stalkers."

"How well did she know him?"

"They worked at the same place, but the odd thing was she couldn't remember ever talking to him because he was a computer geek and shy. He told the cops he was in love with her and was just trying to get her attention. He thought she'd fall in love with him."

"But, that makes no sense. How could he get her attention when she didn't know who he was?"

"Yeah, he was insane, right?" Bonnie looked around the alley.

"Yeah, he was insane and creepy."

They checked inside the jeep and Riki got in.

"When you get back to the Cuicacalli Suites tonight, park as close as you can to the bright lights." She paused a beat. "Drive around the parking lot to make sure he's not there before you park."

"Good idea, I'll do that."

"And, if he leaves anything for you don't throw it away. Save it for evidence."

"Okay."

"Make sure you call me when you get here in the morning so we can go in together."

"But, are you safe here alone?"

"Raymond is coming over later, besides my baseball bat is with me and it has always served me well."

"Great. Bring it tomorrow. See you then, bye."

****

The desk clerk waved her over. "Hey, Riki, you have a delivery here."

At the desk was a bag from See's Candy with her name on it. She placed her groceries on the floor and opened the bag. It held a box of candy and a small envelope with RIKI HOLLIS written on the outside. She pulled out a card that said, 'YOU THINK YOU ARE SO SMART. YOU HAD TO CHEAT TO FINISH FIRST. YOU ARE SO BUSTED.'

"Oh no, I cannot believe this is happening. Who the hell is doing this?" Her hands shook and the note fell onto the desk. "I have to sit."

The desk clerk said, "Hey, are you okay?"

"No, I'm not. Someone is stalking me."

He reached for the phone. "Do you want me to call campus police?" Riki nodded.

A woman from the third floor who always wore several bracelets took Riki's arm. "Let me help you to a chair."

"Thanks."

"I'll wait with you." She pulled up a chair. "What's going on? Are you okay?"

"Someone is stalking me."

"You mean a stalker sent the box of candy?"

"Yeah, and there was a note, too."

"What did the note say?"

Riki lifted her head to tell her when a campus police officer arrived. "Are you the woman I got a call about?"

"Yes, I'm Erika Hollis."

"What seems to be the problem, Erika Hollis?" The officer, who was muscular with curly brown hair, neglected to give his name, but his badge said he was Officer Fowler.

Riki took a deep breath. "I'm being stalked."

"What makes you think that?"

She told him about the man who had followed her around campus and then broke into her apartment. "I didn't want to sleep there, so I came back here only to find he left a box of candy with a note at the desk."

"Where are the candy and the note now?"

"Still at the desk, I guess. After I read the note, I sort of freaked and came over here."

"I understand," he said. "Wait here while I get them for evidence."

The woman with the bracelets said, "You've had such a horrific ordeal today. You can sleep in my room tonight, if you'd like. My roommate is out with her boy-friend, so you can sleep in her bed. It's not a problem."

"Thanks, but I want to be alone. I appreciate the offer, though."

Officer Fowler rejoined them. "They think the candy came around 2:00 and your break in happened around 5:30?"

"Right, he must have dropped off the candy before he drove to Solana Beach."

"How did he know where you live?"

"That's a good question." She scratched her head. "Maybe he followed me into the bookstore and heard me give my address to Ross for a delivery tomorrow. That's the only time I gave out my address."

"You didn't notice him in the store?"

"No, I didn't see him at all after my test. I assumed he left." She put her head in her hands. "I thought it was over."

"This may be just the beginning."

She looked up. "What do you mean?"

"Well, in cases like this, the stalking often gets worse, not better. Sometimes, the stalker gets more aggressive and the incidents escalate and become dangerous. You must be very careful."

"Oh, shit, this is all I need."

He put his notebook away. "If you have any other incidents, please contact me." He gave her his business card. "Even if something happens in Solana Beach, please call me."

"Sure."

"Thanks and good luck".

"Thank you, Officer. Good night."

The woman with the bracelets helped Riki carry her groceries to her room. "Sleep well."

"Thanks." She hugged the woman. "Good night."

Riki closed the door and sagged onto the bed, drained. She stretched out on her back and blinked as tears filled her eyes. She rolled over onto her side and reached for a framed photograph she kept next to her bed. It was of her parents taken the last time they visited her. It was the last time she saw them alive.

Her heart broke as she recalled the fun they had together touring San Diego, but the happiness dissolved the night they left for home. In the middle of the night, she received the dreadful phone call. A strange man's voice said, "Hello, I am Officer Grady of the California Highway Patrol. I am sorry I have bad news for you. Vincent and Jackie Hollis died in a terrible accident on I-5 tonight. It was a five-car pile-up just outside Frenso. Heavy dense fog was to blame. They died at the scene. I am sorry for your loss."

Riki hugged the picture. "I need you so much right now." Her grief was painful, but her fear was crushing. "A crazy man is after me. Why is he doing this? What does he want from me? How do I make him leave me alone? Is he going to kill me? I am so afraid."

CHAPTER 3

RIKI DRAGGED HERSELF out of bed, braided her hair over her right shoulder, and pulled a vibrant pink tee shirt over purple shorts.

Downstairs in the lobby's restaurant, The Dining Room, she sat alone and stared into space as she sipped orange juice and nibbled toast. She was surprised when Dan the drop-dead gorgeous marine biology major from the third floor set his plate of bacon and glazed doughnuts on her table and slid into a seat across from her.

"Hey, how are you?"

"I'm hanging in there."

"I heard about what happened last night."

"Already, who told you?"

He shook his surfer blonde hair out of his bright blue eyes, popped a slice of bacon into his mouth followed by a glazed doughnut and swallowed. "Linda from the third floor said she was there when you got a box of candy with a note from a stalker."

"Oh, yeah, Linda with the bracelets, it was nice of her to stay with me. I was pretty shaken last night."

"Are you jammed by this whole stalker thing?"

"Yeah, this is so insane. And, I have no idea who it is." She looked around The Dining Room. "It could be anyone, anywhere."

"It must be a sicko, I mean, why else would someone do something like this?" He stopped eating and stared at her. "Stalkers can become dangerous."

"Yes, nothing all that bad has happened yet, but it creeps me out that somebody is spying on me and sending me nasty notes. He even snooped through my apartment and touched my things and laid on my bed."

"Are you going up to Solana Beach today?" He stuffed another slice of bacon into his mouth followed by another doughnut.

"Yeah, I'm leaving when I finish here."

He swallowed and leaned toward her. "I could to go with you, as protection."

"Cool, but I will be there all day. I may not leave until after 6:00. Is that okay with you?"

"Not a problem for me. In fact, I'm rock solid with it."

"You wouldn't mind playing my bodyguard?"

"No, I wouldn't mind at all." He lowered his voice to a sexy whisper. "Spending all day with you would be the coolfulness thing ever."

"It may not be all that coolful," Riki said, "but it would be great having you along. I am a bit nervous about being alone." She drank the rest of her orange juice. "Today a man is installing my business sign above the gallery, and I have an order from Blick Art coming sometime this afternoon. I hope you won't be bored."

Dan leaned closer. "I can hang paintings in the gallery, if you'd like."

"Hey, that is a terrific idea. You don't mind if we make a quick stop at the Studio Arts building to pick up some paintings, do you? I've stored eight semesters of paintings there."

"I'm ready whenever you are." He wrapped his last doughnut with his last slice of bacon and shoved the whole thing into his mouth.

"I'm ready." She slid out of her chair and grabbed her purse. "Let's split like a banana."

Dan swallowed. "Oh Riki, you are so corny."

****

Together they peered into the shadowy building.

"Dan, are you going in first to check it out?"

"That is why I came along, right?"

"That's right. You're my hero."

"Don't worry, Riki. I'll search it real good." He went inside while she got back into the jeep and idled the engine, just in case.

Minutes later, Dan appeared at the door and gave a thumb's up. "It's cool."

Riki exhaled. "Super." She turned off the key and opened the back.

Dan carried paintings into the gallery while Riki leaned them against the walls. He placed a large nonrepresentational next to her.

"Is this everything, Dan?"

"No, there is one more. I'll get it and lock up, okay?"

"That sounds good, thanks."

Dan brought in the last painting while Riki shuffled the order of the mix along the wall.

"Dan," she asked, "do you think I should group the abstracts, nonrepresentational, and the few realisms together or separately?"

"I'm not sure I know the difference."

"Oh, sorry, let me give you a quick art lesson." She picked up a painting of a desert valley. "This is 'realism' because it depicts a landscape in a somewhat realistic way."

"Okay, I see that."

"You do? Thanks. I don't do realism well and did this one only because it was a course requirement."

"Is that why there are so few realisms?"

She laughed. "You got that right."

"I like them."

Riki blushed. "You are too kind." She pointed to a painting of giant pink and purple butterflies chasing a herd of blue and green cats. "It's called, 'Attack of the Killer Butterflies.' It is an abstract."

Dan laughed.

"That's right, it is a joke. But, you know these are butterflies and cats even though in the real world butterflies and cats don't look like these." Next, she lifted a painting composed of blobs of yellow and orange surrounded by streaks of red and black. "And, this is nonrepresentational. Can you tell the difference?"

"Aren't they both abstracts?"

"No, not at all, although some people believe anything that's not realism is abstract, abstracts and nonrepresentational paintings are very different."

"They are? I thought they were both abstracts." Dan studied both paintings. "I guess I don't know what abstract means."

"Abstract paintings are always of something real, but painted in an unreal way. Have you ever seen a Rene Magritte, or a Pablo Picasso, or a Henri Rousseau?"

"I guess I've seen some Picasso's, but I've never heard of the other guys."

"No? They are some of my favorite abstract artists. Okay, what about Peter Max, you've heard of him, right?"

"Yeah, he's the guy from the 70's with all the bright colors and people flying around. He was friends with The Beatles, right?"

"Ah, yeah, that's him. His paintings are all abstracts."

Dan rubbed his chin. "Okay."

"You can abstract a chair, an animal, a house, a person. Anything and everything can be abstract, like the butterflies and the cats. They can even be surreal like Peter Max's paintings, but as long as there is something recognizable in the painting, it is an abstract." She picked up the yellow and orange painting. "This is nonrepresentational because it is just that; it represents nothing. Rather, it is a composition made of colors placed in a way pleasing to the eye and speaks to the soul."

"Whizz bang." He smiled at the paintings and then at her. "I can tell the difference now." He looked back at the paintings. "You prefer painting abstracts and nonrepresentational, don't you?"

"You are so astute. Yes, you're right, I'm happiest when I paint abstracts and I don't care if they look cartoonish." She strolled past her collection. "It is what wants to come out. Same with nonrepresentational, it is how my soul speaks."

"So, you find realism confining."

"Yes, I do. Realism takes a lot more time to paint, and I find the details tedious and boring. I enjoy liberation from the constraints of realism to paint whatever I want in any way I want. I guess you could say I like instant gratification."

"I'd say you are a free spirit."

"I'm a free spirit?" She tilted her head. "I suppose I am."

"Well, in answer to your question about how to group them, why don't you mix the three genres together so each artwork stands out in comparison to the others?"

"Good point, let's do that."

"You know, you have more wall space than you have paintings."

"You are so right." Riki walked to the opposite blank wall. "I ordered forty large stretched canvases that Roger will deliver today. Before I open next month, I hope to have a body of work of at least that many paintings. That should fill the walls, don't you think?"

"Yes, I can imagine it already." He fingered a pack of cigarettes in his shirt pocket. "Would you mind if I go outside for a quick smoke?"

"No, take your time and check out my competition. I think everyone on the block sells some kind of art. Well, not Bonnie, she sells only books."

"Wait, Bonnie has a store here, too? What did you guys do, take over the Cedros Avenue Design District?"

"No, it was just luck." Riki gathered her hair in a bun on top of her head. "What happened was there was an ad in The Reader for this place, so I called about it and came up to see it. Bonnie came along for the ride and Kathy the owner showed her the used bookstore two doors down. She took it on the spot."

"No," Dan said, "flaky Bonnie owns a bookstore?"

"She is graduating with a degree in business, you know."

"Is that right? Wow, I didn't know. Sorry, but it seems out of character, that's all."

"I understand what you mean, but I guess the bookstore was an opportunity too good to pass up. The man who used to own it had to go into a nursing home and left all the books behind for whoever rented the shop next. He gave the business to the next tenant and the next tenant is Bonnie."

"Wow, what incredible luck! I'll walk over there and say 'hello.'"

"Great. I forgot to call her this morning. Tell her you're my protector today, okay?"

"Sure, I'll be glad to." Outside, Dan stood on the sidewalk, lit a cigarette, looked around, and leaned against the wall. He noticed a strange woman across the street at The Beach Grass Café staring at him through dark glasses. He stared back until his cigarette burned down to his fingers and he lost interest.

He sauntered down to the bookstore and knocked. "Bonnie, it's me, Dan from school."

Bonnie surfaced from behind a huge stack of old books. "Hi!" She opened the door. "Come in. What are you doing here? Going surfing?"

"No, I'm Riki's bodyguard today."

"You're her bodyguard? Why, what's happened now?"

"Nothing so far today, but last night someone left a box of candy for her at the front desk and it had a note from the stalker. I'm not sure what it said, but Riki freaked out. The guy at the front desk even called the campus police."

"That's toxic." She raked her fingers through her hair. "The stalker is a busy man, isn't he? He follows her around campus, breaks into her apartment, and sends her candy all in one day. I guess he wanted to make a big first impression."

"Yeah, and he may get more aggressive. That's why I came along today to protect her."

"How's she doing?"

"She's good. Want to come back with me?"

"Sure, let's go."

They stepped out of Bonnie's shop just as a truck pulled up and parked in front.

Riki saw them and waved. "Good timing you guys. I would like you to meet Howie Sutherland. He is about to install my fabulous new sign. Wait until you see it. You will love it."

Bonnie shook his hand. "It's great to meet you, Howie. I need to talk to you about a new sign for my bookstore."

"My pleasure, I'll meet with you after I install Ms. Hollis' sign, okay?"

"Perfect, I am two doors down. The name of the place is The Old Bookshop, but I'm changing it to The Cubbyhole Bookstore."

"Okay, I shouldn't be more than a couple of hours."

"No problem. Bye for now, Howie." She turned to Riki and Dan. "I'll see you guys later, I have to get back to work."

"Okay," Riki said, "ciao."

From their vantage point on the sidewalk, Riki and Dan watched Howie remove the new sign from the truck.

"I like how it says The Erika Hollis Gallery in black letters on a white background. That sleek font looks great; it is elegant yet hip."

"I'm glad you like it, but wait until you see it with the light on. It is backlit in blue and will look super cool at night."

Soon the sign hung above the gallery and Howie joined them on the sidewalk.

"Well, what do you think?"

Riki said, "It looks fabulous. I love it, Howie."

"Yeah," Dan said, "it looks great."

"I'm glad you're happy with it." Howie adjusted his hat. "I'll pack up my tools and move the truck. Then I'll visit your friend at the bookshop."

"Okay, thanks."

The truck pulled away from the curb and Dan once again saw the same woman staring at them from across the street. "Do you recognize that woman sitting over there? She's been there for hours."

Riki looked across the street. "What woman?"

"At the sidewalk café, do you see the woman sitting at that table in the hat with the black hair and sunglasses?"

Riki didn't have a chance because the Blick Art truck pulled up and blocked her view.

Through the passenger window, Roger said, "Hi, Riki. Want me to pull around the back?"

"Yes, we'll meet you there."

"Okay."

"Yay, my art supplies are here." They hurried through the gallery to the back-door. "This is great, Dan, everything is going so well today."

Roger drove up and parked behind her jeep, jumped out and opened the back of the truck.

Dan said, "Can I help you, Roger?"

"Thanks, I was hoping you'd offer." He handed Dan an easel and lifted out another.

"Please take everything into the studio." They didn't move, but just looked at her. "That's the room on the left as you go in." They nodded and together they carried in the easels and the rest of her art supplies.

"Riki, I am impressed, this is a perfect location for your art gallery."

"Thanks, Roger. Promise you'll come to my grand opening."

"I'd be honored. When is it?"

"I haven't set a date yet, but I am hoping it will be in about a month."

"You have my email, just let me know when, and I'll be here."

"Thanks. See you then, okay?"

"Depend on it. Adios."

Riki and Dan waved as Roger drove away.

"Dan, I will be busy for hours going through the art materials. Are you hungry? We should have lunch before I get started."

"I would kill for a Western Bacon Cheeseburger right about now."

"Me, too, I love Western Bacon Cheeseburgers!"

"Is there a Carl's Jr. around here?

"But, of course. I couldn't move somewhere without a Carl's Jr. nearby."

"Sweet, this is my kind of place." Dan headed for the jeep. "Let's go."

"Wait. Let me call Bonnie to see if she wants to come."

"Sure, no problem, I am only starving."

Riki speed dialed Bonnie who answered on the second ring. "Hey, we're going to Carl's Jr., want to come along?"

"No, thanks, Raymond is coming by later and he's taking me out to dinner. Cool guy, huh?"

"Very, he sounds like a keeper."

"He's working on it. See you tomorrow either here or at school."

"Okay, later Gator." She clicked off. "We can go now, Dan. She's going out with Raymond."

They jumped into the jeep, turned right on Lomas Santa Fe, and breezed through two green lights, but the last traffic light caught them.

"Do you see anyone following us, Riki?"

She looked in the rearview mirror. "I can't tell. There are several cars behind us." When the light changed, she pulled into the parking lot and parked next to the restaurant's entrance. As they walked to the door, a few cars drove past the driveway; none pulled into the lot.

Inside they inhaled the familiar scents of enticing fast food and ordered their favorite burgers with fries and sodas. While they waited for their orders, the woman from the sidewalk café came in and stood behind them.

When they had their trays, they took their lunch into the dining room and concentrated on eating while the strange woman slipped into the booth behind Riki.

"Oh man, this is so good."

Riki nodded. "Yeah, this hits the spot."

He gulped his soda. "I have to tell you something, Riki. I admire you for opening your own business straight out of college."

"Thanks. That's very nice of you." She ate a fry. "I couldn't see any other way to start a career as an artist. I think this is the best route for me."

"Not everyone is confident and determined to risk going out on their own. You are a special person."

"Stop, you're making me blush."

They went back to munching in quiet bliss. Soon all that remained was a pile of paper and refilled drinks.

"Tell me, Riki, what are your plans for your grand opening?" Dan noticed the woman with black hair sitting behind Riki. She even turned her head to better eavesdrop.

"Plans, what plans? I don't have no stinking plans."

Dan focused his attention on the woman. "Seriously, you are going to have a grand opening, aren't you?"

"I'd like to, but I am not much of a party planner so I don't even know where to begin."

"My mom's the same way. Whenever she has to entertain for my dad's business, she always hires an event planner." The woman behind Riki nodded.

"An event planner, now that is an excellent solution because it is important I have a successful grand opening, but where do I find an event planner? Oh well, even if I could find one, I couldn't afford one, I'm sure their fees are beyond my budget."

The woman nodded her head again. Dan pointed to the booth behind them. "One thing I hate is when people I don't know listen to my private conversations."

"Yeah, me too, that is so rude."

The woman got up and rushed out the door.

"Well, that got rid of her. I knew she was eavesdropping, I could tell by the way she moved her head. Well, that and how she took off in a flash when I busted her."

"What?" Riki turned around, but the woman was gone. "Why would she eavesdrop on us? Who is she? Do you recognize her from school?"

"I have no clue who she is, but I saw her sitting at a table at the sidewalk café across the street from your gallery." He leaned forward. "And now, here she was sitting right behind you listening to our conversation."

"But, why would she care what we talk about? She doesn't even know us."

"What if she's your stalker?"

"Why would she be stalking me?"

"No clue. Besides most stalkers are men, aren't they?"

"Yeah, it seems like stalking is more of a guy thing to do." Riki shrugged. "So are you bored yet? Do you want to go home now?"

"No, I'm good."

"You don't mind going back to hang paintings?"

"No worries, I have all day."

* * * * * * * * *

"Hey, Dan, what time do you have?"

"It's 6:15. Why?"

"I think it's time to call it quits, don't you?"

"That's cool."

"Great, I'm ready. Let's go."

Riki locked the backdoor and turned around. Dan stared at the jeep's windshield. "What now?"

"Look." He pointed to a piece of paper under the windshield wiper.

"Super," Riki didn't move. "Another note from the stalker, that's great."

"Well, aren't you going to read it?"

"You do it."

"Okay." He snatched the note out from under the windshield wiper and ran his fingers through his hair as he read. "Oh, man."

"What does it say?"

"It says, 'I LIKE YOUR APARTMENT BUT NOT YOUR BOYFRIEND. YOUR BED IS MORE COMFORTABLE WITHOUT HIM. DID I SCARE YOU WHEN I LEFT THE DOOR OPEN? YOU SHOULD BE MORE CAREFUL. I HOPE YOU LIKED THE CANDY.'"

"Oh, my God, the stalker was here."

"Yeah, your stalker was definitely here. Think we should call the cops?"

"No." She took the note from Dan. "But, I'll keep the note just in case something else happens."

Dan hugged her. "I'm sorry, Riki, I thought the stalker would leave you alone if I were with you."

CHAPTER 4

"RIKI, ARE YOU there? Open the door, okay?"

"Okay, okay, I'm coming." Riki threw back the covers, stumbled to the door, and opened it. "What time is it?" She yawned.

"It's almost noon."

"What are you doing here? I thought you were in Solana Beach."

"Raymond and I came back this morning." She strode in and dropped her purse on Riki's desk. "His parents wanted to take him to breakfast before they leave for New York this afternoon. They won't be here for his ceremony tomorrow so he thinks they'll give him his graduation present today at breakfast."

"You woke me up to tell me that?" Riki dragged herself back to bed and gave Bonnie a dirty look.

"I wouldn't have, but I ran into Dan a few minutes ago and he told me about the note on your car yesterday. He said you kept it."

"Yeah, I did."

"Can I see it?"

"Sure, it's over there in my purse."

Bonnie rummaged through Riki's purse and found the note. "This is serious. What are you going to do?"

"I don't know. What can I do?"

"Well, I think at the moment all you can do is keep a record of everything that's happening."

"Yeah, but I need a new notebook to start a journal. All of mine are pretty much used up with class notes."

"Well, let's go to the bookstore for the notebook and then we can go to East Commons for lunch."

"Food is just the motivation I need to get out of bed. I'm hungry." Riki flipped off the covers and headed to the bathroom. "I'll be ready in a sec."

"No worries." Bonnie's phone rang. "Hi, Raymond, what's up?" She listened. "We'll be there in about a half hour, okay?" She listened some more. "Okay, see you then."

Riki came out of the bathroom and pulled a purple tee shirt on over black shorts. "These are pretty much my only clean clothes."

"What are you going to wear to the frat party tonight?"

"I guess I'll have to do some laundry this afternoon." She pointed to the corner. "That mountain of dirty clothes represents endless hours of boredom. And, I still need to pack up the rest of my stuff and clean the room, too."

"So do I, Monday is the move out day, right?"

"Yeah, that's why I hope to get it all done today. I'd like to finish moving to Solana Beach tomorrow after your graduation."

"What?" She looked up from her phone. "You're not coming to my mom and dad's after the ceremony? They're having relatives over and it will be so boring without you. Please come, please."

"I don't think so. It doesn't sound like much fun to me, besides I have to move."

"Think about it, please, pretty, please?"

"Sorry, I can't. I have too much to do."

"Oh, okay." They left the dorm and headed across campus to the bookstore. "Oh, I forgot to tell you, Raymond wants us to meet him at Vinnie's for pizza. He said he had something exciting to tell us."

"Like what?"

"I have no idea, but I got the impression he received a cool gift."

"Like a new car?"

"I don't think it is that cool, but it could be knowing his parents, they give interesting gifts. In any case, we'll find out soon. I told him we'd meet him there in about thirty minutes."

"Great. That gives us plenty of time to go to the bookstore first."

They ambled over the footbridge, past the Student Union, and along the tree lined lawn that fronted the Student Services building.

"You know, this may be the last time we will ever walk here."

"Yeah, it's hard to believe we're graduating this weekend and will never come back." Bonnie wiped away the tear that slithered down her cheek.

"Well, you can always come back for your MBA."

"Ha! Not a chance, are you serious? I've had enough school to last the rest of my life."

"I know what you mean. I doubt I'll ever come back either." Riki looked at the familiar buildings and gardens. "But you know, this has been my home for the past four years and it is where I grieved for my parents. I have some strong emotions tied to this campus. I'm going to miss it."

"Oh, come on, don't be so sentimental. Do you really think you'll miss it when you're in Solana Beach with your own gallery and studio in the heart of the artsy Cedros Avenue Design District? Get real."

"Well, maybe I won't miss it for long, but I will miss it. Won't you?"

"Yeah, right, for about a minute and a half."

They made it to the bookstore and Riki bought a notebook with pockets to hold the stalker's notes. "This gives me a strange feeling of power over the stalker because I am going to save all and tell all. Maybe it will be evidence someday, and as hard as it is to consider, if something should happen to me, it could be useful."

"Nothing will happen if you take control. You can't let him get inside your head. Be strong."

They went around the corner to Vinnie's and took seats at a table outside. Riki opened the notebook and took a pen out of her purse. "Okay, I guess I should start with the Unabomber's twin brother sitting next to you on the bench the other day? That was Wednesday, right?"

"Yeah, it was the last day of finals, remember?"

"That's right, it seemed like he was following me all over the place that day."

"That is because he was following you all over the place that day. Record everything that happened that day and since, even if it seems small and insignificant, because it could be important later."

"What do stalkers do when they get tired of leaving gifts and notes?"

"I guess the next step is to get close to you, talk to you, and maybe even touch you."

"Yuck! That is toxic. How do you think he'll do it, just come up and start talking to me and then try to touch me?"

"Well, he'll make up an excuse to talk to you. He may want you to go somewhere with him. Whatever you do, don't get in his car. You have to be careful not to trust anyone because it could be someone you already know or someone new."

"I get what you're saying."

Raymond and Dan slid into seats across from them.

"Hi, guys. Look who I ran into on my way here."

Dan said, "Hi, Riki, how's it going?"

"Hi, I'm doing better today."

Raymond beamed. "You guys will never believe what I got for graduation."

"Sounds intriguing, I can't wait."

"Tell us now." Bonnie grasped his hand.

"No, you have to wait until I order, okay?" He waved a server over. "We'll have a large Hawaiian pizza, a pitcher of beer and diet cokes for the ladies, please."

"It'll be about fifteen minutes for the pizza." The server put the pad in his pocket and stepped back. "I'll get the drinks right away."

Dan took three sheets of paper out of his backpack. "My parents gave me the best graduation present ever, and it includes you guys." He handed a piece of paper to each of them.

Dan squinted. "I don't have my glasses with me, Dude. What is this?"

"Ladies and Gentlemen, you are holding your very own ticket to The Rolling Stones concert next week!"

Riki stared at her sheet of paper. "No, I cannot believe it, are you serious?

"Yes. That's your ticket."

"Oh, my God, thank you, Raymond. Everyone is talking about the concert. Everyone wants to go, but not everyone has tickets. Now, we do."

Dan shook his head. "Wow, I am amazed your parents gave you four tickets to The Rolling Stones concert."

Bonnie kissed him. "This is totally fantabulous."

Riki's ticket read, The Rolling Stones Zip Code. Section UI306, Row 17, Seat 13. Location Upper Infield Reserved 306. On May 24th at 7 p. m., nothing would keep her from sitting in that seat at PetCo Stadium, not even the Unabomber's twin brother.

"A reporter once asked Mick Jagger, if he wasn't Mick Jagger who would he be?"

Dan cleared his throat. "And, he said, 'I'd be someone else.'"

"That's amazing." Riki sipped her soda. "You must be a big fan."

"Yeah, I grew up listening to The Rolling Stones all my life. My parents have all their CDs and still listen to them."

"They must have all their videos, as well." Riki sprinkled parmesan cheese on her pizza.

"Of course, they do. I've seen them all a gazillion times."

Bonnie pulled a piece of pineapple off her pizza and popped it into her mouth. "You know, I didn't realize until I saw the video of their 2013 Hyde Park concert that the 1969 concert at Hyde Park was just two days after Brian Jones died. When I first saw the video of the '69 concert years ago, I wondered why they seemed so glum. Now it makes sense."

"Yeah, Mick Jagger was crying before the concert, he felt really bad because they had just kicked Jones out of the band."

"Hey," Raymond asked, "is it true someone murdered Brian Jones?"

"In the movie Stoned the handyman drowned him in the swimming pool," Riki said. "Apparently, he confessed on his deathbed."

"So they didn't know that in 1969?"

"No, it didn't come out until sometime in the '90's. At the time, everyone assumed Brian Jones had overdosed on drugs and alcohol, passed out in the pool, and drowned."

Dan said, "Keith Richards said he was not surprised Brian drowned even though they did not find large amounts of drugs and alcohol in his system because he had a troubled past as a substance abuser. Passing out and drowning seemed to fit and they never investigated further."

Bonnie pulled her phone out of her backpack and scrolled the screen. "This is all very interesting, but I have stuff I have to do this afternoon, like move out of the dorm."

"Me, too, I have tons to do."

Dan asked, "Riki, would you like me to walk you to the frat party tonight?"

"No thanks." She gathered her purse and notebook. "I'll meet you there."

****

"So, why didn't you want Dan to take you to the party?"

"I like him a lot, but I don't want him to get too serious about me. Know what I mean?"

"No, I thought you liked him," Bonnie said.

"He's a nice guy, and I think he's hot, but I don't have time for a boyfriend. I have to give all my attention to being an artist and gallery owner if I want my business to succeed." She adjusted her purse on her shoulder. "Besides, I don't plan to stay at the party for more than an hour or two. I have to get up early tomorrow in time to make it to your graduation."

"I sort of understand, I guess."

Later that evening, Bonnie knocked on her door and walked in. "Are you ready? Want to go with Raymond and me?"

"No, I'm not ready yet. I'm going through all these textbooks and school papers. I can't decide what to keep and what to throw away. Are you saving all of yours?"

"It's hard to toss everything, so I'm keeping my research papers and the text books I can use for future reference."

"Good idea. That's what I'll do, too."

"Isn't it strange on Monday we won't be students anymore?"

"Yeah, this is our last weekend as students. Can you believe it? Monday we'll be college graduates. It will be the first day of the rest of our lives."

"Hey, I just realized that I have been a student since I was five years old. I've been a student for almost my entire life."

"Yeah, and I started preschool when I was three. I have been going to school longer than you have. But, now it's over." She jumped up and grabbed Bonnie's hands. "Happy dance, happy dance."

"School is over forever! WE'RE FREE! WE'RE FREE!" They held hands and danced around in circles. "NO MORE SCHOOL FOREVER!" They danced around the room until they were out of breath and sank onto Riki's bed.

Bonnie caught her breath and stood. "Well, I guess I'll meet you at the party."

"Okay. I'll see you guys in about an hour or so."

"Okay, catch you later."

Riki put on earphones and cranked up The Rolling Stones on her MP3 player. She danced and sang, and sorted research papers, old notebooks, and textbooks. When she had made progress, she pulled off the earphones, changed into blue jeans and a green tee shirt, fluffed her hair, and left for the party.

Half way across the footbridge, she looked over her shoulder, but there was no one behind her. On the other side of the footbridge, she passed the deserted construction site on her way to the well-lit transit center, no one suspicious there. She left the safety of the bright lights and looked over her shoulder once more and although she saw no one, she heard faint footsteps.

She hurried along the dark stretch of lawn that led to Fraternity Row. The footsteps mirrored hers on the grass. She stopped and listened, but when she stopped, so did the footsteps.

She stifled a scream when she heard excited breathing coming from somewhere in the shadows. She turned, and retraced her route back to the bright lights and safety of the transit center and found it deserted. Footsteps came closer, louder, threatening her. Fear propelled her. The approaching footsteps quickened to match her own. She ran, but she tripped over her flip flops and fell. The menacing footsteps accelerated, coming closer. She kicked off her shoes, sprang to her feet, and broke into a frenzied run. She neared the Student Union and was almost to the footbridge when a man sprang out of the shadows and blocked her path. She came to an abrupt halt.

"Ah!"

"Riki, it's me, Officer Fowler. What's wrong?"

Her hand on her chest, she bent over panting. "Oh, Officer Fowler, thank God it's you."

"Riki, what's happened?"

"He's chasing me."

"He's chasing you right now?"

She nodded.

He took her to a bench. "Sit here." He turned on his flashlight and searched the darkness. "Where were you when you were aware of him stalking you?"

"I was on my way to Fraternity Row, and he followed me. I could hear him behind me, but I could never see him." She gasped. "When I was almost there, he got much closer. It sounded like he was walking opposite me on the grass, but it was so dark, I couldn't see him. That's when I freaked and turned around to go back to the dorm. I walked faster and faster, but so did he, so I ran."

"Was he close behind you?"

"Yes," she wheezed, "he almost caught me."

"Your feet are bloody. What happened to your shoes?"

She looked at her bare feet. "My shoes, where are my shoes? Oh, I lost them somewhere. I took a dive and had to run barefoot."

"Are you injured? Are you in pain?"

"No, not much, I'm just banged up a little."

"Sit tight while I call for help."

Riki nodded and wrapped her arms around herself. Numb, she didn't think, but kept her eyes on Officer Fowler.

He finished his call and stood in front of her. "They'll find him if he's still out there, but chances are he's long gone by now. Let me walk you back to your dorm. I want to make sure you make it there safe."

"Okay." She limped beside Officer Fowler into the dorm's lobby. "Thanks for walking me home. I'll be fine now."

"Has anything else happened since we last spoke?"

"Ah, yeah, I forgot to tell you, when I was in Solana Beach yesterday, I got a note on my jeep."

"What did it say?"

"It said something about being in my apartment and the candy and leaving the door open."

"Do you still have the note?"

"Yes, I have it in my room. Want me to get it for you?"

"Please, I'll add it to the other evidence. I'll wait for you here in the lobby."

"Okay, I'll be right back." Minutes later, she handed him the note.

He put it into a plastic evidence bag and examined it. "Where was your jeep parked?"

"I parked in the usual spot behind my building. My friend Dan and I were working inside and when we went out to the jeep we found the note under the windshield wiper."

"Obviously you didn't see anyone around your jeep."

"No, we saw no one behind the buildings at all."

"Do you think you will be all right now?"

"Yes, I'll be fine. Thanks for rescuing me."

"Glad I was there when you needed me."

Sleep that night eluded Riki, but sometime in the early morning, she drifted off to a dark place. Someone chased her. Fear engulfed her. She was in imminent danger. She raced against the unseen stalker. Suddenly, there were loud noises and something wet enveloped her face suffocating her. She bolted upright covered in sweat.

CHAPTER 5

RIKI STRETCHED, YAWNED, and looked at the time. "Oh, shit, it's 7:30." She threw back the covers, leapt out of bed, brushed her teeth, splashed water on her face, pulled on the clothes she wore the night before, flew downstairs, and joined the throngs of students heading for Viejas Stadium.

Bonnie's graduation ceremony was boring. Riki yawned, but stayed. When the last student received a diploma, she made her way to where a group milled around the new graduates. She found Bonnie and gave her a big hug.

"Congratulations, Girlfriend! You did it!"

"Thanks. Did you change your mind about coming to my parents? I'd love it if you did."

"Um, I don't think so. I'm still freaked about what happened last night."

"What do you mean? What happened?"

"On my way to the party, I was chased by the stalker."

"Oh, my God, so that's why you didn't make it? I was wondering why you didn't show. What happened?"

"I was almost to Fraternity Row, when I heard someone tailing me, so I turned around to go back and he chased me. I started to run, but I was wearing flip flops and I tripped and fell on my knee." She reached down and touched the rip in her jeans. "I had to run barefoot. Oh, my God, there is dried blood on my feet."

"Holy shit! That must have freaked you out big time."

"Yeah, I was very scared. He was so close behind me, I thought he was going to catch me, but just as I got to the footbridge, the campus police officer rescued me."

"That was lucky."

"Yeah, I practically ran into his arms."

"Wow, he saved your life?"

"Yeah, I'm not sure I could have made it all the way back to the dorm."

"That is horrific. I guess the officer didn't spot him?"

"No, no one ever sees him."

"Toxic. So, what are you going to do today?"

"I'd like to go back to bed, but I have to move out of the dorm so I'm taking the rest of my stuff up to Solana Beach. Tomorrow after my ceremony, I am leaving and never coming back."

Bonnie looked over Riki's shoulder. "There are my parents."

"Okay, have fun. Tell them 'hi' for me, till later, bye."

"Okay, bye."

Riki walked back to the dorm and intended to have breakfast at The Dining Room, but when she entered the lobby, the woman at the desk called to her. "Hey, Riki, we have a special delivery for you, it came about an hour ago."

Riki dropped onto a chair with the special delivery envelope. On the front printed in block letters it said, 'RIKI HOLLIS.' She slid her finger under the flap, ripped open the envelope, and pulled out a simple white card. It said, 'Congratulations, Graduate' and inside it said, 'Great things await you.' It had no signature, but printed in the same block letters, 'THE MORE I WATCH YOU THE BETTER I LIKE YOU. I KNOW YOU'RE A FAN. ENJOY THE CONCERT. P.S. DID I SCARE YOU LAST NIGHT? I JUST WANTED TO GO WITH YOU. IF THAT WAS WRONG OF ME, I AM SURE THE ENCLOSURE WILL MAKE IT RIGHT.'

Inside the envelope, she was amazed to find another ticket to The Rolling Stones concert on May 24th at PetCo Stadium.

The paper fluttered to the floor. Her shoulders drooped.

"Riki, are you okay?" It was Linda with the bracelets.

"No, it's the stalker again." She stared at the floor. "Now he is trying to trap me."

"Oh my God, what did he send you?" Linda picked up the papers and placed them next to Riki.

"He said he followed me to the frat party last night because he wanted to go, too. And, now he gives me a ticket to The Rolling Stones concert. I know he wants to get near me. And, at The Rolling Stones concert where it will be super crowded, he could easily overpower me and no one could do anything. What if he wants to kidnap and kill me?"

"Wicked, can I call someone for you?"

"Yes, please call campus police and ask for Officer Fowler."

Riki had just finished telling Linda everything the stalker had done when Officer Fowler arrived. He sat with her in the lobby and studied the card and the concert ticket through a plastic evidence bag.

"What if I use the ticket to see what happens? I could end up sitting next to this jerk. Let's see what he says then."

"Better you than I." Riki folded her shaking hands in her lap. "I don't want to be anywhere near him let alone talk to him."

He scrutinized the ticket. "It's interesting he blacked out his name and customer number."

"What do you mean?"

The officer held up the evidence bag. "You see the blacked out areas? He bought the ticket online with a credit card so his name and credit card info would be on the ticket. At least, until he blacked it out. This guy is serious about stalking."

"Oh, that's just great. He's a savvy stalker." She put her head in her hands. "Now, I'm petrified."

"Don't be. I will sit in your seat." He looked at the ticket in his hand. "And, I get to go to The Rolling Stones concert. I'm excited." He glanced at her. "Oh, sorry I'm taking your ticket."

"That's okay, it's not a problem." She looked up at the officer. "I'm already going with friends. I just don't want him to see me there."

"Where are you sitting?"

"My seat is in section UI306."

"This ticket is in section UI311, which is several sections away from yours. With the crowd of people there, no way he will ever see you."

"Can you promise that?"

"Yes, I promise I won't let him get near you."

"So, you'll be there undercover?"

"Yes, of course. That is, if my supervisor will let me go in your place." He gazed at the ticket. "She might want to go instead. She's a big Stones fan."

"Yes, isn't everybody?"

"I'll get back to you later with the details, okay?"

"Okay." She handed him one of her newly printed business cards. "Here's my cell number and email. I'm leaving here right after graduation tomorrow morning and I don't plan on ever coming back."

"I understand. I'll get in touch with the latest plan."

"Okay."

****

What was true for Bonnie's graduation was also true for Riki's, except it was even more boring.

Finally, it was over. Bonnie found her in the crowd, and gave her a tight hug.

"Now it is official, we are both college graduates."

"Yeah, we made it."

"And, tomorrow we'll be part of the business scene on South Cedros Avenue just like the big kids."

"We are totally awesome."

"Want to have brunch?"

"Thanks, but no thanks. I can't wait to live west of I-5."

"Oh, right, because there is 'no life east of I-5.' Okay, I'll meet you there later."

"Okay, bye."

****

She parked in her usual spot next to the backdoor and sat for a few minutes. Nothing happened. She turned off the engine, slowly opened the door, and got out. Her hand shook when she inserted the key, unlocked, and opened the backdoor. She turned on the lights, and went inside.

After a quick walk through all the rooms, she wandered into the studio and smelled the enticing scent of canvas and paint. She threw out her arms and twirled through the studio and gallery. She danced over to the staircase and scooted up the stairs.

She changed into an old tee shirt and shorts and spent what remained of her graduation day in the studio. Spray bottle in hand, she saturated the first canvas with water. A passionate release of kinetic energy surged through her as she applied red, orange, purple, and black paint in quick sweeps and bold slashes. On to the second canvas, she painted blue, green, and purple in swirls, splashes, and waves. Her phone rang, but she ignored it.

On the third canvas, she slapped on yellow, orange, and black in clumps and streaks with her fingers. The painting took on a sinister composition and needed nothing more. She moved it to a corner.

On the last canvas, she squeezed purple, blue, and pink straight from the tube onto the canvas and slashed the paint with a comb. She added orange and yellow. The colors lifted her mood as she expressed her deepest emotions in bold strokes through the paint. She worked until dawn. Entirely drained, she dragged herself up the stairs and crashed onto the bed, asleep within minutes.

CHAPTER 6

RIKI FUMBLED WITH her phone. "What is it?"

"I'm at your backdoor. Let me in."

"I'm still sleeping." Riki yawned. "I was up all night painting." Riki yawned again. "My eyes aren't quite open yet. What time is it?"

"It is a little after one in the afternoon."

"Oh, okay, I guess I might as well get up now."

"Great, I'll wait here."

Riki poured herself a glass of orange juice before she sauntered downstairs. She cracked open the backdoor and Bonnie burst in.

"I didn't want to tell you on the phone, but this was under your windshield wiper."

"What, another note?"

"Here, you have to read it." Bonnie pushed the note into her free hand.

Riki read, 'WHAT WAS YOUR BIG HURRY? YOU FORGOT TO PICK UP YOUR FLOWERS.' "What the hell does this mean? What flowers?"

"Don't know. Maybe he sent flowers to Cuicacalli Suites. Why don't you call the dorm and find out?"

"Do I want to know?" Riki finished her juice.

"Of course, you do."

"Okay, but I have to go upstairs to get my phone."

"Here, use mine. I have it on speed dial."

"Oh, okay." Riki took her phone and called the dorm.

"Cuicacalli Suites, Paula speaking."

"Hi, Paula, this is Riki Hollis. Do you have something for me?"

"Yes, I do. I have a dozen red roses waiting for you."

"Is there a card?"

"Yes, there is. Want me to read it to you?"

"Yes, would you please?"

"Okay, it says Congratulations. That's it, no signature."

"Okay, thanks Paula. Officer Fowler from Campus Police will be by to collect them."

"Officer Fowler? Why, is there a problem?"

"Yeah, someone is stalking me."

"Oh, that's wicked. Do you know who it is?"

"No clue. Did you see who delivered the flowers?"

"No, they were already here when I came to work today."

"Okay, thanks again." She hung up and ruffled her hair. "He sent a bouquet of red roses with a card that said only congratulations."

"No shit? What are you going to do?"

"I'm calling Officer Fowler." The call went to his voicemail. "This is Riki Hollis. I found out he left flowers for me at the dorm yesterday. I told the desk clerk you'd pick them up. Call me."

* * * * * * * * * *

"Riki, this is Jim Fowler."

"I beg your pardon, who?"

"Jim Fowler. Officer Jim Fowler."

"Oh, sorry, I didn't know your first name."

"You shouldn't call me Officer Fowler, at least while I am undercover."

"Oh, okay. I get it, Jim. Did you get the flowers from the dorm?"

"Yeah, the flowers and the card are in evidence. My supervisor approved the plan for The Rolling Stones concert, but there is one condition."

"Oh, what's that?"

"We have to meet with a detective from the Encinitas Sheriff's Station."

"Why? I thought you'd be handling it."

"So did I, but you moved out of the area so we have to let the San Diego County Sheriff's North Coastal Station take over. I hope I still get to go to the concert."

"So, the Encinitas Sheriff's Station is handling it now?"

"Yeah, the detective and I want to meet with you tomorrow. Can we drop by your gallery?"

"You guys aren't going to wear uniforms, are you?"

"No, we'll be in regular street clothes."

"Okay, let's say 3:00? Do you have my address?"

"Let's see, your card says 501 South Cedros Avenue."

"That's it. See you then."

****

A woman in a black Honda snapped a photo of a large man with dark hair just before he entered the gallery. A few minutes later, a woman with short curly hair wearing a navy blue pants suit also went into the gallery, but not before the woman in the car took her picture.

She got out of the Honda, crossed the street, and strolled by the gallery, but it was empty. She crossed the street to The Beach Grass Café, took a seat at her usual table, and ordered a cup of tea. Bonnie entered the gallery. Her tea arrived. She took a sip, crossed her legs, and jiggled her foot.

****

Detective Stanton said, "Ms. Harrison, tell us about when you found the note."

"Well, there isn't much to tell. When I tossed a bag of trash in the dumpster, I noticed the note on Riki's jeep. I took it and read it, and then I gave it to her."

The detective examined the note now held in a plastic bag. "Okay, do you have anything to add?"

"No, just that I wish this guy would disappear."

"Our objective is to arrest him."

"That works for me." Bonnie stood. "I guess that's it then." On her way out, she turned to Riki.

"Want to get together later?"

"Sure, I'll call you when we're finished here."

"Okay, later."

"Bye." Riki looked at the detective. "So, what's the plan for the concert?"

"Jim will sit in your seat and take pictures of the people sitting around him. He will have no contact with you. I will sit nearby."

"I'll be just another fan enjoying the show taking lots of pictures," Officer Fowler said. "But if he wonders who I am and why I'm sitting in your seat, we could have a problem."

The detective tapped her pen on the table. "I don't expect that to happen. That would mean exposing his identity and he is keeping that secret, at least for now."

Hunched over, Riki wrapped her arms around herself. "What if he sees me?"

"That is unlikely because you will be so far away and he'll be watching Jim's seat expecting you to sit there. Besides, we'll have an officer keeping an eye on you, too." Detective Stanton closed her notebook and stood.

Jim said, "I'll call you later that night to tell you what happened, okay?"

"Great, I'll come right home after the concert."

****

On the afternoon of May 24th, Riki and Bonnie walked across Lomas Santa Fe to the Solana Beach Amtrak Station. After they bought their tickets, they started across the footbridge to the southbound side of the tracks. They were almost to the elevator that would take them down to the departure platform when Riki stopped. "This bridge is creeping me out."

"Why?" Bonnie stared at her. "This is clean and safe. What is bothering you?"

"It's so strange." She looked around. "I feel as if I've been here before like in a déjà vu experience, only the stalker is part of it, too."

"Well, get over it." Bonnie put her hands on Riki's shoulders and looked into her eyes. "We will have a blast tonight, okay? The stalker will never see you so don't get weirded out."

"Yeah, okay."

They walked across the rest of the bridge and pushed the button for the elevator. "After the concert Raymond is driving us home so when we get back you and Dan go to your place, okay?"

"Um, no, I don't think so. I'm not interested in sleeping with Dan. He is a nice guy and cute too, but he's too young for me."

"What do you mean? He's our age."

The elevator door opened and they got in and pushed the button to go down to the southbound departure platform.

"Yeah, but he's immature. For example, he says things like 'coolful' and 'whizz bang.' He even eats glazed donuts and bacon for breakfast, and he shoves them in his mouth at the same time. Do adult men do that?" She tucked her hair behind her ears. "Besides, I'm expecting Officer Fowler to call me after the concert to tell me what happened with the stalker sting."

"Oh, come on, if Dan is with us, Raymond can't spend the night with me. He said he had something important to ask me after the concert."

The elevator slowed to a stop, the door opened, they exited, and stood waiting.

"Oh, my God, do you think he's going to ask you to marry him?"

"I don't know, yeah, maybe."

"Oh, Girlfriend, that's fantastic. What are you going to say?"

"I'm going to say yes. Please, Riki." Bonnie pressed her hands together. "Do it for me."

"Sorry, but the answer is no. You and Raymond will have to work something else out."

The Coaster arrived and they boarded the train, settled into their seats, and relaxed as the train zoomed south out of the Solana Beach Amtrak Station. It stopped at Santa Fe Depot in downtown San Diego where Raymond and Dan waited on the platform.

"Did you have a good trip?" Dan smiled into Riki's eyes.

"Yes, I enjoyed the scenery from the train. It was cool."

Raymond said, "Let's go to Dave's Last Resort on 4th Avenue. You'll enjoy it. The food is great and the service is off center and crazy."

"I've heard how fun and outrageous it is." Bonnie took his hand. "I've always wanted to go there."

They walked a few blocks to the restaurant, took seats at a picnic table on the patio, and chilled with strawberry margaritas while they perused the menu.

Riki asked the server, "What is this dish called Dolly?"

The server illustrated with both hands cupped on his chest. "Think of Dolly Parton, two grilled chicken breasts."

She laughed. "Okay, I'll have that." She glanced up at the high rise across the street. "Hey look, those guys are mooning us."

They all stared up at the apartments. In one window, there were two bare butts. Then one butt moved to another window and swished back and forth.

"Hey look at that, he's cleaning the window with his bare ass."

It was too funny. They were in high spirits when they joined the long line leading into PetCo Stadium.

* * * * * * * * *

The woman in the black wig made her way to Section UI311 and found her seat. Riki's seat was four seats to the left in the row in front of her. Four teenage boys came down Riki's row and sat left of Riki's seat. Fifteen minutes later, an older couple took the two seats to the right of Riki's. The next person to come down Riki's row should have been Riki, but it was not. It was a man and he sat in Riki's seat.

She stared at him as he took pictures of the people sitting around him, but when he pointed his phone in her direction, she pretended to look in her purse.

Gary Clark, Jr. opened the show with blues that captivated the audience, except for the woman whose attention remained on the man sitting in Riki's seat. When the set was over, the man stood and looked at the people sitting in the row behind him including her. Again, he pointed his phone in her direction, and again, she looked in her purse.

The man stopped taking pictures when The Rolling Stones took the stage. They broke into Jumpin' Jack Flash and the audience went wild. Everyone was dancing and singing except the woman. She glared at the man. Four songs later during Doom and Gloom she remembered where she had seen him. He looked like the man she had seen at Riki's gallery the other day.

She scrolled through the photos on her phone. She was right. She had a picture of him going into Riki's gallery. The next photo was of a woman dressed in a navy blue pants suit who looked like a cop. Now that she saw the man up close, he looked like a cop, too.

It was apropos the next song was Bitch. The woman stood and pushed her way out.

****

After the concert, Raymond drove them to Solana Beach and parked behind Bonnie's bookstore. They got out of the car and Riki kissed Raymond on the cheek.

"Thanks so very much for taking me to the best concert ever. I will always remember it."

"You are welcome. I'm glad you liked it."

"Liked it? I loved it!" Riki fished her keys out of her purse and kissed Dan. "See you."

"Ah, wait. Don't you want me to check your place to make sure it's safe?"

"Thanks, but no. The stalker was at the concert, not here. Besides, Officer Fowler will call me soon and I don't want to miss his call."

Behind Dan's back, Bonnie mouthed, "What the fuck?"

Riki smiled at her. "Good night." She had just enough time to change into her pajamas before Office Fowler phoned.

"I'm sorry, Riki. We didn't spot him tonight."

"He wasn't sitting next to you? No one approached you or acted suspicious? The officer watching me didn't see him, either?"

"No, damn it. No one came to our attention, but wasn't it a great concert?"

"Yeah, it was fabulous."

CHAPTER 7

RIKI GOT INTO bed, put on her headphones and MP3 player, and listened to The Rolling Stones at Hyde Park in 2013. Soon, Mick Jagger sang her to sleep.

In her dream, as if she were at the concert, colorful lights flashed, and the music pulsed. Then, the dream shifted and she was in a dark sinister place and she was running, running for her life! The stalker ran right behind her, but she slugged along. He would catch her soon! She thrashed about and the sheets entangled her legs. Her earphones slid onto the floor. Terror gripped her. She tried to scream, but her voice froze. She ran and ran until she found herself in a maze of gray shapes and flashing lights. Loud sounds thundered. Moisture coated her face.

A rattling roar awakened her. She bolted upright in bed, her heart pounding. She looked around the bedroom before she recognized the sound of the late night train as it roared past her building.

She took a deep breath and got out of bed, slipped into her paint splattered clothes, and padded downstairs to the studio. She put a fresh canvas onto an easel and grabbed a clean palette onto which she squeezed red, black, yellow, orange, and white paint. She put some water in a spray bottle with water, selected a variety of brushes and paint combs, and began to paint. She got into the zone and let her subconscious take control as she attempted to replicate her dream on canvas.

Angular shapes in gray and black with circular shapes of white and yellow emerged on which she misted bright red paint. The fine droplets snaked down the canvas. She added a little black paint to the red and sprayed the darker mixture onto the wet canvas. It merged with the bright red and trickled onto the floor. Next, she applied her final application of orange mixed with dark red and misted close up and far away, at the top, the bottom, and the sides.

She washed her palette and brushes, climbed the stairs back to bed, and slept well the rest of the night.

****

"Riki, are you here?"

"Just a second, I'll be right there." She placed her loaded paintbrush on the palette and walked into the gallery to greet the woman who stood just inside the doorway.

"Hello, I'm Riki. Can I help you?"

"Don't you remember me, Riki? I'm Nancy Thomason. We were friends at Kearny High School."

"Oh," Riki stammered, "right. How are you?"

"You don't remember me, do you?"

"Yes, I, ah, remember you, but you look so different now. I don't think I would have recognized you if you hadn't told me."

Nancy blinked. "I look that different?"

"Yes, quite."

"Well," she admitted, "I have gained twenty pounds since high school."

"That must be it." Riki crinkled her brow and tilted her head. "I just moved here, how did you know I was here?"

Nancy coughed. "Oh, I was shopping when I noticed The Erika Hollis Gallery sign. Since you are the only Erika Hollis I know, I assumed it was you. I hope you don't mind my dropping in. I thought it would be cool to see you again."

Riki raised her eyebrows. "Why would you think it would be . . ." She stopped. "I mean, it's cool to see you, too."

Nancy studied a painting near her. "This is your art gallery with only your art and no one else's?"

"That's right. I open in a few weeks. Right now I am in a time crunch."

"You are? Why?"

"Well, I need a large body of work when I open."

Nancy gestured at the paintings. "But, you have quite a few already."

Riki fluffed her frizzy auburn hair. "Yes, but I need at least thirty new paintings. I will have to paint nonstop if I hope to be ready in time for my grand opening. And, that is something else I don't have time to do, even if I knew how to organize such an event."

"You need an event planner to handle the grand opening. That would take a lot of pressure off you."

"You are so right. A friend of mine suggested the same thing." She tucked her hair behind her ears. "I could use the help."

"You're in luck." Nancy shrugged her left shoulder. "I'm an event planner, and I will plan your grand opening for free because you're an old friend."

"That's amazing. How lucky for me. Come on back to my studio and we'll talk."

Nancy followed Riki into the studio, but as soon as she saw Riki's nightmare depicted on canvas in the corner, she stopped and stared. "This is me."

"I beg your pardon?"

"I cannot explain it, but this painting expresses my soul." She studied it. "What is it called?"

"I call it, The Swirling Red Mist."

"It is strange, but this painting conveys something deep inside myself." She bit her lower lip as she studied the artwork. "Sometimes I feel as if I am swirling inside. How much is it?"

"I've priced it at twelve hundred dollars."

"I'll take it." Nancy couldn't take her eyes off the painting. "It's strong and powerful and emphatic."

"Emphatic?" Riki looked at the painting and then back at Nancy.

"Yes, in the sense you can predict the results of certain actions, like I can."

Riki looked back at the painting. "You are perceptive."

"Yes, I suppose, I am. I must have it." She opened her purse. "Do you take Visa?"

"Yes, I do."

"What luck I ran into you today. It's been great seeing you after all these years and now I own one of your paintings, too."

"Thanks, I am glad you identify with The Swirling Red Mist. I hope you will enjoy it."

"Oh, don't worry. I am enjoying it already."

Riki heard light rapping. "Oh, there is someone at the backdoor. Excuse me for a minute, I'll be right back."

As soon as Riki opened the door, Bonnie burst in. "You'll never guess what Raymond wanted to ask me."

"Oh, my God, you're getting married?"

"No, I am not! He's leaving for New York next week, because his parents want him to take over the family business and he wants me to go along as his private secretary. Can you believe that?"

"He wants you to be his private secretary? That sucks big time. What did you say?"

"What do you think I said?" Bonnie crossed her arms. "I said, no. What else could I say?"

"You're staying here while he goes there?"

"Yeah, I told him what I thought about his 'offer' and we had an argument about it. So, we are officially no longer together."

"Wow. That is not what I expected."

"Yeah, me neither." Bonnie sighed and let her arms drop to her sides.

"But hey, wasn't the concert last night fabulous?"

"Yes, I had a great time, until Raymond told me his plan of my working for him."

"But, did he hint at a future wedding?"

"No, he did not." Bonnie put her hands over her eyes. "He wanted me to work for him, not marry him."

"Come in here." Riki walked into the studio and Bonnie followed. "I have a surprise for you."

"So, what's the surprise?"

Riki said, "Well, I sold a painting. Isn't that amazing?"

"Yeah, who bought it?"

Riki nodded toward the corner. "Do you remember Nancy Thomason from high school?"

Bonnie spun around. "What the hell are you doing here?"

Nancy pulled her eyes away from The Swirling Red Mist. "Nice to see you, too, Bonnie."

"You came here to buy a painting?"

She shrugged her right shoulder. "No, I was shopping, but when I saw Riki's gallery, I dropped in to say hello."

"What else did you buy besides the painting?"

"The painting is my first purchase today."

"Oh, right." Bonnie's eyes strayed to the painting behind Nancy. "That's the painting you bought?"

"Yes, isn't it exciting?"

Bonnie turned to Riki. "When did you paint that?"

"I painted it last night after I had a bad dream. Why, don't you like it?"

"It's creepy. It reminds me of dripping blood. What is it called, Murder After-math?"

"I don't think the painting is creepy, at all," Nancy said. "I love it. It is so mean-ingful."

"Yeah, I bet it is, to you."

"Did I hear you say you both went to The Rolling Stones concert last night?"

"Yeah, and it was wonderful!"

"I was there last night, too. They were great, weren't they?"

"Yes," Riki said, "they were so hot. I thought it was the best concert ever."

"So, you two went together?"

"Well," Bonnie said, "we double dated as my mom would say. Did you have a date?"

Nancy cleared her throat. "I, um, planned to meet a girlfriend there, but she didn't show. A guy I didn't even know sat in her seat."

"Oh, that's strange." Riki raised her eyebrows at Bonnie.

"Yeah, after she stood me up, I got disgusted and left during the fifth song."
Riki shook her head at Bonnie.

Bonnie nodded. "That's too bad you left so early because it got better and better, didn't it Riki? We had a fantabulous time. But, then I guess you didn't mind missing most of the concert, right?" Bonnie tossed her hair over her shoulder. "I don't remem-ber you as being much of a Rolling Stones fan."

"I guess you don't remember me well, Bonnie, because I love them." Nancy pulled her keys out of her purse and moved toward the door. "I have the Honda today, Riki. Is it okay if I pick up the painting tomorrow? I can use my grandma's Mercedes, it's larger."

"Sure, that's fine."

"We'll discuss your grand opening then."

"Perfect."

Nancy strode out of the gallery and thought: okay Riki had a date last night and she gave her ticket to that man. He must be a friend of hers and not a cop. It wasn't a setup after all.

An old woman blocked the sidewalk. "So, are you through spying on her now?"

"What?" Nancy stopped. "I beg your pardon. I don't know what you're talking about."

"Don't play dumb with me, Missy. I have watched you spy on that nice young artist every day this week."

"No, you're wrong."

"I am not wrong and I want to know why you are spying on her. And, if you don't tell me, I will walk in there right now and tell her what you've been doing."

"Oh all right, you figured it out." Nancy shrugged her right shoulder. "I am doing surveillance for a private investigator."

"Why?"

She rubbed her left eyebrow. "I can't tell you, but I would appreciate it if you didn't say anything to her."

"Yeah, I bet you would, but fat chance of that happening."

"Please, it would be better if you didn't."

"Better for you, I'm sure." The old woman stomped off.

Nancy crossed the street to her car. "You got that wrong, you old bitch."

The woman traipsed past the shops as Nancy drove down the block to The Antiques Warehouse and parked. When the woman marched by, Nancy got out of her car, crossed the street, and followed close behind.

At the corner, the light was red. The woman pushed through a group of tourists to the curb and Nancy sidled up right behind her. When a car was about to turn in front of them, Nancy pretended to sneeze while she pushed her right knee into the crook of the woman's right knee. The woman toppled into the path of the turning car. She screeched, "Oh!" and the car hit her.

The group on the corner stood dumbstruck as they watched the woman fly onto the hood and smash into the windshield. Helpless, they watched her roll off and bounce into the gutter in front of them.

Everyone focused on the dead woman while Nancy stepped backwards unobserved. She paused for a moment on the sidewalk. No one noticed her. Delighted, she walked away from her first murder.

CHAPTER 8

MURDER EMPOWERED HER. She burst out laughing and started her car, but instead of driving by the murder scene, as she wanted, she turned left. When she stopped at a red light on Via de la Valle, she turned on the radio and heard the old Beatles song Maxwell's Silver Hammer. Oh, my God, she thought, how perfect! She sang along with Paul McCartney. The song seemed to be about her debut as a murderer. Even The Beatles said it was okay.

The next day, she found nothing suitable to wear in her closet except an ugly faded black suit she had last worn to Todd's sad wedding. She twisted her lifeless mousy brown hair into a tight French roll. She was unhappy when her ears poked through stringy strands, and after she applied blush and lipstick, she frowned.

To compensate, she stopped at Office Depot and bought a laptop computer, a black computer bag, a notebook, a package of black pens, and a daily planner. When she reached Solana Beach, she strapped the laptop in the computer bag and stuffed the rest of the office supplies in the various pockets and compartments.

She got out of the car, stood tall, slung the bag over her shoulder, and marched across the street to Riki's. Inside, she found a small group of women chattering in the middle of the gallery and shuffled to one side unnoticed.

A hippie-like woman, who wore a long skirt and clunky boots, crossed her arms. "It is hard to grasp, isn't it?"

Sandra, the owner of the café across the street, pulled a tissue out of her pocket and dried her eyes. "Yes, I talked to her just yesterday morning and now she's gone."

Bonnie asked, "Does anyone know why or how she fell?"

A woman in a leotard and leggings said, "One of my students said Ophelia was standing on the curb and fell in front of the car just as it was turning."

Sandra blew her nose. "It is so tragic poor Ophelia died that way."

"So, no one witnessed what happened?" Bonnie asked.

"That's right. There was a group of people standing on the corner with her, but no one saw her fall."

Bonnie said, "Could she have had a heart attack or fainted or something?"

"Perhaps, but at least she wasn't pushed." Sandra clasped her hands at her waist.

"Yeah," said the woman in long skirt and boots, "the way she treated people, I wouldn't have been surprised if someone pushed her." She nodded to the others. "That was my first thought when I heard about it."

Riki's jaw dropped. "What do you mean? You thought someone pushed her in front of the car on purpose?"

"She was not well liked on the block," said the woman in the skirt and boots, "was she?"

"Well, she did have a somewhat caustic personality." Sandra glanced at the other women. "We all know she liked dogs better than people."

The woman from the gym rubbed her chin. "It could have been on purpose I suppose, but the medical examiner determined it was an accident."

Sandra looked at her watch. "Oh, it's time for Tina's break. I have to go now."

"I have to leave, too," said the woman in the long skirt.

"Yeah, me too, I have an aerobics class to teach in five minutes, I have to run."

Riki walked them to the door and saw Nancy standing off to the side. "Sorry," she said, "have you been waiting long?"

"No, I just got here. I hope I didn't come at a bad time."

"No, of course not, we were just talking about our neighbor who died yesterday. A car struck and killed her right after you left."

"Oh, no," Nancy shook her head. "I am so sorry."

"Yes," Riki said, "it was quite a shock." She opened the door for the women.

Bonnie said, "Are we still on for dinner tonight?"

"Um, no, not tonight, I want to put in some serious time painting. Let's make it tomorrow."

"Okay, I'll see you then if not before." Bonnie waved to Nancy and left.

Riki headed for the studio. "I guess you're here for The Swirling Red Mist."

Nancy followed her into the studio. "Yes, and we need to discuss your grand opening." She scanned the room until her attention focused on The Swirling Red Mist standing on an easel in a corner. She stood in front of the painting with her back to Riki. "I take it the woman who died had a shop on this block?"

"Yes, she owned the dog groomer's business a few doors down. Why do you ask?"

"Oh, I was just wondering if maybe a storefront would be available now." She turned toward Riki. "Oops, sorry, I don't mean to sound insensitive and self-serving, but I guess I am. I was hoping to find a place where I could set up my event planning business."

"I get where you're coming from. Ophelia's daughter was her partner and will keep the shop, as far as I know."

"Oh, that's too bad." Nancy let the computer bag slide off her shoulder onto the table.

"Where do you work now?"

She coughed. "Um, at the moment I'm working out of my house." She fiddled with her earring. "I, um, meet my clients at their homes or their places of business so, uh, not having an office has worked okay so far. But if I had actual office, I would get more clients."

"Yeah, you're right, a real office would help." Riki scratched her head. "You know, Kathy has a small office building down the street and she said the other day someone moved out. It would be advantageous for you to have an office in the center of the Cedros Avenue Design District, wouldn't it? It is such a hot location."

"Yes, I love it here. It would be perfect. How big is the office? Is it big enough for me to live in, do you think?"

"I haven't seen it, but if you're serious, I can introduce you to Kathy right now and you can take it from there."

"Okay, that would be great."

On their way to Kathy's Hair Salon, they walked by The Cubbyhole Bookstore and through the window saw Bonnie sorting a mountain of books.

Nancy shook her head. "Bonnie has all the luck, doesn't she?"

"Yeah, Bonnie needs something solid to anchor her. She's been searching for the right thing since high school and I think she's found it in the bookstore."

On the other side of the neighborhood pub The Belly Up, Riki pointed to an upstairs window. "There is the future home of the Cedros Avenue Design District's new event planner."

"I like that it is so close to your place, it is ideal."

Kathy, busy cutting hair, greeted them with a smile. "Hey Riki, are you finally going to let me cut your hair?"

"Sorry, but not today." Riki tried to smooth her wild and fluffy hair and glanced at the woman standing next to her. "This is Nancy Thomason. We knew each other in high school. She's interested in renting the empty office next door to The Belly Up."

"Hi."

"Hi Nancy, I'm Kathy Morris. I own most of the block. Why do you want the office?"

"I am an Event Planner."

"That's interesting." She combed and snipped. "Like what kind of events do you plan?"

"I plan mostly weddings, reunions, and parties." She cleared her throat. "But I also do commercial type events like grand openings, conventions, and specialty fairs."

"I see. Who are your current clients?"

"Um."

"I'm one of them," Riki said. "She's planning my grand opening in three weeks."

"Oh, that's cool."

"Yes, Riki is my most recent client."

Kathy nodded. "Okay, when I finish this cut, I'll take you to see it. I don't have another appointment for an hour."

"Super." Nancy and Riki took seats around a large coffee table that held stacks of hairdo magazines. Riki reached for the one on top.

She flipped through the magazine and contemplated how she would look with the various extreme haircuts at her grand opening. Would she look amazing and spectacular or would she look crazy and weird? She wanted to appear fabulous not peculiar.

"Riki, how's everything shaping up at your place?"

"Great, except I have a lot of work to do. Thanks for reminding me." She closed the magazine and stood. "I should go back to the studio and get some painting accomplished today. Good luck, Nancy."

"Thanks for everything. See you later."

Riki strolled down South Cedros Avenue and ducked inside The Cubbyhole Bookstore.

"Hey, guess who our new neighbor's going to be."

Bonnie groaned. "Nancy?"

"You guessed it. She's renting an office."

"You mean she's going to work on this block next to us?"

"Yeah, and she wants to live in it, too."

Bonnie narrowed her eyes. "You told her about the office for rent, didn't you?"

"Well, yeah."

"What were you thinking?"

Riki looked at the floor. "I was just trying to help."

"That's just super." Bonnie sighed. "At least The Belly Up puts some distance between us."

CHAPTER 9

"RIKI, ARE YOU there?" Nancy peered through the window, spotted her, and waved. "Hi, I have good news."

Riki opened the door. "Hi. Come in."

"Hey, I am moving into the office! I hope it isn't too late for dinner." She held up white bags. "I brought food to celebrate and to thank you for your help."

"Oh, you didn't need to do that."

"I wanted to. You haven't eaten already, have you?" She strode past Riki into the gallery toward the studio.

Riki followed her, "Um, no, not yet."

"I dropped by earlier, but you weren't here so I went shopping for furniture and brought back take-out." She stopped and looked at Riki. "I hope it's all right."

"Um, sure, I guess."

"Good. I'm hungry." She continued into the studio and unpacked the bags. "You do like Rubio's fish tacos, don't you?"

"Who doesn't?"

"I know, right? Let's eat them while they're hot." Nancy splashed a taco with green salsa.

"Good idea."

They ate without talking until they were both satiated. Riki stretched, yawned, and yawned again. Nancy sipped her drink. Riki gathered their trash and yawned some more.

Nancy leaned back. "I bought spectacular furniture for my new office. It is going to be fabulous. I chose the colors of The Swirling Red Mist for the decor."

"That sounds exciting."

"You are so right, it is very exciting. I bought a black lacquer coffee table and some modern chairs in a vibrant red and orange print for the outer office. For the inner office, I bought a black leather sofa that makes into a somewhat comfortable bed, and a desk chair and a reading chair both in vivid red and orange, a black lacquer desk, and a matching credenza I can use as a dresser. I am going to put The Swirling Red Mist on the wall opposite the window so I can bask in the vivid red. It will brighten my living space, so I, ah, won't slip into darkness." She lowered her head.

Riki drifted around the studio inspecting her paintings in progress. "What do you mean you won't slip into darkness?"

"I just get down sometimes and everything around me loses color, everything seems dull and colorless. I don't know how to explain it, but everything looks gray to me."

"You mean like in that old Rolling Stones song Paint It Black?"

She nodded. "Yeah, I guess so, sort of. It is as if I am enveloped in darkness, and everything around me becomes dark and gloomy." She gazed at the painting. "I hope the intensity of these colors will keep the darkness away."

"You really think this painting will keep you from getting depressed?"

"I hope so."

"Yeah, me too, I mean, that would be great."

"Anyway, the office is going to be radiant. I'm moving in tomorrow."

"Wow. That was fast."

"Yeah, I am so excited about it, I can't wait."

"Congratulations."

"Thanks. This is a new direction for me, so to speak, in the middle of the affluent Cedros Avenue Design District." She opened her purse. "This is a fantastic opportunity for me to break into upscale north coastal events. You've helped me a great deal."

"Oh, it was nothing, but thanks for dinner."

"It was my pleasure." Out of her purse, she took a notebook and a pen. "Now what did you want for your grand opening?"

Riki yawned. "Well, I want a lot of people to come who will buy my art or at least tell other people who will buy my art."

"So, you want to invite local community leaders, your friends and family, and persons in the media?"

"Yes, everyone you can think of." Riki lowered her head. "My parents passed away last year, but I'll give you my cousin Cherry's address, she's my only family now."

"Okay. What about food?"

Riki tucked a loose strand behind her ear. "I would like to use someone local. Perhaps, The Beach Diner; they have great food and I think they cater, too."

"Great idea, I will check it out." She made a few notes. "Like you, I like keeping the business local so I'll use the printer on the other side of Lomas Santa Fe for your invitations. I will drop by there tomorrow to get some samples from which you can choose."

"Super. Bob the owner and I are good friends."

"Who would you like to use for entertainment?"

"There is a hot jazz ensemble that performs around State that would be perfect."

"That's great, Riki. Jazz is the perfect complement to your artwork."

"Yeah, I think so, too. The name of the group is Jazz Matters and I'll send their email address to you tomorrow along with Cherry's, and the emails of my friends and college professors."

"Great, email invitations will keep the cost down." Nancy got up to leave. "I won't disappoint you, Riki, I promise. Your grand opening will be fabulous."

"I am glad to hear it." Riki yawned. "I didn't know how I was going to get it done and still paint thirty or forty canvases. You've made it possible for me to have it all."

****

The man behind the counter said, "Hi, I'm Bob. Can I help you?"

"Yes, please. I am Nancy Thomason. I'm an Event Planner and I'm planning the grand opening for The Erika Hollis Gallery. Would it be possible for me to borrow examples of invitations from which Riki can choose?"

"We have several binders full of samples." He placed three overstuffed binders on the counter. "But, these contain the most recent popular designs. I'm sure Riki will find something in these that will reflect her artistic flair."

"Thanks." Nancy lifted the binders. "I'll return them in a few days when Riki decides."

"No worries."

Ten minutes later, Nancy traipsed into the studio, and dropped the binders onto the table next to Riki. "Here you go, have fun choosing."

"Oh, my God," Riki flipped through the pages, "there are so many cool designs. How can I choose just one?"

"It will be a hard choice, but you can take a couple of days to decide before I need to place the order. I am going to order three hundred and hope fifty people will come. That would be a successful turnout, if they are the right fifty people."

"You mean fifty influential people?"

"Exactly," Nancy said. "If we get fifty people with influence, clout, and money to come, it would be a very successful grand opening, wouldn't it?"

"Yes, it would!"

****

"I need to order three hundred invitations and I would like to order a thousand business cards."

"Not a problem," Bob said, "I can have both orders ready next week."

"That will be perfect."

When Nancy returned to her office, she sent Jazz Matters an email requesting they perform for the grand opening of The Erika Hollis Gallery in Solana Beach on June 27 from 7 p.m. until 10 p.m. An hour later, she received their enthusiastic confirmation.

That afternoon she ate lunch at The Beach Diner. When the check came, she said, "I'd like to speak to the manager, please."

"Is there something wrong?"

"No, everything's fine. I would like to discuss something with the manager."

"I'll get her for you."

Soon a stylish woman came to her table. "I'm Grace Paige, the manager. How can I help you?"

"Hello, my name is Nancy Thomason and I'm planning the grand opening of The Erika Hollis Gallery. We'd like you to cater the event."

"We'd be happy to. I love Riki's art. I saw a painting through her window that would look amazing in here. I hope she still has it."

"I'm sure she wouldn't mind if you dropped in. Do you happen to have a catering menu I can show her?"

"But, of course. Actually, we have four catering menus. Let me get them for you."

Nancy perused the menus as she walked to the gallery. She found Riki in the studio and dropped the menus next to her palette.

"Riki, all four of these menus look delicious. It will be a hard choice."

"You are so right. I love their food. I'll let you know when I've decided."

"Okay, but you'll need to tell me within a couple of days."

"I'll decide by tomorrow. I may have to have dinner there tonight to sample some of these entrees."

"I just had a wonderful lunch there. I'm sure you'll enjoy it."

"I know I will." Riki resumed painting. "What else is new?"

"Well, I've placed advertisements in all the local newspapers inviting the community, plus I hired a professional art salesperson so you'll be free to enjoy the event. He'll handle all the sales while you mingle."

"Wow, I'm impressed Nancy. The grand opening is coming together so well. You're doing a great job."

Nancy blushed. "Thanks."

****

"I'll be right there." She put down her brush and entered the gallery. "Hi, Bob. What's up?"

"Hi, I'm sorry to disturb you, Riki. No one was at Nancy's and I didn't want to leave the invitations and her business cards outside her door. Would it be okay if I leave them here with you?"

"That's not a problem at all. She comes by here every day, so I will make sure she gets them."

"Great, thanks."

"You are coming to the grand opening, aren't you?"

"Am I invited?"

"Everyone's invited. Please come and bring your wife and friends."

"Okay, thanks, I will." His eyes drifted to the artworks. "You have some outstanding paintings here. That blue and green wavy one is quite nice. What is it called?"

"I call it, How Music Flows."

"It is very tranquil and serene. My wife would love it. How much is it?"

Riki looked at the card taped to the back. "It's $1800."

"I'll take it. Can I come back later with my credit card?"

"Sure, I'll put a SOLD sticker on it. Thank you, Bob. I'm glad you like it."

"No, I love it."

"Well, you know what they say, 'if it speaks to you; you must have it.'"

"That's it, it speaks to me."

CHAPTER 10

"HEY, SURPRISE, YOUR business cards are here and the invitations, too. Bob stopped by your office, but you weren't there so he dropped them off here."

"Cool." Nancy inspected the invitations satisfied they were as she ordered. "I will get these addressed this afternoon; I have all the addresses already uploaded in my computer so I just need to print the envelopes and stuff them. They will be ready to mail tomorrow."

"Terrific. Did you find three hundred people to invite?"

"Oh, easily, we are inviting everyone on this street, plus the business owners and government officials in Solana Beach and Del Mar as well as in La Jolla, Pacific Beach, and Ocean Beach and all the beach cities up the coast as far as Oceanside." She took a breath. "I'm also inviting the major players at the local TV and radio stations and the arts and society reporters at the local papers. And, that's just the three hundred who will get snail mail invitations. I've already sent over a hundred emails inviting your friends, your cousin, and your associates including your professors at San Diego State. I can't think of anyone I've overlooked, can you?"

"No, you have it covered."

Nancy grinned as she opened the box of business cards and pulled one out to inspect. But when she read it, her face turned red. "How could he be so stupid? What an imbecile!" She slammed her fist on the table. "Damn!"

"Why, what's wrong with them?"

Nancy handed her the card she still held in her hand. "What a horrible way to begin! Shit! Shit! Shit!"

"What? I don't see it."

"My name," she snapped. "Look at my name!"

Riki read, Nance Can Plan It, followed by Nance Thomason, Event Planner, her address, email address, and her phone and FAX numbers.

"The guy can't even get my name right. I might as well give up now. I'm doomed." Nance put her head in her hands. "Nothing I do turns out right. I fail at everything."

"I don't think it's all that bad. In fact, I think Nance Can Plan It sounds better than Nancy Can Plan It."

"You think so?"

"Yes, and changing your name to Nance is a great idea. You'd have a new personal name as well as a new business name to go with your new office. Everything new, that has to be good."

"Yes, I can see that."

Riki slid the card into her daily planner. "I remember in school when you started going by your middle name and everyone had to stop calling you Nancy and start calling you Lynn. Then the next year, you stopped going by Lynn and we had to go back to calling you Nancy again. It was confusing."

"Yeah, that was a weird time for me."

"I always wondered what that was all about. I mean, why did you decide to go by Lynn instead of Nancy in the first place?"

"I wanted to be someone else, someone different. I thought if I changed my name, my life would change."

"Did it work?"

"No, not so well, that's why I went back to Nancy."

"Well, I like the name Nance. It suits you and your business. From now on, you're Nance, okay?"

She pulled another card out of the box. "A new name may be just what I need. I feel better about this now."

"That's good. I'm glad to hear it, Nance. Now, please get these invitations sent and let me get back to work."

Nance, formerly known as Nancy, picked up the boxes. "Okay, I will see you later."

She strode out of the gallery and down the street, but stopped short when she caught her reflection in The Cubbyhole Bookstore's window. Her shoulders slumped as she stared at her ears poking through thin stringy strands of mousy brown hair.

"Hello, Nancy." Kathy stopped on the sidewalk next to her. "How's it going? Is everything okay? Is there a problem?"

"No, no problems except for my ugly hair." Nance turned to Kathy. "Is there anything you can do to give it some body? I hate seeing my ears stick out like this."

"Not a problem." Kathy fingered Nance's hair. "We can add a great deal of volume if we layer and perm it."

"Sounds perfect, can we do it now?"

"Well, I have to take care of a few things first, but if you meet me at the shop in about an hour, I will perform my magic and you'll have big beautiful hair tonight."

"Okay, see you in an hour." She returned to her office and dropped the boxes onto her desk. She said to the mirror, "I'm Nance Thomason, Event Planner and I own Nance Can Plan It."

****

She put a frozen dinner into the microwave and as she waited for it to heat, she admired her full curly hair in the bathroom mirror. Then, she wandered in front of the picture window watching the passersby.

Across the street, Bonnie and Riki came out of the bakery with a big brawny man walking between them. Nance attracted to his powerful muscular build, his dark skin, and nearly shaved head, forgot her dinner, grabbed her purse, and raced out the door just as the microwave dinged.

Up ahead the threesome looked in shop windows as they strolled and Nance rushed to catch up until she was two shops behind. Then, she slowed to match their pace.

Minutes later, Riki glanced over her shoulder and walked back. "Hey, Nance, what have you done to your hair? It looks fantastic! Did you go to Kathy?"

"Yes, Kathy is a genius isn't she?" Nance patted her new hair. "Who knew my thin stringy hair could be so full and thick?"

"It's amazing. I love it." Riki touched Nance's arm. "You have new hair for a new life. How cool is that?"

"Thanks. I'm glad you like it."

"We're on our way to eat at Veggie Delights. Would you like to join us? You can show off your new hair and tell Bonnie and Sam about your new name."

"Well, I don't want to impose or anything."

"Don't worry, you won't be imposing."

"Well, if you're sure. Thanks."

"Super, come on, let's go. Sam and Bonnie are already there. So, how are the invitations coming along? How many have you have addressed so far?"

Nance shrugged her left shoulder, "Great, they are all addressed and ready to mail tomorrow."

"That was fast. How did you find time to get a perm and print and stuff three hundred envelopes?"

She coughed. "Just good time management, I guess."

"Well, aren't you full of surprises? Well done."

Bonnie and Sam sat at a glass topped wicker table on the patio surrounded by potted palms. While they studied the menu, Riki and Nance walked up to their table and stood. When they didn't look up, Riki picked up a spoon and clicked it on the side of Bonnie's water glass.

"Attention please, I would like to present Nance, the event planner we once knew as Nancy." Bonnie and Sam looked up.

"Wow," Bonnie's jaw dropped, "your hair looks great. It really does!"

Nance's smile froze.

"Yes, your hair looks nice," the handsome man said. "I like it."

Nance's smile warmed. "Thank you."

"I'm Sam Collins. I own Bread Temptations across the street from your office."

"It is a pleasure to meet you Sam. I'm planning on visiting the bakery tomorrow to drop off your invitation to the grand opening of The Erika Hollis Gallery."

"I'll look forward to your visit. Would you care to join us for dinner?"

"Thank you, I would be delighted." She and Riki slid into wicker chairs.

Bonnie said, "Did Riki say you've changed your name to Nance?"

"That's right. Bob the printer made a mistake on my business cards, and although I wasn't too happy about it at first, Riki convinced me to change my name and keep the cards."

She handed cards to Bonnie and Sam.

"What do you think?"

"It looks professional." Sam tucked the card inside his shirt pocket.

"Thanks so much."

"Yeah, it's nice." Bonnie tossed the card onto the table. It landed face down. Nance frowned.

"Sam," Riki said, "have you heard anything new about poor Ophelia's accident?"

"No, just that she fell into the path of an oncoming car."

Nance reached across the table and turned her business card face up.

"Did you know her well?"

"I knew her well enough. She was a cantankerous old gadfly and was always gossiping and pissing people off."

Nance tapped the business card with her index finger. "So you won't miss her?"

"Few will."

Her napkin hid the smile she couldn't control.

****

Nance sat at her desk, and began the tedious job of printing and stuffing envelopes while she gazed out the window at Bread Temptations in the hopes of seeing Sam, but an hour later, a woman walked up to the bakery and knocked on the front door. In the dim light, Nance couldn't tell who she was, but when Sam opened the door, the light spilled onto Bonnie. Sam put his arms around her, pulled her inside, and closed the door. Nance clenched her fist and swept the invitations onto the floor.

CHAPTER 11

INTENT ON SCRATCHING Bonnie's BMW, Nance bolted into the alley with her keys in hand and stomped to the bookstore. The backdoor was ajar. A wicked smile played on her lips and by the time she climbed the stairs to Bonnie's apartment, her fury had transformed into saturnalia. In a state of frenzied delight, she trashed the living room and danced into the bedroom. After she threw the mattress off the bed, she ripped all the clothes out of the closet and dumped the contents of the dresser drawers on top of the growing heap. She stomped on them, wiped her feet on them, spit on them, and for a final insult, she peed on them.

Consumed with laughter, she staggered into the kitchen, opened the cabinets, and swept everything crashing to the floor.

Before she left, she found a red lipstick on the bathroom counter and wrote in block letters WHORE on the mirror. Satisfied she made her point she threw the lipstick into the toilet and skipped down the stairs singing Maxwell's Silver Hammer.

****

"Hey, what's going on?"

"Hi, Nance, you haven't heard?" Sam rubbed his jaw. "Someone broke into Bonnie's apartment last night and ransacked it."

Nance turned to look at the building. "No, you're kidding?" She cleared her throat. "I thought this neighborhood was safe from burglars."

"There are bad people everywhere."

She nodded. "I am sure you are right. Did it happen while we were at dinner?"

"No, it happened after dinner, but Bonnie was with me." Sam put his hands on his hips. "We had an impromptu late date."

"That was, ah, fortunate for her, wasn't it?"

"What do you mean?" Riki took off her sunglasses.

"Um, well, if she had been there, with the intruder, I mean, she, ah, could have had a violent confrontation with a maniac."

"You're right, Nance." Sam shifted his weight from foot to foot. "Being with me may have saved her life."

"Lucky for her, wasn't it? Do they, ah, know how he got in?"

Sam said, "I heard one of the deputies say that there was no forced entry."

"Oh, so what do they think he did, just walk in?"

"They don't seem to know, but they are surprised he didn't touch the bookstore, because he went up to the apartment and tossed it and nothing else."

She rummaged in her purse. "Do they have any idea who did it?"

Riki said, "No, but someone said there was a witness."

Nance's head sprang up. "A witness, a witness to what? How could anyone see into her apartment from the street?"

Riki put her sunglasses on top of her head and stared at Nance. "It wasn't someone on this street. They say it was someone walking his dog on Highway 101. No clue what he saw, if anything."

"Oh, right." Nance pulled her keys out of her purse. "Well, I am on my way to the post office, so I'll catch you later."

****

"I propped the door open with a rock when I left last night."

"You did what?" Riki stared at her. "After what happened to me?"

"You don't have to say it." Bonnie looked at the floor as she braided her hair over her shoulder. "I knew it was stupid when I did it."

"Then, why did you do it?"

"Well, Sam called about an hour after I got home and wanted to know if I would join him for a drink at his place." She looked up and met Riki's eyes. "I was so excited that I couldn't find my keys, so I used a rock to hold the door open in order to get back in."

"So it was some bum walking by?"

"Well, no. There is another detail no one knows but me, the police, the person who broke in, and now you."

"What's that?"

"He took one of my lipsticks and wrote on the bathroom mirror, WHORE! The deputies said it might be someone I know."

"Yeah," Riki agreed, "it doesn't sound random, does it? What about an old boyfriend?"

"Like who? I have thought of everyone I've dated and no one comes to mind."

"Well, does Sam have a jealous girlfriend or ex-wife?"

"He hasn't mentioned anyone."

"Maybe he's just being polite."

"I hope that's not it." She looked out the window. "What if it was Nance?"

"Nance, why do you think she did it?"

"Because it is something she would do if she were jealous." Bonnie tossed the braid over her shoulder.

"You mean she has the hots for Sam?"

"Well, she stared at him all during dinner, didn't she? And, her place is right across the street from his, so she has a perfect view of his front door. Last night when I went over there, her light was on. It's possible she saw me go in and not leave."

"So?"

"So think about it; if she wanted to vent, all she had to do was run over to my place, trash it, and then run back to her place."

"You have a point. But how would she know your backdoor wasn't locked?"

"Oh yeah, I hadn't thought of that, I guess she wouldn't."

****

The woman at the counter said, "Hello, I'm Mary. What can I get for you today?"

"I would like to talk to Sam."

"I'm sorry, but today is not a good day for Sam. You heard about the break in down the street, right?"

"Yes, I heard about it."

"That's his girlfriend's place, The Cubbyhole Bookstore. You'll have to excuse him today. He's pretty upset about it."

"Yes, I am sure he is. Well, um, I'll take a Brazilian coffee. Please tell Sam I was here, and I'll come back later." Nance handed Mary a business card and took the coffee outside. She sipped the rich brew, made a sour face, tossed it in the trash, and strode toward Lomas Santa Fe.

She invited the owners of every eatery, furniture store, antiques store, clothing boutique, gym, salon, garden shop, and art gallery on South Cedros Avenue. Her last stop before heading home was The Bike Guy. The owner was good looking with curly brown hair and deep blue eyes.

"Hello, I'm Mark, is there something I can help you find?"

"I'm Nance Thomason of Nance Can Plan It. I'm an event planner. Here's my card. And, here's your invitation to the grand opening of The Erika Hollis Gallery."

"Erika Hollis? Is she that cute redhead who's been tripping around South Cedros Avenue the past few weeks?"

Nance raised her eyebrows. "You've noticed her in the neighborhood?"

"Who could not notice her? She's hot!"

"She's a good friend of mine and a great artist."

"She's an artist? That's interesting." He glanced out the window and then back at Nance. "Sure, I'll go to her grand opening."

Before Nance stopped for the day, she decided to drop in the bakery again. As she entered, Sam came out of the kitchen.

"Hello, there. Come on back. Want some coffee?"

"I'd love some." Nance settled into one of the comfortable chairs arranged in a corner of the kitchen.

Sam handed her a hot cup. "This is Brazilian coffee. Have you tried it before?"

She shrugged her left shoulder. "Um, no, I haven't." She took a sip. "Yum, this is very good. I like it."

"My specialty after bread is coffee."

"You're a man of many specialties, I'm sure." Nance's hand shook as she handed him the envelope. "This is your invitation to Riki's grand opening." She looked into his eyes. "You are planning on coming, aren't you?"

"Of course, I wouldn't miss it."

She fastened the flap on her tote bag. "What's new with Bonnie's break in?"

"They don't seem to know much about what happened."

"But, I thought there was a witness."

"Some witness. All he saw was someone run out her backdoor toward the train station."

"He can't describe anyone?"

"No, he didn't see anything useful."

She shrugged her left shoulder. "That is too bad." She set her cup on the table. "Bonnie must be upset."

"I should say so. She's trembled all day."

"Poor, Bonnie." She shook her head. "I hope she feels better."

"She's pretty strong willed. She'll be fine."

"Is she closing her shop again tomorrow?"

"Yes, she plans to open the day after tomorrow."

She picked up her cup and held it with both hands. "Well, it's good to bounce back." She drank her coffee.

"Yeah, she's resilient, isn't she? I just wish there was something I could do to make her feel safe again. But short of finding this asshole and beating the shit out of him, there isn't too much I can do."

Nance sputtered into her coffee.

CHAPTER 12

"YOU CLUMSY IDIOT, you are such a klutz!"

Riki rushed to the studio expecting a huge calamity, but it was nothing. Steve, a political science student and part of the work crew, had dropped a painting.

Riki walked past Nance. "No harm done. Go ahead and take it out front, okay?"

When Steve left, Riki said, "I don't want to hear you speak to Steve or anyone else like that ever again."

"He works for me, don't tell me how to talk to my workers."

"Wrong, he doesn't work for you, he works for the agency you hired, but I am telling you how to talk to the workers the agency sent. This is my gallery and you are disrupting the peace and harmony. Either lose the attitude or get the hell out." Riki marched away. Nance fumed.

****

That evening, Kathy came over, and applied Riki's makeup and styled her hair in a fabulous mane of lovely auburn curls.

"Well, how do I look?"

"You look sensational."

"Wait till you see my dress."

With Kathy's help, Riki slipped into a long white gown. "Do you like it?"

"I love it. It is sleek and sophisticated and looks great with your tan. You will complement the artworks."

"That is what I am aiming for. I want people to notice the paintings, not me. They're for sale and I'm not."

"Good point."

"Well, I have to go downstairs to check on how things are coming along and you still have to get ready, Girlfriend. See you later."

"Okay, till then."

****

Nance waved her over. "Erika Hollis, let me introduce you to Mr. Adams. He will handle all the sales this evening. He'll take the checks and credit cards, write the receipts, provide the certificates of authenticity, and arrange the crating and delivery. You don't have to do anything, but talk to the guests and have a good time."

Riki shook his hand. "It's nice to meet you, Mr. Adams."

"The pleasure is mine, Ms. Hollis."

"I am so relieved to have a professional handle this part of the evening for me."

"Is this your first exhibition?"

"Yes, this is my first gallery and my first solo exhibition. I am excited and a little nervous."

"Just enjoy your special evening." He glanced around. "I venture to say you'll do well tonight." Mr. Adams opened a program and adjusted his reading glasses. "Now if you'll excuse me, I will take myself on a self-guided tour."

Soon the gallery filled with guests who enjoyed the jazz, food, and art. The party was in full swing when Dan touched her shoulder. "Riki, I'm sorry I'm late."

She smiled and turned. "That's okay. I'm glad you made it. It's been weeks since I last saw you."

"I know. I'm sorry about that, too." He looked into her eyes. "I have something I have to tell you."

"You're so serious." She took his hands in hers. "This doesn't sound good."

"I got a job."

"But, that's great! Aren't you happy about it?"

"It's on a ship, as a researcher, I'll be at sea for weeks, maybe even months, at a time."

"Oh, but that's good. It's in your field doing what you want to do. What's the problem?"

"Yeah, well, since I won't be here much, I want you to know I don't mind if you date other guys."

"Oh, I see your point." She looked at the floor. "Don't worry, I understand."

"Sorry if I upset you tonight."

She met his eyes. "No, on the contrary, I wish you luck and adventure."

"Thanks." He pulled at the collar of his tee shirt. "Well, I guess I'll be going."

"Okay, take care of yourself. Bye."

Riki watched Dan walk out of her life.

Sam touched her arm. "Riki, I'd like you to meet my friend, Mark McDonald. He owns The Bike Guy."

Mark studied her face when he took her hand. "It is a pleasure to meet you, Riki."

"Mark." Tingles raced up her arm. "I'm so glad you came tonight."

Bonnie whispered in her ear, "I thought you didn't have time for a boyfriend."

"Mark is a man, not a boy," Riki whispered back, "and I have plenty of time for a man."

At the end of the evening, Mr. Adams took her hand. "Ms. Hollis, I sold twenty-two of your wonderful paintings."

"That is fabulous." Riki glowed. "Thank you so much for your help tonight, Mr. Adams."

"You are most welcome, Ms. Hollis. You are such a talented artist the artworks almost sold themselves." He handed her the paperwork. "I'll be here with my crew on Monday to handle transporting the paintings."

"Thank you. I will look forward to Monday." She looked over his shoulder. "Please excuse me. I need to say good night to Mr. McDonald."

Nance touched his arm. "You are a pro, Mr. Adams. I appreciate the great work you did this evening."

"Anytime you need me, Ms. Thomason, just call." He bowed and departed.

Sam and Bonnie slipped out.

Nance grabbed her bag and headed for the door. "Riki, the cleaning crew will be here in the morning around 9:30 and I'll be here to supervise. Bye."

Not far ahead, Sam and Bonnie ducked into the bookstore.

Nance stomped up to her office, grabbed a piece of paper and a red marker, and wrote in large block letters, SHE'S A WHORE.

She replaced her glittery evening dress and blazer with black jeans and a black tee shirt, but kept her curly hair held back with a sparkly clasp. She crept downstairs and stood in the shadows. She stepped up to the curb and was about to cross the street when a car sped past her. She drew back into the shadows and another speeding car raced down the street, but this car had its siren blaring and red lights flashing.

"I'll take that as an omen," she said under her breath.

Instead of going to the bakery, she walked toward the beach. At the intersection of Highway 101 and Lomas Santa Fe, she waited on the corner for the traffic light to change and glanced across the highway where an old man with a dog faced Highway 101. The man had a clear view of the backs of the buildings on South Cedros Avenue. Yes, he could have witnessed her crime.

The dog walker and his dog were halfway across the parking lot toward the northern bluff when the light turned green. Nance hurried across the highway and followed them. When they began trekking up the bluff, she circled above them to the top, and waited.

The man and his dog climbed the path that skirted the edge of the cliff and headed toward the tree where Nance hid in the shadows. When they got to her tree, she sprang onto the path. "Excuse me, do you know the time?"

The man jumped. "What?"

She pointed to her wrist. "Do you have the time?"

"Oh, I see, ah, yes, I do."

His eyes went to his watch and Nance yanked the leash out of his other hand.

"Hey! What the hell do you think you're doing?"

"This." She put both hands on his chest, and with one quick push, she shoved him off the cliff. "I don't like witnesses."

The dog walker's face registered surprise, then shock, and as he fell backwards, he looked terrified. He grasped at air and thrashed as he tipped further back, screamed, and vanished. The crashing waves drowned out his last pathetic shriek.

She looked over the cliff and saw nothing but churning waves and foamy white-water. She laughed and skipped back to her office singing her personalized version of Maxwell's Silver Hammer.

CHAPTER 13

NANCE SPRANG OUT of bed, showered, dressed, and walked to the Solana Donut Shop. She bought two dozen donuts for the cleaning crew and on her way back, she stopped at Bread Temptations.

Mary handed her a steaming cup of Brazilian. "Here's your favorite."

"Thanks." She was about to turn away when Sam walked into the kitchen. "Good morning, Sam. How's it going?"

"Hi, Nance, I'm great, how are you?" He carried his coffee around the counter. "Let's sit by the window." He led the way to an empty table. "Have a seat."

"Thanks, I don't have much time, but I can always make time for you."

"Have you recovered from the grand opening?"

"Oh, yes." She nodded. "I feel fantastic this morning. The evening came off well last night, don't you think?" She sipped her coffee. "Riki sold twenty-two paintings. And, even the mayor and city councilors came. Isn't that wonderful?"

"Yeah, and the mayor said he wanted to commission her to paint something for city hall."

"How great is that?" She took another sip. "Did you like the food and the music?"

"The food was delicious, and the jazz was the perfect music for the occasion. You did a terrific job putting it all together."

She blushed. "You think so, Sam?"

"Yes, you should be very proud. It was an impressive evening."

"Thanks, Sam. It means a lot to me to hear you say that." She glanced at the clock over the sink. "Oh, it is getting late. It's been great having coffee with you this morning. I'm sorry, I hate to leave now, but I'm meeting the cleaning crew at Riki's in a few minutes." She lifted the boxes of donuts in her arms. "Bye-bye."

* * * * * * * * * *

"Good morning," Nance sang. She breezed past Riki into the studio where she placed the donuts onto the table.

"Good morning to you, too, you are in a good mood today. You must have slept well."

"Oh, I did sleep well. I slept very well, in fact. I feel energized, even revitalized. The grand opening was fabulous, don't you think?"

"Yes, it was fantastic. I sold more paintings than I had hoped and it was a lot of fun, too. I had a wonderful time. You planned a great grand opening."

"Thanks so much. I'm glad you're happy with the event." Nance blushed as she arranged napkins. "I had coffee with Sam this morning and he said it was impressive."

"I agree the grand opening was most impressive. We should both benefit."

"I hope you're right."

"I am right. You made a smashing impression."

"Thanks, Riki."

The cleaning crew arrived and Riki ushered them into the studio where Nance waited.

"Please enjoy the donuts, everyone. Thank you for your hard work to help make Riki's grand opening such a huge success. I foresee using your services again. Now, take your time and when you're ready, let's make this place sparkle for Riki."

The cleaning crew finished the donuts in minutes, had everything cleaned by noon, and by 12:05 they were gone.

"Riki, I would like to take you to lunch."

Riki looked out the window and rolled her eyes. "I'll pass on lunch today. Thanks, anyway."

"Okay, see you later."

****

Riki headed for Fletcher's Cove, but before she reached the entrance to the parking lot, she saw Sheriff's vehicles and pockets of onlookers in the parking lot.

She approached two women. "What's going on? Did a surfer have an accident?"

The woman closer to her said, "No, it was an older man who slipped off the cliff."

"Oh, no, that's awful."

"Yeah, the lifeguards said the old guy was out walking his dog when he slipped over the edge. When the dog showed up at home alone, his wife went looking for him and when she couldn't find him, she called 911."

The other woman said, "Somehow he was trapped by the rocks under water until the tide subsided. That's when they spotted him."

"How sad," Riki said. "When did this happen?"

The first woman said, "It was last night. From what I overheard the lifeguards saying, the man was in the habit of walking his dog when he couldn't sleep."

Behind her, Riki overheard two men talking. One said, "I saw a woman leave the parking lot around 11:00 last night. She sang Maxwell's Silver Hammer as she skipped away."

"Wait a minute," the other man said. "You mean, just like the woman you saw the other night behind those buildings?"

"Yeah, it looked like the same woman. She behaved the same way and had the same build. Her hair was different though. Instead of a wild mane, a shiny clasp held it at the back of her neck. It glittered in the lamplight."

"She may have pushed the man off the cliff thinking she was getting rid of the witness to her crime."

"You mean, she thought she pushed me off the cliff?"

"Yeah, I think the wrong dog walker got whacked."

"In that case, let's get out of here."

Riki turned around, but the two men had their backs to her, one of whom accompanied by a brown dog on a leash.

Riki bit her lip and turned away as the stretcher wheeled up the slope. She headed back to the gallery, but when she reached The Bike Guy, Mark opened the door. "Hi, Riki, come in for a minute."

"Sure, I'd love to." Bonnie and Sam were already inside. "Hi, guys!"

Mark said, "We were talking about what to do for dinner tonight. Would you care to join us? We're going to The California Pizza Kitchen across the highway."

"I'd love to."

"Great, we'll just walk over," Sam said. "Can you two meet us here around 7:00?"

Riki nodded first at Bonnie who nodded back, and then at the men. "Okay, it sounds good. See you then."

On the way back to their shops, they stopped for a frozen yogurt.

Riki stirred chocolate chips into her cherry yogurt. "Did you hear about the old guy who fell off the cliff at Fletcher's Cove last night?"

"No. What happened?"

"He slipped off while walking his dog last night. They were bringing his body up when I was there just now."

"Wow. That's two deaths since we've been here."

"It's creepy, isn't it?"

"Yeah, two people are dead, but the good news is you're not being stalked anymore, at least for now."

"You're right, nothing has happened since The Rolling Stones concert."

"He must have freaked when he saw the cop sitting in the seat meant for you."

"Yeah, I bet he realized it was going nowhere fast, so he dropped the whole stalking thing."

"I'm not sure stalkers just stop."

"What do you mean?"

"I don't know, but from what I've read, stalkers don't give up."

"But you just said the stalking had stopped."

"I said that it stopped for now, not that it was the end. You must still be on guard."

****

At the traffic light, the friends crossed Highway 101, but as they walked toward the restaurant, Riki happened to glance back and there was Nance waiting at the light. When they reached the restaurant's door, Riki looked back again; Nance had crossed the highway and sauntered towards them. Seated next to a wall of windows, Riki kept an eye on the sidewalk and watched Nance walk by three times.

Bonnie nudged her under the table. "These pizzas look amazing, don't they, Riki?"

Riki turned away from the window. "Yes, they look great." She put a slice on her plate, started to eat, and didn't look out the window again.

After dinner, Mark said, "Why don't we go to The Lavender Moon Lounge on the other side of the plaza for a drink?"

"Sounds great, how about you ladies?"

"I'd love to," Bonnie said.

"Me, too, I've wanted to go to The Lavender Moon Lounge for a month."

"Well, tonight's your lucky night, Riki. Let's go."

****

"Riki, Bonnie?"

"Todd Cummings?"

"Hey, how are you guys?"

"Is it really you?"

Bonnie said, "Oh, my God! We haven't seen you since high school. How's life?"

"I'm hanging in there."

Riki said, "These are our friends Mark and Sam."

"It's a pleasure, what can I get you to drink?"

The women ordered white wine coolers, and the men ordered beers.

Todd set their drinks in front of them. "It's been a long time. What's new?"

"We moved to Solana Beach about a month ago."

"Hey, that's cool. You'll love living here."

"Yeah, and we have shops on South Cedros Avenue now. I have an art gallery and Bonnie has a bookstore."

"No shit? So, you are business owners in Solana Beach. That is way cool. I am impressed."

Bonnie said, "Well, are you married? Do you have any kids?"

"I'm divorced with no kids."

Riki sipped her drink. "I'm so sorry, what happened?"

"It's a long story. I don't want to bore you."

"Do you remember Nancy Thomason?" Riki asked. "She also has a business on South Cedros Avenue."

"Oh, man." Todd ran his hand through his hair.

Riki said, "What?"

"Is that right? She has a business here, too?"

They all nodded.

"Look, I don't want her to know I work here. She is nothing but trouble."

A young woman hurried behind the bar. "Sorry I'm late, Todd. My car stalled at the intersection and it took forever get it started."

"No worries." He turned to Riki. "My bartender got here so I can take a break now. Let's go over to a booth where we can talk."

"Great idea," Riki said, "you guys coming?"

"No, I'll stay here and watch the game."

"Same here."

"Bonnie?"

"Um, no thanks, I'll stay here with the men."

"So tell me," Todd said when they were seated, "how did Nancy get a business started here in Solana Beach?"

"Well, she came by my gallery one day and said she was an event planner and offered to plan my grand opening, which was last night, by the way."

"Oh yeah, I heard about that. My boss attended it. He said it was a great party with great art." He paused. "That was the grand opening of your gallery?"

"Yes, and she did a good job, too."

"Wow, and Nancy organized it? That's amazing, I never knew her to organize anything." He rubbed his chin. "But, I'm glad she's found a niche for herself."

"She needed an office, and there was one for rent next door to The Belly Up, so she rented it. She lives in it, too."

"Oh, that is just great." Todd frowned. "Now I'm bound to run into her."

"Why? What happened between you two?"

"More than you want to know. It's just that she is so evil, I don't want to see her again."

"I thought you guys planned to get married after high school. Not so?"

"We were just dating, and I never asked her to marry me no matter what her warped brain thinks. She assumed that I would marry her if she planned a wedding. It was her way of manipulating me, but when I found out what she did at UCLA, I didn't want to have anything more to do with her."

"UCLA?" Riki leaned back. "She never mentioned going to college." Riki sipped her drink. "What happened?"

"She got kicked out when she got busted for plagiarizing her roommate's assignments."

"Oh, my God," Riki said, "no wonder she never mentioned it."

"I am sure she isn't proud of it."

"How did she manage to steal her roommate's assignments?"

"She lived in the dorms and had a roommate who was taking the same course from the same professor, but at a different time, so even though they weren't in the same class, their assignments were the same. Somehow, Nancy found out that the professor didn't read the assignments himself, but used readers who graded the papers, and he used different readers for each class. She figured she could turn in her roommate's papers without the professor ever knowing and ace the class. So when her roommate wasn't around, Nancy would sneak into her computer and copy the finished assignment on a flash drive. Then, she'd rewrite it a little, and turn it in for a better grade than she could have gotten on her own."

"So she stole her roommate's assignments and turned them in?"

"Yeah, and it would have worked, but she ran into trouble when the reader for her class was in a car accident and the reader for her roommate's class took over her class. Nancy was unaware of the change and the fraud fell apart when the new reader noticed how similar Nancy's papers were to her roommate's and took it to the professor. The professor determined the original was by her roommate, but rather than come clean, Nancy denied it. That pissed off the professor, so he turned her in to the Dean of Students who didn't believe her either and expelled her sorry ass."

Holy shit, she was expelled from UCLA. That is huge. I mean, I don't know anyone else who has been expelled from anywhere until now. Wow, wow, wow, wow."

"Yeah, she tried to make it sound as if it didn't matter to her one way or the other, but I knew it cut her to the core because she had always planned on getting a college degree."

"I never imagined she would do something like that. I mean, she's weird and I knew she snooped in high school, but I didn't figure was she a thief."

"If only snooping and stealing were the worst of it."

"What do you mean?"

"I mean, she's vindictive and vengeful."

"Like what did she do?"

"Well, the day they expelled her, Nancy wanted to get even, which is a normal reaction for her. She wrote an anonymous letter saying she witnessed the Dean of Students going into a public restroom with a bunch of little boys."

"You mean she made it sound like the Dean was a pervert? She made it up?"

"Yeah, she anonymously sent the letter to the president of UCLA and to each department head. She even sent it to the police, the newspapers, and the local TV stations."

"That's horrible. She tried to destroy the man's reputation?"

"Yeah, that was her intention."

"But, how could she lie about the Dean of Students?"

"I asked her the same thing when she told me about it. She said it didn't matter if it were true or not. No one could prove she sent the letters and even though it was all a lie, it would still kill the Dean's career, which was what she wanted."

"Did it, kill the Dean's career, I mean?"

"I don't know. I never heard. Once Nancy told me what she had done, I stopped seeing her."

"Well, I guess that explains why she didn't apply to any other universities."

"Oh, yeah, no college would accept her except those online degree mills."

"Wow, she was really out for revenge, wasn't she?"

"But, that's not all she did."

"What, there's more?"

"Yeah, when the shit hit the fan and her roommate found out what she had been doing, she kicked Nancy out of their room. So, as long as she was writing bogus letters, she wrote one to her roommate's boyfriend claiming her roommate had screwed every guy on the football team and had STDs five times. She dropped off the letter at the boyfriend's dorm and left campus. That was how her college career ended."

"It also ended your relationship with her?"

"Yeah, that's what happened." He bent his head over his folded hands.

"And then you married someone else?"

He looked up. "Yes, after we split up I met Krissy, a very sweet Japanese woman. We were happy." He looked down at his hands again. "But it wasn't long before Nancy ruined it. She's responsible for the breakup of my marriage."

"Oh, no, what did she do?"

"Well, for starters she came to my wedding dressed in black."

"Don't tell me you invited her to your wedding."

"Believe me, she was the last person I wanted at my wedding. She showed up uninvited wearing black as if she was going to a funeral." He rubbed his neck. "The wedding was at Kate Sessions Park on the way to Mt. Soledad. I don't know how she even knew about it, but she showed up in black and stood next to some trees in the distance. People told me later that she cried through the whole thing."

"Did she continue to harass you after you got married?"

"Oh yeah," he said, "big time! She sent cards and letters to our house as if she and I were having an affair. I suppose she hoped Krissy would see them, but I always got rid of them as soon as I got them. When Krissy got a job at Kyocera, Nancy got a job in the same department and they became friends."

"Kyocera, isn't that a manufacturer?"

"That's right. Krissy worked as an assembler and Nancy somehow got a position on the line right next to her."

"Why would she do something like that?"

"Nancy did it so she could tell Krissy lies all day. She pretended to be having an affair with a man who managed a bar and had a dumb Japanese wife."

"You mean, she told your wife she was having an affair with you?"

"That's right, in a round-about way, she did. She used her middle name at work so when Krissy talked about Lynn, I didn't know she was really talking about Nancy."

"Incredible. So she changed her name again. She goes by Nance now instead of Nancy."

"No shit? It is the same old, same old. Some people never change." He paused and shook his head. "Anyway, Nancy didn't tell Krissy my name until later, but she dropped enough hints about me and my job for Krissy to get suspicious. But, on the day Nancy was due to leave on vacation, she dropped my name."

"You have got to be kidding."

"No, that Friday afternoon Nancy told Krissy she was taking three weeks off so she could spend all day with her boyfriend Todd while his oblivious Japanese wife was at work. Nancy filled her head with so much erroneous information it seemed plausible. All the pieces seemed to fit together as Nancy wanted. Krissy wouldn't believe me when I told her it wasn't true, so she left me."

"What happened when Nancy went back to work after her vacation?"

"That's the funny thing. She never went back. She got revenge, caused a great deal of pain, and destroyed my marriage, then disappeared."

"Has she stopped bothering you?"

"Yeah, but I'd appreciate it if you didn't tell her you saw me here."

"I won't say a word." Riki sipped her drink. "Thanks for telling me, Todd."

CHAPTER 14

MR. ADAMS ARRIVED early Monday morning with his crew, and went to work. Riki stood back, watched, and then moved into the studio. She lost track of the time and didn't realize it was almost 4:00 until Mr. Adams came to the studio door.

"We loaded the paintings onto our truck scheduled for delivery tomorrow morning." He handed her a file folder. "These are the documents associated with the sales. I am sure you will find them in order. So, if there is nothing else, we'll be off now."

Riki held the folder to her chest. "Thank you for selling so many paintings. And, thanks for taking care of the details. I appreciate everything you've done."

"It is my pleasure, Ms. Hollis. Please call me again if you should have a need for my services."

"Yes, I will. Good bye."

After Mr. Adams and his crew left, Riki put her 'closed until sometime tomorrow' sign in the door and dashed down to The Cubbyhole Bookstore. Devoid of customers, Bonnie sat in a corner reading.

"Hey, Girlfriend, I want to celebrate! Mr. Adams took off with the paintings. I'm a real artist now. And, I'm rich." Riki grabbed Bonnie's hand and pulled her to her feet. "Come on. Let's walk to Which Wich for sandwiches, my treat."

"Ouch, okay! You don't have to twist my arm."

They walked down to The Belly Up and Sam came out of the bakery across the street. He called to them, "Hi, Ladies, where are you off to?"

"We're going to Which Wich, would you like to come? It's my treat."

"Sure! I'd love to." Sam locked the door, and glanced across the street at Nance's window before joining them on the sidewalk. "Hey, I sense Nance is spying on us."

Bonnie took his hand. "So, what else is new? She always was a spy and a snoop. Why do you think no one likes her?"

"Is that right?" Sam looked from Bonnie to Riki. "No one likes her?"

"She has no friends, does she?" Bonnie looked at Riki. "Well, do you like her?"

"Um, well, not very much."

"Do you like her, Sam?"

"I don't know her like you two do, but she doesn't seem so bad."

"Just wait until you get to know her better," Bonnie said, "you won't like her, either. No one does."

They continued walking down the street and when they got to The Bike Guy, Mark came out. "Hey, guys. Where are you going?"

"We're off to Which Wich. I am celebrating the success of my grand opening. I'm buying. Why don't you join us?"

"It's about time to close up, anyway. Okay, I will. Thanks."

****

"Would you like to take them with you?"

"No, please deliver them to Sam at Bread Temptations at 448 South Cedros Avenue."

"Okay."

"Can you deliver them now?"

"Not a problem."

"Perfect." She printed on the card: TO MY FAVORITE BAKER, LOVE FROM YOUR #1 FAN.

****

"Good morning, Mary." Nance sniffed the bouquet. "What beautiful roses! What's the occasion?"

"No occasion. Someone sent them to Sam to tell him she likes his bread."

"That is so nice of someone."

"Yeah, and we have no clue who sent them, just someone who is his number one fan."

"That's interesting."

"It's weird she didn't sign her name. I mean, why the big mystery?"

"Maybe she's shy."

"Yeah, it is possible she's shy, or perhaps she's just sly."

Nance cleared her throat. "I don't understand what you're talking about, but I think it's nice someone sent him flowers to praise his bread. Sam's my favorite baker, too."

"Interesting you should say that."

Nance took her coffee to her usual table where she would see Sam should he walk into the kitchen, but he didn't. When the coffee went cold, she tossed it in the trash and left.

Her car was stifling hot, so she twisted her hair into a knot at the back of her neck. She turned on the air conditioner, put her car in gear, drove to Sweet Dreams in Del Mar, and ordered a two-pound box of chocolate creams.

The clerk wrote up the order. "What is your name, please?"

"My name is Lynn, but I want it to be anonymous. It's an inside joke."

"Sure, don't worry."

She wrote on the card, SWEETS FOR THE SWEETEST MAN IN SOLANA BEACH. LOVE FROM YOUR #1 FAN. "I want them delivered to Sam at Bread Temptations in Solana Beach."

****

"Who sent this?"

"She said her name was Lynn, but she wanted to remain nameless because it is an inside joke, so don't tell Sam, okay?"

"What did she look like?"

"She was sort of plain looking, actually."

"What was she wearing?"

"I don't remember."

"What did her hair look like?"

"I don't know, it was ordinary I guess."

Mary handed Sam the package. "This came for you."

"I don't believe it, another delivery?" Sam lifted the package. "What the hell is this, anyway?"

"It came from Sweet Dreams in Del Mar. I asked the delivery woman if she knew who sent it and she said the woman's name was Lynn. I bet Lynn is your secret admirer and your number one fan."

"Oh, jeez, you think?"

"Well, open it. Maybe there's a card inside."

Sam tore off the paper and read the note. "You're right, Mary. It's from my number one fan, but who is Lynn? I don't know anyone named Lynn."

"Sam, this is getting weird."

"It sure is." Sam sighed. "And I don't like it. How do I make it stop?"

****

"Riki? Riki Hollis? Is that you?"

She looked up from her shopping cart at two women smiling at her.

"You don't remember us, do you? We graduated from Kearny High School in 2011."

Riki studied their faces for half a minute. "Yes, I remember you two. Charlene and Debbie, right?"

"Yes! You do remember us." Debbie laughed and hugged her. "How's it going?"

Charlene hugged her, too. "Are you married? Have any kids?"

"No, no husband and no kids, but I just graduated from State."

"Wow, good for you."

"Thanks."

"Yes, that is a great accomplishment."

"And, after graduation I opened an art gallery studio in Solana Beach. It is in the center of the Cedros Avenue Design District."

"That is so cool. What's it called?"

"It's called The Erika Hollis Gallery, what else?"

"That's a great name, Riki." Debbie said, "It is very creative."

"Thanks, I thought so, too."

Charlene said, "We must come by sometime to see it."

"Yes, you must come by. Please do."

"Riki, you didn't recognize us at first," Debbie said. "Do we look that much different?"

"No, in fact, you guys look the same. I am surprised that's all, especially since I ran into Todd Cummings the other night. Do you remember him?"

"Sure," Charlene said, "he used to go with Nancy Thomason."

"Right, you'd never guess, but she has a business down the street from mine."

"Oh, that is too bad." Debbie said, "I wouldn't want her anywhere near me."

"That's what Todd said, too. He said she stalked him and broke up his marriage."

"What a shame, poor Todd."

"I feel sorry for him," Debbie said. "She does despicable things."

"What did she do to you guys?"

"She stalked us all over Europe, and ruined our trip."

"She stalked you in Europe?"

Debbie crossed her arms. "Yeah, the three of us were going together until we caught her snooping through our backpacks the night before we left, so we told her she couldn't go with us."

"But she did, in a way."

"What do you mean?"

"She was on all of our flights, but she changed her seats so we didn't have to sit with her. That was nice, but after we got there, she would take the same trains and stay in the same hotels as we did and followed us everywhere like on tours and in museums."

"She would even sit with us in restaurants uninvited. Can you imagine the gall?"

"Wow, seriously, that took real nerve, didn't it?"

"It didn't seem to bother her as much as it bothered us." Charlene sighed. "She was a real pain in the ass. We wanted to ditch her, so at first we just ignored her. We even walked out of restaurants when she sat with us. Several times, we told her to go away, but she wouldn't. When we couldn't take it anymore, we had a screaming fight with her at a train depot in France."

"Yeah, it was an ugly, public scene. People stood and stared. It was so embarrassing. We couldn't help but lose it."

"Yeah, it was bad."

"We didn't want it to get to that point," Debbie said, "but she pushed our tolerance to the breaking point. It was the last few days of our trip and we wanted to enjoy them without her bothering us incessantly, but she would not stop."

"She wanted to be friends again. Can you imagine being friends with someone who would do something like that? I remember saying to her, or rather screaming at her, that she wasn't the type of person I wanted to know let alone have as a friend and to leave us alone. She said that she would never leave us alone."

"And she didn't. When we got back, she broke into our apartments and left gifts and notes and moved things around. Then, the notes became threatening."

"Threatening, how?"

Charlene said, "Well, the notes said things like: You'll be sorry you treated me this way, and Driving can be dangerous to your health. We had to have our cars inspected before we could drive them again."

"Had they been tampered with?"

"No, she was just trying to freak us out, and it worked."

"We both had to get restraining orders against her."

"So did that end it?"

"Oh no, it never ends with that one!"

"She still calls me at work sometimes and hangs up."

"Yeah, she does that to me too, but I haven't had one of those calls in a while. Have you, Charlene?"

"No, as I remember the last one I had was a month or two ago. Could she have forgotten about us?"

"We could only be so lucky." Debbie sighed. "She's a psychopath." She looked at Riki. "Has she acted crazy in Solana Beach, yet?"

"Oh, yeah," Riki nodded, "she is being herself as you would expect."

CHAPTER 15

"HI, MARY," RIKI said, "what pretty flowers. Where did they come from?"

"Sam's number one fan sent them."

"Who sent them?"

"Sam's number one fan, at least, that's what she calls herself. She didn't reveal her true identity."

"What do you mean? These were sent anonymously?"

"Yeah, Sam has no clue who sent them." Mary took a deep breath. "And yesterday, Sam received another delivery. This time from Sweet Dreams in Del Mar. His number one fan sent him a two pound box of chocolate creams."

"How weird is that?"

"I'll say it's weird." Mary whispered, "And, I think I know who it is, too."

"You do, who?"

"The woman over there who lives in her office; she has a crush on Sam and this is her way of getting his attention."

"You mean Nance Thomason, the event planner? You suspect she's behind the flowers and the candy?"

"Yes, I do. And, I'll tell you something else, she makes my skin crawl."

"But, if she wants to get Sam's attention by sending him gifts, why doesn't she tell him who they're from? Why keep it a secret?"

"I asked her the same thing."

"So, what did she say?"

"She said maybe the woman was shy."

"You think she meant herself?"

"Probably, yeah, I think so. And, she also said Sam was her favorite baker, too."

"So?"

"So, that's what the note with the flowers said, but she couldn't have known that unless she wrote it herself because I told her the flowers came from someone who said she was Sam's number one fan, not that he was her favorite baker."

As they stood at the counter, Nance drove up and parked across the street. They watched as she gathered her things.

"But, it isn't her. The candy delivery person said it was from someone named Lynn."

"Did you say Lynn?" Nance had gotten out of her car and stood staring back at them.

"Yeah, but Sam doesn't know anyone named Lynn." Mary looked at Riki. "But you do, don't you?"

Riki nodded at Nance. "Yeah, her, it's her middle name."

"Are you kidding?"

Riki shook her head. "No, she even went by Lynn in high school for a year."

Mary looked straight at Nance. "Seriously, she is Lynn? That makes sense, doesn't it? Why am I not surprised?"

Nance turned and stomped into her building.

"Holy, shit! Did you see that? She read my lips, didn't she?"

"Possibly, well, yes, probably."

"That woman is insane." Mary rubbed her arms. "She gives me the heebie-jeebies."

"Yeah, she creeps me out, too. Be careful, okay?"

* * * * * * * * * *

"Mary, look at this." Sam handed her the note.

It said, I WISH YOU WOULD NOTICE ME. I LOVE YOU, YOUR #1 FAN.

"Sam, this is getting weirder and weirder."

"I have an idea how to tell whoever it is to stop." Sam went into his office and came back with a sign. It said, No NUTS and No FRUITCAKES, please.

"This sign will make her stop sending you stuff?"

"Yeah, I think the whacko will stop now. She knows she's a nut and a fruitcake. Now I'm telling her to stop sending me crap like this."

"I guess it's worth a try." Mary taped the sign in the window and glanced up at Nance before she turned away.

"She'll get the message," Sam said, "you'll see."

****

The sign in the window pissed her off, but when Mary had the nerve to look at her, it sent her into a fury. That afternoon when Mary got off work, Nance followed her to The Tropicana Trailer Park in Leucadia. Mary parked on the quiet tree lined street and walked in. Nance parked down the street and waited.

It was just turning light when Mary walked out. Nance yawned and started her car, put it in gear, and stomped on the accelerator.

Mary looked up as the car sped toward her. She froze. She didn't even scream. Seconds later, Nance smashed into her at high speed and propelled her into the trunk of a big tree. Her bones broke. Her heart stopped. She bounced off the tree. Nance squealed to a stop, backed up, and idled while she stared at the lifeless body lying in the dirt. There was no sign of movement, not even a twitch.

Nance left singing Maxwell's Silver Hammer as she drove to a self-serve car wash. Remarkably, her car suffered no damage, not so much as a dent. She turned her clean car in the direction of Solana Beach and drove back to South Cedros Avenue singing the song that expressed her so well, the song that kept repeating itself in her head, the song that made her feel like a success.

****

"Hi, Sam, why are you on counter duty?"

"Mary didn't show this morning and when I call her cell, she doesn't answer."

She cleared her throat. "Well, I hope everything's okay." She left with her coffee, crossed the street, and skipped upstairs to her office. She dropped her purse on the desk, paused at the window, drank her coffee, gazed at the bakery, and laughed.

Intense fatigue overwhelmed her when she finished the coffee. She craved rest. She closed the blinds and stripped off her clothes. She tossed the cushions off the couch, pulled the bed out in one quick snap, flopped down, and instantly fell into a deep sleep.

Voices from the street below awoke her. She got out of bed and peeked through the mini-blinds at a group of mourners gathered on the sidewalk in front of Bread Temptations. Sam was actually crying.

She threw on a tee shirt and shorts, and hummed the catchy tune of her favorite song as she skipped downstairs. But before she reached the group, she stopped humming.

"Nance, have you heard what happened to Mary? It is so horrible!"

Nance coughed. "No, what happened?"

Riki said, "She's dead."

Nance's hand flew to her mouth. "What?"

"She was killed this morning. Someone hit her and drove away!" Riki blinked away tears. "Sheriff's deputies were here talking to Sam a while ago."

"Did anyone see anything?"

"No, it was so early in the morning, no one was up. Some people heard the sound of the car when it hit her, but no one saw anything."

"What did they hear?"

"Apparently, some crazy driver going really fast hit her, screeched to a stop, backed up, and idled for a moment, and then kept going at normal speed."

Bonnie joined them. "People are speculating that the driver stopped to see if Mary was dead before driving away. That would make it deliberate."

"Yeah, it sure sounds like it was on purpose."

Bonnie nodded. "But why would anyone want to kill Mary?"

"It's senseless." Riki wiped a tear away from her cheek.

"How's Sam taking it?" Nance asked.

"Hard," Bonnie said. "Mary worked for him for five years. They were good friends."

"What a shame. He must feel awful. Poor, Sam. Was Mary married?"

"No, she lived alone in a little trailer park in Leucadia." Bonnie blew her nose. "As far as I know, she had no family. I think her closest friend was Sam."

****

Nance returned to her room, and sat in the dark. She was so tired she was dizzy. She slept again and felt better, and opened the blinds. The group outside Bread Temptations had dispersed, but in its place was a shrine to Mary. People dropped off flowers, stuffed animals, signs, and cards.

Nance decided that she should contribute something to the shrine and walked down to The Cubbyhole Bookstore. There were no customers.

"I know, it's just horrible," Bonnie said into her phone. "I can't believe she's dead." After a pause, "I hate to complain, but it puts me in a very bad position. Mary helped me on Friday nights with the pajama parties. With so many kids coming, I need another adult. Now I can't find anyone to help me." Pause. "No, Riki has something scheduled late Friday afternoon and won't be back in time." Pause. "I know, I feel awful about it, but what am I going to do? There are too many kids and not enough adults." Pause. "Yeah, most of the kids are dropped off here and their parents pick them up later."

There was another pause. "I guess I'll have to cancel the party this week, but it will be a big disappointment for Toni Wood. For weeks, she has been looking forward to her chance at being the storyteller. You see, the authors sell a lot of books at the kiddie parties and Toni has been counting on this opportunity to get her books into the hands of children and to make some money."

Bonnie looked up and saw Nance. "Listen, I have to go now. Talk to you later, bye."

Nance perused a display of tiny stuffed animals.

"Hi, Nance."

"Hi. Isn't a shame about Mary?"

"Yes, it is devastating."

"I saw a shrine outside the bakery and I want to get something to add. Would you happen to know if Mary had a favorite animal?"

"Well, I think she liked cats."

Nance found a stuffed yellow cat. "This is sweet." She shook her head. "Just like Mary. I'll take it."

Bonnie took it to the register and rang it up. "This is so thoughtful of you, Nance."

"Thanks. Ah, did I hear you say you needed someone to help you on Friday night? What was it that Mary did?"

"She mainly supervised the snacks table. You know, she poured the punch and set out a plate of cookies and cupcakes. She also kept the kids from going wild during the break. That was about it. It doesn't sound like much, but she was a huge help."

"I could help you this Friday night. I'm not doing anything anyway."

"Really, you would do that, Nance? I'll pay you what I paid Mary."

"No, it's my pleasure. You don't need to pay me."

"That's nice of you, thanks."

"Oh, you are most welcome. What time should I be here?"

"Toni will be here around 6:45 and will start the story at 7:00. It would be great if you could be here at 6:30 to set the table with the refreshments and arrange the little chairs around the story rug."

"Okay, see you Friday at 6:30."

"Thanks again, Nance."

Nance walked out with the little stuffed cat, which she threw onto Mary's shrine.

CHAPTER 16

BY 7:15, THE story circle was full of children entranced by Toni Wood's magical mystery story, all except one restless little boy who wandered around the bookstore unnoticed.

Bored, Nance drifted away from the refreshment table and snuck past the workroom where Bonnie chatted with another woman, and crept up the stairs. Neither the women, nor Nance, were aware of the little boy tiptoeing behind her.

She made it to the landing eager to get inside Bonnie's apartment when shuffling feet startled her. She spun around. The little boy stood behind her. His long golden curls glowed around his head like a halo.

Nance bent over. "Well, hello. Who are you?"

"You're not supposed to be up here. My mom told me no one could come up here. That means everyone, even you." He pointed at her. "You better leave right now."

Nance edged closer to the boy. "So, what are you doing up here? You're not supposed to be up here, either."

He jabbed his finger at her. "You have to go downstairs."

"But, I am not ready to go downstairs." Nance inched closer.

"You better go down, or I'm telling my mom you're bad."

"Nance took another step. "I'm not the bad one, you are. You are in trouble, not I."

"No, I am not." He backed up closer to the railing. "You're a bad lady."

Nance took another step closer. "What's your name?"

"My name is Billy." He crossed his arms and stared at her.

She inched closer until she was within arm's reach of him. "My name is Nance. Don't worry. I won't tell on you."

"You better go downstairs now."

"I will later."

"But, you're supposed to go now. You're not allowed up here." Billy stepped backwards and pressed against the balusters.

Nance stepped closer, bent down to Billy's level, and gripped the balusters on either side. "I have you trapped. Now what are you going to do?"

"You're bad. I'm telling on you." He tried to make a break, but Nance grabbed him, and put her hand over his mouth.

"You're not telling anyone anything, you little snitch."

Billy squirmed as she lifted him onto the banister. She whispered into his ear, "I bet you've always wanted to slide down a banister, right? All brats like you want to slide down banisters."

He thrashed and she tightened her grip. "Stop fighting. This is the best ride you've ever had in your short worthless life." Billy struggled and almost broke free.

"Hey! Don't do that!" She shook him. "You'll fall off!" She whispered, "Like this," and gave him a shove.

Billy shrieked as he plummeted to the floor.

Nance stifled the urge to laugh. Instead, she screamed, "Oh, no, no, no!" and ran down the stairs. When she reached the women already gathered around the boy's body, she covered her mouth with both hands and smiled.

Bonnie, the other woman, and Toni Wood all looked at her when she joined them. "What the hell happened?" Bonnie demanded.

She cleared her throat. "I, ah, I was setting the table, and I saw him sneak up the stairs."

"So, what did you do?"

She shrugged her right shoulder. "I had a feeling he wanted to slide down the banister like all kids, so I followed him." She cleared her throat again.

"What happened when you got there?"

"I was too late. He was already on the banister and when he saw me coming he lost his balance and slipped off."

Toni Wood bent over Billy's lifeless body and felt for a pulse. Next, she checked his heart and lungs. "He's not breathing and his heart stopped."

"Oh no," Bonnie gasped, "he can't be dead. Please say he's not dead."

"I'm sorry, but he's gone."

"I couldn't get to him sooner." Nance shrugged her right shoulder again. "I tried."

"I'm sure you did your best." Bonnie led her to a chair. "Sit here while I call the police." Bonnie pulled her cell phone out of her pocket and punched in 911.

"What is your emergency?" the dispatcher asked.

Bonnie walked back to the women and the body. "I need help right away. A little boy fell off my second floor banister. He's not breathing and we can't find a pulse."

Nance pressed her lips together as she listened to the rest of Bonnie's conversation. Without moving a muscle, she stared into space as if in shock.

The children went outside with the adults to wait for their parents to pick them up. Nance didn't move, but stayed in her chair near Billy's body. When Sheriff's deputies and paramedics filled the bookstore, no one thought it was strange that this unrelated woman sat alone with the dead little boy. They bagged the body and wheeled it away as Nance watched out of the corner of her eye.

A woman who looked familiar dressed in a plain navy blue pantsuit walked up to a man who Nance assumed was the medical examiner. She overheard the woman say, "Dr. Ruffner, was this an accidental fall?"

"I believe so, but I have to perform an autopsy before I will be certain." Nance stifled a smile as adrenaline surged through her body.

* * * * * * * * * *

Detective Barb Stanton of the San Diego County Sheriff's North Coastal Station stood at the edge of the activity in the bookstore, surveyed the scene, and noticed Bonnie pacing wringing her hands.

The detective walked up to her. "Excuse me, Ms. Harrison, do you remember me?"

"Yes, I think so."

"I'm Detective Barb Stanton from the Encinitas Sheriff's Station."

"Of course, I remember now, we met when Riki was being stalked."

"Yes, that's right. I know you're upset about what happened tonight, but can we talk?"

"Of course, let's go up to my apartment."

When they reached the landing, Detective Stanton looked over the banister to the floor below where a puddle of blood remained. "So this is where Billy started his slide?"

"Yeah, I guess so. I wasn't here. Nance Thomason said she saw him come up here and followed him in case he planned to try sliding down the banister." Bonnie crossed her arms. "She was right, unfortunately. He went for it and fell off."

Bonnie led Detective Stanton into her living room.

"Tell me what happened."

"Okay, well I was in the workroom downstairs talking to Patty, one of the kid's mothers, when Nance yelled something like, 'No, you'll fall off.' And, Billy screamed and fell to the floor."

"Did Ms. Thomason say anything else?"

"Oh, yes. After he fell, she screamed, 'Oh, no, no.'"

"Then what happened?"

"Patty and I ran out and found little Billy on the floor. Next, Toni Wood ran up, and then Nance." Bonnie put her head in her hands.

"Go on."

"Toni felt for a pulse and couldn't find one and he wasn't breathing."

"What happened next?"

"I called 911. Then Toni, Patty, and I took the kids outside and I called their parents to come get them." She folded her hands in her lap and lowered her head.

"How often do kids wander up here and slide the down the banister?"

Bonnie raised her head. "As far as I know, it has never happened."

"How often does Ms. Thomason help out on Friday nights?"

"This was her first and only time."

"Okay, Ms. Harrison. I think I have enough for now. If I have more questions, I have your number."

"Yes, call me anytime."

"Thanks. Now I need to talk to Ms. Thomason." They descended the stairs and approached her where she still sat in the same chair.

"Nance," Bonnie said, "can you hear me?"

She didn't move. Bonnie touched her shoulder. "Nance, there is a Sheriff's detective here who would like to speak with you. She wants you to tell her what happened to Billy."

Nance blinked and looked at Bonnie and then at Detective Stanton. "I tried to stop him, but he let go."

"Nance Thomason, I am Detective Barb Stanton from the Encinitas Sheriff's Station. Please tell me what happened tonight."

Nance cleared her throat and repeated the same story she told the women. "He saw me coming, let go, and fell." She shrugged her right shoulder.

"Well, okay, that's enough for now. I may want to talk to you again in a few days, okay?"

Nance covered her mouth and nodded. The detective walked away. As familiar elation surged through her, she stood and left The Cubbyhole Bookstore.

****

Riki and Sam waited at Bread Temptations for the deputies to leave and watched Nance leave the bookstore and breeze down the street past her office.

"Wow," Riki said, "that's kind of strange, don't you think? Where do you think she's going?"

"Yeah, that is weird. Why would she walk right by her place?"

"Did you notice how she was walking? Not slow and sad like you'd expect."

"No, you're right. She had a spring in her step like something great had just happened instead of something tragic."

"Let's follow her and see where she's going, okay?"

"Now you're talking."

They sprang out the door, jogged to Lomas Santa Fe, turned the corner, and stopped. Nance waited at the intersection at Highway 101 for the light to change. They slipped into the shadows behind her and heard her singing Maxwell's Silver Hammer. When the light turned green, she crossed the highway and headed toward the plaza.

"I think I better warn Todd just in case The Lavender Moon Lounge is where she's going." Riki took out her phone.

"Good idea, but you'd better make it quick because she's almost there."

Riki speed dialed the lounge. "The Lavender Moon Lounge, how can I help you?"

"I need to speak to Todd Cummings right away, it's an emergency." Nance was minutes away from the bar.

"This is Todd, who's this?"

"Hi, Todd, this is Riki. It looks like Nance is on her way to your bar right now. I wanted to warn you."

"How do you know she's coming here?"

"I don't, but I'm walking behind her, and she is heading your way. In fact, she's crossing the parking lot right now. She'll be opening your door within minutes."

"Thanks, Riki. I'll handle it." He hung up before she could tell him about the accident at the bookstore.

****

"Let's talk in my apartment," Bonnie said.

They sat on the couch and Bonnie handed them each a cup of herbal tea. She told them moment by moment what happened to poor little Billy. "It was horrible to call the parents to come get their kids." She covered her eyes. "I had to tell them what happened." She looked at them. "I couldn't call Billy's mom though. I left that for the deputies."

"How awful for you, it must have been hard." Riki patted Bonnie's hand.

"So," Sam leaned forward, "what do the deputies think happened?"

"They think Billy accidentally fell off the banister when he tried to slide down." She put her hands over her ears. "I can still hear him screaming in my head."

"So afterwards Nance just sat there?" Riki asked. "That's weird."

"Yeah, I sat her down in a chair and she seemed to sort of shut out what was going on around her. It was odd. She seemed to be somewhere else, you know?"

"You mean, like she spaced out?"

"Yeah, I had to touch her shoulder to get her attention when Detective Stanton wanted to talk to her."

"What did she say?"

"Not too much, so the detective told her she'd get back to her later."

Sam said, "What do you mean she didn't say much?"

"She zoned out, I guess. And then she left." Bonnie looked at Riki and Sam. "What?"

"She looked upbeat and happy when she breezed past us."

"She sure did, so we followed her! She didn't know we were even there, did she, Sam?"

He shook his head.

"When it looked certain she was going to the lounge, I called Todd to warn him. I hope nothing bad happened when she got there. He didn't want her to know he worked there, but she will now."

"It's strange, after witnessing the accident she was in such shock she couldn't talk, but then recovered enough to bounce over to the bar. She looked as if she was out to have a good time."

"She sure didn't look upset about Billy, that's for sure. She almost skipped there."

Bonnie said, "That is so wicked, I mean, she sits practically comatose for over an hour and then she gets up and dashes off to have a drink? I wonder if her story about Billy sliding off the banister is even true. She's the only one who knows what happened, isn't she?"

* * * * * * * * * *

Todd left the lounge area and stood in the shadows near his office. He watched Nance come in, take a seat at the bar, order a split of champagne, take a sip, and look around.

Their eyes met so he walked over to her. "Hello, Nancy. How are you?"

"Todd!" Nance jumped off the barstool, threw her arms around his neck, and kissed him on the cheek. "How nice it is to see you! What a surprise!"

He grabbed her wrists and pushed her away. "It's a surprise to see you, too."

"I never imagined I'd see you here." Nance reached out to touch his face. "Do you live in the area?"

Todd brushed her hand aside. "No."

She settled back on her barstool. "You work here?"

"Yes, that's right. I'm the manager."

"That's super." She looked into her bubbling drink. "How's Krissy doing these days?"

"I have no clue. We split up a long time ago."

She looked up with a smile. "Is that right?" She nodded her head. "I hope it wasn't anything I did."

"Oh, come on. You don't expect me to believe that, do you?"

"Oh, so it was because of me." Nance sipped her drink.

"Of course, it was because of you."

"I'm sorry. I don't know what came over me, Todd. I was possessed with an uncontrollable desire to hurt you. It was an irresistible impulse." Nance reached out for his hand, but he pulled away. "I just couldn't stop myself. Please forgive me."

Todd said nothing.

"Seriously, Todd, I know it was wrong." Nance sipped her champagne and made eye contact over the rim of her glass. "Can we talk?"

Todd clenched his jaw. "Sure, let's find a booth."

Nance sat across from him and gazed at his face. "I'd like us to be friends again."

"I make no promises." He crossed his arms. "So, what have you been up to?"

"I'm a professional event planner now. I plan fabulous parties, weddings, and conventions." She gave him one of her business cards and told him about her fictitious clients and successful events. "I live in my office on South Cedros Avenue. I have a couch that makes into a bed. It's quite comfortable. If you'd like to come over when you get off work tonight, I'll be waiting."

"I have other plans tonight."

"Oh, okay." Nance finished her drink. "Call me sometime"

She left the lounge and walked home alone.

CHAPTER 17

"YOU'RE QUIET THIS morning, Todd." Craig put the newspaper down. "Is there something on your mind?"

"What?" Todd looked at his roommate.

"You seem preoccupied about something. Care to talk about it?"

"Yeah," Todd ran his hand through his hair, "something totally weird happened last night. One of my old girlfriends came into the lounge." He picked up his mug, but did not drink. "It shocked me to see her again."

"Why were you shocked? Had she gained 100 pounds or grown a beard or something?"

"I wish. No, it was that crazy woman who keeps bothering me, the one who broke up my marriage."

"She's stalking you again?"

"Yeah, could be, hell, I don't know. She seemed surprised to see me, so it may not have been deliberate this time. But now that she knows where I work, she will be a problem again. I just know she is going to ruin my life."

"So how did it go with her last night?"

"She apologized for what she had done to Krissy and me. She said it was just something she couldn't control because it was an irresistible impulse."

"Wait, did she actually say it was an irresistible impulse?"

"Yeah, those were her exact words. Why?"

"Hey, don't you get it? Don't you watch old movies?"

Todd shook his head.

"In the old movie Anatomy of a Murder the man gets away with murder because he said it was an irresistible impulse. It was his excuse for murder because he had an uncontrollable impulse to kill the man, so he got away with it. This chick is doing the same thing to justify breaking up your marriage. She thinks saying it was an irresistible impulse makes it okay to do what she did because it was beyond her control. It is all about her and not what she did to you."

"Yeah, and the bad news is that she has her own business in the Cedros Avenue Design District and is doing quite well."

"Don't tell me she's in the neighborhood now." Craig rubbed his chin. "Todd, that's all you need."

Todd ran his hands over his face. "It's toxic, and it gets worse."

"How does it get worse?"

"She lives in her office."

"No, shit? Only a few blocks away?" Craig poured himself more coffee. "That is way too close. I mean, you are sure to run into her around town."

"I want to avoid her, but how can I?"

"Yeah, even if you don't run into her at CVS or Rubios, she can go to the lounge any time and hang out all she wants."

"She wants to get back together. She asked me over to her place after work. I cannot believe she would think that I would be interested in starting a relationship with her again. She is such a loser. I wish she would just go away and leave me alone."

"I hear you." Craig drank his coffee. "You suppose it pissed her off that you turned her down?"

"She seemed okay when she left. That is, she wasn't screaming or throwing things or anything. But, give her time, you never know."

"She doesn't know where you live, does she?"

"No, and I want it to stay that way, too."

"But with her living and working so close, that is one secret that will be hard to keep."

Todd sighed. "At least I'm off tonight so I won't see her until tomorrow night."

"Well, that buys you some time."

He stared at the horizon. "Maybe something will happen by then."

"Like what?"

"I don't know." Todd rubbed the back of his neck. "It'd be great if she would just move somewhere else." He looked at the view. "Or better yet, what if she landed in jail? If she were locked away, it would be perfect."

"How would she manage that?"

"Hell, anything works for me." He finished his coffee. "I don't want her near me. I don't want her in my life."

"So, what are you going to do? Hide in the apartment until you go to work tomorrow?"

"No, I'll take my chances at the beach. I'm going down to the cove to do a little body surfing."

"I take it you don't expect she'll be there?"

"I hope not. Want to come?"

"I'd like to, but I have to work today. Enjoy."

****

"Hey, you guys. Taking the day off?"

Riki shielded her eyes with her hat. "Todd, hello, how are you?"

"Do you mind if I sit down for a minute?"

"Of course not, have a seat."

He tossed his towel onto the sand, dropped onto it, and crossed his legs. "Why aren't you two working today?"

"Oh, we're here for an hour or two and then we're going back to our shops." Riki adjusted her sunglasses. "After what happened last night, we needed a break."

"Yeah, I am not eager to spend much time in the bookstore today." Bonnie pulled her hair into a ponytail. "I'll have to call someone to come in and clean it. I'm just not up for it."

Riki bent the brim of her hat. "What happened with Nance last night?"

"Well, it was unexpected, that's for sure. Thanks for the forewarning."

"Did you talk to her?"

"I did. I am still plenty pissed at her, so I was not real friendly." He watched an old man throw a frisbee to a kid. "She told me about her new business."

Riki and Bonnie dropped their jaws.

"What's wrong?"

Bonnie said, "Nothing seemed to be bothering her?"

"No, not at all, in fact, she seemed buoyant, which for her is unusual, unless she's done something aberrant."

They both gawked at him. He looked first at Bonnie and then Riki. "She did something aberrant, didn't she?"

"I'd say there is a good chance of that. Last night before she went to your lounge, and I mean right before, like not even two hours before, she was at my bookstore when a little boy fell to his death off the second story banister."

He stared at them. "She never said a thing."

"That is so weird because she was with Billy when he fell. She was the only witness and afterwards, she was so upset she couldn't speak."

He rubbed his chin. "She didn't say a thing about the little boy. Oh, man, I can't believe it. She was quite proud of herself and bragged about how well she's doing with her business, if you can believe that."

"How crazy is she?" Bonnie said.

"She is totally insane." He took his hat off and ran his fingers through his hair. "How else could she act as if nothing had happened?" He put his hat back on. "What kind of a callous person behaves like that?" Todd tweaked the bill of his baseball cap as he gazed at kids jumping waves. "She is a psycho."

"You are so right, she's heartless, and that is a kind of crazy, isn't it?" Bonnie leaned on her elbows. "She seemed upset at the time and I fell for it. What an idiot I am. It was all an act."

Todd said, "Only a psychopath can switch from catatonic to chatty like that."

"You're right," Riki said, "I recall from Psych 101 that psychopaths lack empathy and are narcissistic. That fits her, doesn't it?"

Todd nodded. "Yes, it sure does."

"She's always been like that. In school, she seemed weird and offbeat, but at the same time almost invisible. I mean, I knew her, but I didn't notice her much."

"No one paid attention to her." Bonnie sat up and brushed sand off her hands. "Nance wanted to be different and accepted but instead, she turned people off by being weird and obnoxious."

"Yeah, she would do some real crazy shit. That's why I could never trust her." Todd stood and grabbed his towel. "I am sorry about the little boy, Bonnie. See you later, bye."

"Okay, see ya."

"Bye."

He dragged himself down the beach.

"He looks so depressed."

"Yeah, he was pretty shaken up." Riki watched him walk across the sand, "Hey, look, he's going up the cliff stairs to the condos above. He must live there."

Bonnie shielded her eyes. "Yeah, he lives here in Solana Beach."

"I just hope Nance doesn't find out."

CHAPTER 18

AFTER PAINTING FOR hours, Riki grabbed her purse, and flew out the door. She walked towards Lomas Santa Fe and just as she passed The Belly Up, Nance bounced onto the sidewalk right in front of her.

"Hi, Riki, how are you?"

"Oh, hey, Nance, how's it going?"

"It is going great. Guess who I ran into last night."

"Last night? You mean, after what happened to Billy?"

"Well, I was so upset I needed a drink, so I walked over to The Lavender Moon Lounge."

"Oh, right."

"And, I can't believe it, but I met Todd there."

"No kidding?"

"Yeah, I never expected to see him in Solana Beach, but he works at The Lavender Moon Lounge. Did you know he works there? You've been there, right?"

"Yeah, it's nice."

Nance beamed with pride. "He's the manager." She lowered her voice and leaned closer. "He wants me back again."

"You think so?"

"I know so. I'm going over there for a drink. Want to come with me?"

"Thanks, but I'll pass."

"Okay, whatever, but how about tomorrow night?"

"Tomorrow afternoon is Mary's funeral."

"Oh, yeah, Mary's funeral, so you're going?"

"Yes, aren't you?"

"I hadn't thought about it."

"If you'd like, you can come with us. Mark's taking Bonnie and Sam, and all our beach gear in his SUV. There is room for one more."

"It's at the beach?"

"Yes, at Moonlight Beach, it is casual dress, and we're going to scatter her ashes over the ocean."

"So you're throwing her ashes into the water, huh? Yeah, maybe, okay I will join you. See you then."

Riki walked on to Arturo's in peace and ordered two chicken enchiladas with spicy hot carrots on the side. After she picked up her order, she took it to a picnic table and dived in. When she lifted her head, she noticed Todd getting out of a sexy red sports car in the parking lot. As she munched, he walked up to the order window and placed his order.

He turned around and Riki waved. "Hi, Todd, care to join me?"

"Hi, Riki, how's it going? Did you have a nice day at the beach?" He sat across from her.

"Yes, it was great. I love the beach." She pushed the small container toward him. "Here, have some hot carrots. They are extra spicy tonight."

"Thanks, I love these."

"I bumped into Nance on my way over here. Luckily, she didn't ask to join me, right?"

"No, shit? Did she say anything about me?"

"As a matter of fact, she did. She told me she was happy she saw you last night and she thinks you are interested in her again."

He groaned. "Oh, no, I was afraid of that." He put his head in his hands. "I just moved here and I have a great condo with a great roommate and a job I love. And now she has to come along and spoil it all."

"What do you mean, she'll spoil it?"

"She does it every time. She always finds a way to ruin my life. She is evil and vindictive." He ate a hot carrot. "I want her out of my life."

"I'm sorry she found you."

"I'm going to have to quit my job and move now."

"Maybe she's matured and gotten over being petty." Riki ate a carrot. "She is going to the lounge tonight, and she plans to go tomorrow night, as well."

"That's just great." He ground his teeth. "Thanks for the tip." When his order was ready, they finished their dinner in silence.

Riki ate the last hot carrot, drank the last of her soda, cleared the litter, and stood. "Well, good luck tomorrow night. It sounds like you're going to need it."

"Thanks." Todd looked around the lot. "Where's your jeep?"

"I needed the exercise so I walked over."

"Would you like a ride home?"

"Sure, I can show you my gallery."

"Cool, I've been meaning to drop by to see it."

"Great."

"Super, let's go."

****

"Where's Todd tonight?"

The bartender wiped the counter. "Tonight's his night off."

"Is that so?" She licked salt off her margarita glass. "I'll have another, please. I will be right back." She slipped off the barstool and dashed into the restroom, pulled her phone out, and speed dialed.

A man answered, "The Lavender Moon Lounge. How can I help you?"

"Is Todd there?"

"No, Todd's not here tonight."

"Will he be in tomorrow night?"

"Yes, would you like to leave a message?"

"No." She finished her drink and left.

****

Nance had just parked her car in front of her building when Riki zipped past in the passenger seat of a red sports car. As Nance watched, Todd got out and opened the door for Riki.

Jealousy consumed Nance. She watched the lights go on in the gallery and the studio. Then, the upstairs lights went on.

Furious, Nance seethed in her car, but fifteen minutes later Todd was still there, so she dialed Riki's number and waited. It rang three times before going to voice mail. Nance didn't leave a message. She preferred to make a statement by saying nothing and hanging up.

"Oh, man, Nancy must know I'm here. That's her signature hang up phone call."

"Really, that's her?"

"Yeah, it is one of her ways of upsetting things. If it's Nancy, it will happen again."

"You seem well acquainted with her silent phone calls. Does she do this to you?"

"She hasn't in a long time because she doesn't have my number." Todd rubbed the back of his neck. "But, I expect she'll start calling me at the lounge now."

"She doesn't know you live on South Sierra, does she?"

"No, and I hope she never finds out. Even though my complex is gated and secure, let's face it, if Nancy wants in, she'll find a way."

"Well, she won't find out from me."

The phone rang again, and again, and again. Each time Riki let it go to voice mail. And again, and again, and again, Nance hung up without saying anything.

Riki was incensed. "How dare she disrupt our peace? This is enough."

"Get used to it. This could go on all night. You might as well turn off your phone."

"No way, I have an idea." She searched in her junk drawer and came back with a whistle. "I learned this in college. It's supposed to put an end to these kinds of phone calls."

When the phone rang again, Riki answered. "Hello?" Silence on the line.

"Hello? Who's there?" Again, silence. "Okay. I guess you want to hear this." Riki blew the shrill whistle long and hard. "Get the message?" She hung up and laughed. "That should stop the calls."

"And her hearing, too. That was wicked cool Riki. I like a woman who takes decisive action."

Down the street Nance screamed, stomped upstairs, and took four ibuprofen.

In the morning, the pain in her ear had worsen. She swallowed five ibuprofens and trudged downstairs. Outside, she saw Todd's red sports car still parked outside Riki's gallery. "Shit!" Then, she noticed Sam had closed the bakery because of Mary's funeral. "Shit! Shit!"

CHAPTER 19

MARK BEEPED HIS horn and Riki dashed out the door and stopped. Nance stood at the curb holding a bouquet of daisies.

"Hello, Riki."

"Oh, you decided to join us?"

"Yes, if that's okay."

"Um, sure, I guess."

They got into the car and Mark drove to the bakery where Bonnie and Sam waited with their gear. He popped open the back and got out.

Nance rubbed her ear. "I have a terrible earache today."

Riki looked out the window. "Why is that? Do you have an ear infection?"

Nance unsnapped her seatbelt and leaned forward. "You know damn well I don't have an ear infection."

"No, I don't think I do." Riki stared straight ahead and braided her ponytail. "Why don't you tell me?"

She pounded her fist on the back of Mark's seat. "You blew a whistle into my ear last night."

Riki pushed her sunglasses onto her head, turned around, and glared. "So, that was you! Why didn't you tell me you were on the line before I blew the whistle? I gave you a chance, didn't I?"

"Yeah, but I had no idea you were going to do something so painful."

"That's what you get for what you were doing, don't you think? By the way," Riki said, "why were you calling me and hanging up in the first place? Why didn't you say something? What was that all about?"

"That was about your screwing Todd, you cheating slut! He's my boyfriend and yet you took him upstairs to your apartment and fucked him!"

"That's enough!"

"Ha! You don't want Mark to know Todd spent the night with you. Well, he will now, won't he?"

"Okay, that is enough."

"His car was still parked right outside your place this morning. Are you denying it?"

"That's it. Get out of the car." Riki shot out of her door and opened the passenger rear door. "I said, get out."

"Fine, I'll get out!" She slid across the seat, burst out of the car, and faced Riki. "So?"

"Let's get something straight right now, Nance." Riki put her hands on her hips. "You do not tell me what to do. You do not tell me whom I can entertain in my apartment. You do not tell me with whom I can have sex. It is none of your business who my friends are or when they come over to my place or if their car is still out front in the morning."

Nance held her arms tense at her sides, the daisies crushed in her tight grasp. "Todd is my boyfriend and you're trying to steal him from me! I lost him once already and I will not lose him again. Back off."

"No, you don't get it. You cannot own people. You don't own Todd and you do not own me. You cannot tell me what to do. I do what I want, and I see whomever I want, whenever I want. My life is my business, and you have nothing to say about it. Stay out of my life, Nance."

"No, I won't let you take him away from me!" She waved the daisies. "He's my boyfriend. I won't give up."

"What, Todd's your boyfriend? Look, you've seen him once and you think he's your boyfriend? Nice try, but it isn't so."

"He wants me back! I know he does. I can tell."

"Seriously, you are too funny."

"What the hell do you mean?"

"I mean, he's not your boyfriend, and he doesn't want to be."

"That's not true. He does want me back. He's mine and no one else's."

"This isn't high school, Nance. Grow up."

"I am grown up!" Nance screamed.

"Is that right? Like now? This is how you think an adult should behave? You could have fooled me. Because you are not behaving like an adult, you are behaving like a child, a ridiculous child."

"How can you say that?"

"Think like an adult for a change. Why would he want you back after what you did?"

Nance lowered her voice. "What do you mean? I didn't do anything."

"Breaking up his marriage is nothing?"

"I did not break up his marriage. Who told you that?"

"He did, of course."

"He didn't mean it. I told him I couldn't help it and I was sorry. He understood."

"Yeah, he understood that he never wanted to see you again, that's what he understood."

"No, that's not true."

"Well, has he called you? Has he asked you out?"

"No, he hasn't, but so what?"

"Has he been to your place?"

"No, not yet, but he will, I know he will."

"No, you are wrong there. He won't ever, I can assure you."

"How dare you get between Todd and me?"

"You just don't get it, do you? There is no 'Todd and you.'"

"You're supposed to be my friend, but you're not. You are nothing but a whoring slut! I hate you!"

"You think we're friends? You cannot be serious. We are not friends."

"How can you say that to me? I am your friend."

"No, you have never been my friend. You don't know how to be a friend, because you are too narcissistic to be a friend."

Nance took a step toward Riki. "But we were friends all through school."

Riki took a step backwards. "No, we weren't."

She took another step toward Riki. "But, we've known each other for years."

"That doesn't make us friends though, does it?" Riki backed up another step. "Just leave me alone, Nance."

"Leave you alone?" Nance took another step towards her. "I will never leave you alone! Do you hear me?"

"Back off or I'll call the police."

"Call the police for what?"

"For harassing and threatening me, that's what. Look, don't talk to me. Don't call me. As far as I'm concerned, I don't know you and I will never speak to you again." Riki started toward the car.

"Oh, you will talk to me again! We are not done here! Don't worry about that!"

Riki walked past her friends. "Let's go."

Bonnie, Sam, and Mark looked at Nance and then followed Riki to the SUV and got in. Before Nance could say, 'hey wait for me,' Mark drove down South Cedros Avenue and left her fuming on the sidewalk.

"Grow up my ass!" She threw the daisies on the ground and stomped on them.

****

On the way to Encinitas, Riki was beyond talking, so they drove to Moonlight Beach in silence. But, after Mark had found a place to park, she was calm. "What if Nance goes to the lounge to confront Todd. She knows he works tonight."

Mark said, "Shouldn't you call and warn him?"

"I don't have his number. I just have the number to The Lavender Moon Lounge."

"Well, leave a message with whoever answers," Bonnie said. "They'll contact him."

"Yeah, that should work." She called the lounge and a man answered. "Hello, I'm Riki Hollis. I'm a friend of Todd's."

"Hi, Riki, this is Dave. I'm one of the managers. Todd's told me about you. What's up?"

"I'd like to leave a message for him. It is very important he gets this message."

"Sure, no problem, what is it?"

"Tell him that his ex-girlfriend is pissed off and I think she might go over there tonight. She is in a rage because she thinks he spent last night at my place."

"Ah, I see. I know about his crazy ex-girlfriend."

"She's furious because she saw his car parked outside my place this morning and jumped to conclusions. Actually, Todd walked home last night, but I didn't tell her that because he doesn't want her to know he lives just a few blocks away. Anyway, I want to warn him she might be over to see him tonight insane and in a hateful mood."

"Okay, I'll tell him. Thanks for calling."

"Tell him 'good luck' for me, I think he's going to need it."

"Why is that?"

"She was screaming her head off the last time I saw her which was about five minutes ago. She is a real nutcase."

"Yeah, she sure sounds like one."

CHAPTER 20

SAM SAID, "I don't think it is legal to scatter someone's ashes over the ocean without some sort of permit, but what the hell? Let's throw caution to the wind along with Mary's ashes."

The group followed Sam to a secluded spot where there were no sunbathers. He scooped sand into a mound, into which he pushed a picture of Mary smiling from behind the bakery counter. "Let's place our chairs and towels in a semi-circle around Mary's picture."

Riki covered her beach chair with a towel and sat. "She looks so happy in that picture."

"She loved working the counter. She loved talking to the regulars and welcoming newcomers. But, she was also a great singer. Did you ever hear her sing?"

They shook their heads.

"Well, she stopped singing when her boyfriend dumped her for a man." Sam sighed. "That rocked her world big time. It made her feel like a failure in life, as if she was less of a woman, she felt worthless. I guess that's why she didn't mind working at the bakery when she had a MSW."

"That is so sad. I never heard her sing and I didn't know she had an advanced degree. She was a cool person and I really liked her."

"Yeah," Bonnie said, "she always brightened my day."

"I can't imagine what kind of monster would do something like this," Mark said.

"Yeah, it sure looked deliberate."

Riki stared at Mary's picture. "Her life was so short."

Sam held the bakery box of the ashes on his lap. "Well, are we ready to set her free?"

"Okay." Bonnie twisted her hair into a knot at the base of her neck. "What do we do?"

"Just dip your hand in and scoop up some ashes and then toss them over the ocean." Sam carried the box in both hands into the shore break. "Or, let the wind lift the ashes off your hand so she can fly away." Sam opened the box and offered it to each of them. They each took a handful.

Riki looked at the ashes in her hand. "I don't know about you, but this feels creepy."

"You'll feel better about it when you release her." Sam opened his hand and the ashes blew away. "Mary, you are free now."

Bonnie tossed a handful of ashes into the water. "Farewell, Mary, rest in peace."

Riki walked further into the small waves. "Nothing can hurt you now." She tossed the ashes as tears trickled down her cheeks and rejoined the others.

Mark put his arm around her and kissed her on the cheek. He scooped up another handful of ashes and let them flutter out of his hand like angel wings. "She is blowing in the wind. Good bye, Mary."

Sam lifted the box in the air and the rest of Mary's ashes took flight. "Good bye, Mary, I will miss you."

Back on the sand, Bonnie asked, "So, what was Nance's problem?" She released her hair and let it fly about her face.

"Do you really want to know?"

"You know I do, come on, tell all."

"Well Mark, of course, already knows the story, but last night Todd came over and Nance somehow found out and started calling and hanging up. So, I found my old college safety whistle and put a stop to the phone calls."

"Oh, no, what did you do, give her an earful?"

"Exactly right, I did. I gave her a brief, but loud rendition of my extra special earsplitting whistle blast. Was that a mean thing to do?"

Bonnie laughed. "No way, you didn't."

"Ouch!" Sam put his hands over his ears. "That had to hurt."

"I hope it did, seriously. She said she had a terrible earache. Isn't that a shame?"

"Yeah, that's a real bummer, alright. Sorry, but I think it is hilarious. She's pissed off at you for hurting her ear when she made silent phone calls. Isn't turnabout fair play?"

Sam said, "Is that what you guys were fighting about, the whistle?"

"Well, that's what started it, but it escalated to Todd. Last night, he was still there when Mark came over with some great Chilean wine, so we drank and talked. It got late and Todd was pretty much wasted. So instead of driving, he left his car in front of my place, and walked home. But when Nance saw his car still out front this morning, she figured he had spent the night with me."

"Oh," Sam said, "so that was why she was so crazy?"

"Yeah, she accused me of sleeping with Todd and trying to steal him from her. That's when I told her to get out of the car." Riki paused. "You guys know the rest."

"Oh, Riki, you know how she takes revenge when someone crosses her. What are you going to do?"

"Nothing, I'm not afraid of her." Riki shook her hair out and fluffed it with her fingers. "She thinks she can control everyone with her narcissistic nastiness, but she doesn't control me and now she knows it. Besides, I will never speak to her again."

Mark squeezed her hand. "Maybe you should move in with me."

"Are you serious?"

"Of course, I'm serious. I love you and I want you to live with me. And, I want to protect you from Nance if she should try to hurt you."

"It's tempting, I love you too and it would be amazing to live with you, but it won't be because I'm afraid of that crazy whacko."

Sam clapped his hands. "Well, I'm hungry. Let's eat somewhere cool. How about Las Olas, their food is always great."

"Yeah, okay!" They packed up their stuff, hiked back to the SUV, and headed south on the old coast highway.

Minutes later, they parked in the sand lot and checked out the beach on the other side of the highway.

Riki said, "I just love living at the beach."

"Me, too," the others said together. They all laughed.

Inside, they sat at a spacious table with a view that overlooked San Elijo Lagoon. They drank margaritas, munched on tortilla chips and salsa, and ate spicy Mexican food.

Bonnie asked, "The name of the place is Las Olas. Does anyone know Spanish? What does it mean?"

Mark said, "It means 'the waves.'"

"That makes sense since its right across the highway from the ocean."

They heard a familiar rumble in the distance and watched the Coaster whizz past destined for Solana Beach Amtrak Station on the trestle that stretched across the inlet.

"I sometimes hear trains going by late at night. I thought they stopped around 11:00 or so, but sometimes I hear them much later."

"After a while you won't even notice them," Sam said.

Mark sipped his margarita and licked the salt off his lips. "The trains you hear after midnight are freight trains. They run two or three times a week and sometimes two or three times a night. They go straight through Solana Beach without stopping."

"Ah, freight trains, of course." Riki sipped her drink. "You know, they sound louder than the regular trains during the day."

"Yeah, they can be pretty loud at night."

"Yes, loud and ominous."

"Ominous?" Mark took Riki's hand. "The sound of the freight trains frightens you?"

"Well, in a way, yeah. Sometimes they trigger a strange recurring dream I have of someone chasing me."

Bonnie said, "Like what happened after the frat party?"

"Yes, that was a scary night, and when these dreams started. Once when I had the dream, I got out of bed in the middle of the night and painted that weird canvas Nance bought. That in itself is odd." She shuddered. "Anyway, the sound of trains gives me an uncanny feeling something bad is going to happen."

Mark said, "You should be sleeping at my place. Nothing bad will happen to you as long as you're with me."

"That's a great idea." She gave him a quick kiss.

"I've heard those trains a few times," Bonnie said, "but not often. I must be a deep sleeper."

"Yes," Riki said, "you can sleep through anything."

"So, what do you think Nance did after we left?"

"I think she went to The Lavender Moon Lounge. Why don't we stop by for a drink? I'd like to know what if anything happened."

"Yeah, let's do that."

Mark said, "Is that a good idea? What if she's there?"

"We have as much a right to go there as she does," Bonnie said.

"That's not the point. The point is do you want to be involved in this melodrama?"

The women said, "Yes!"

Mark shook his head. "Well Sam, do you want to go by the lounge to see what's happening?"

"I don't think it'd hurt. I'm sort of curious myself about what she did after we drove away and left her standing there crazed and screaming."

"Okay." Mark chuckled. "Let's go."

They drove the short distance to Solana Beach and pulled into The Lavender Moon Lounge's parking lot crowded with Sheriff's vehicles.

Sam said, "Could this be about Nance?"

"I bet it is," Bonnie said. "I wonder who she killed this time."

"Don't say that." Riki folded her hands under her chin.

"What do you think happened?" Sam said.

"Let's find out."

They walked to the perimeter of the yellow crime scene tape. Sheriff's deputies stood around and a squad car waited nearby with its backdoor open.

"Look! There she is."

They stood transfixed as they watched Nance struggle with two deputies who escorted her to the squad car where she slumped in the back. The door slammed shut. As the squad car pulled away, Riki met her eyes. Nance hung her head and her hair covered her face.

"Holy, shit!" Bonnie grasped Sam's hand. "What did she do?"

"It had to be something pretty bad for her to be arrested and hauled off to jail."

"Yeah," Mark said, "she must be on her way to Las Colinas."

"I hope they keep her there a long time," Riki said. Two men left the bar and walked toward the deputies gathered in the parking lot. "Hey, there's Todd. And, I think the woman he's talking to is Detective Stanton."

CHAPTER 21

DETECTIVE STANTON ASKED, "You arrived after the meltdown was over?"

"Yes," Todd said. "Dave gave me the night off."

Dave joined them. "Man, I'm glad this night is just about over."

"So," Detective Stanton said, "you were here the whole time?"

"Yes, that's right."

"You witnessed everything?"

"Yeah, well there were a few times when I went into the office to make some phone calls, but most of the time I was in the lounge."

"Tell me what happened from the moment she entered until now."

"Well, a friend of Todd's called and told me his crazy ex-girlfriend could be coming by in a mean mood, so I hung in the lounge and waited for her. A few minutes later, she walked in and sat at the bar. She ordered a Long Island Iced Tea and told the bartender to keep them coming because she planned on being here a long time."

"Did you notice anything unusual?"

"Well, if you consider she drank half of a Long Island Iced Tea in one gulp. That was a bit unusual; not many people do that. I would say she was intent on getting drunk, because five minutes later she finished it and ordered another."

"You say she was drinking Long Island Iced Teas? That's a pretty strong drink, isn't it?"

"You bet it is. The way we make them, they are almost all liquor."

"Okay, what happened next?"

"She asked Jane the bartender what time Todd was coming to work. Jane told her Todd's shift started at 8:00."

"What time was this?"

"Oh, it was around 4:00, I guess. She told Jane she wanted to run a tab and then, she moved to a booth."

"She sat in a booth for how long?"

"About an hour, I'd say. I stayed in the lounge and watched her pretend to be interested in the sports on TV. She kept looking around I guess to see if Todd would magically appear or something. When Jane served her a fifth Long Island Iced Tea, she was in a foul mood and demanded to know how much longer it would be before Todd came to work."

"She had five drinks? She must have been intoxicated by then."

"Yes, she was quite drunk. Jane told her Todd wasn't due for another three hours and asked her if she was waiting for him. That's when the trouble started." He rubbed his forehead.

"I know this is stressful for you, but please go on."

"She got totally loud and belligerent. She screamed, 'yeah, that's right! I'm waiting for him! He screwed my best friend last night and I have something to say to him, the fucking son of a bitch!'"

"That's not true," Todd said. "I didn't spend the night with Riki. Her boyfriend was even there."

"I understand," the detective said. "Please continue, Dave."

"Jane didn't know what to say, so she said, 'Oh, I see.'"

"So, at this point, Ms. Thomason was still reasonably under control?"

"No, not at all, she had already lost it by then and got louder and more belligerent with every sentence. She shouted, 'Do you? Do you see that Todd is a fucking asshole?' I decided things were on the verge of getting out of hand, so I went over to her booth and said, 'Excuse me. Is there something I can help you with?' She forgot about Jane and turned her wrath on me. She said, 'Who the hell are you?'"

"She was getting more agitated?"

"Yes, she was extremely agitated. I told her that I'm the manager and she said, 'You're not the manager, Todd is the manager.' I told her that I am the other manager and she said that she'd wait for Todd. Then, I went in the office and called our part time manager Mike to cover for Todd tonight. Next, I called Todd and told him not to come in tonight because his crazy ex-girlfriend was getting out of control."

"How long were you in the office?"

"Just a few minutes and when I was still on the phone with Todd I heard yelling coming from the lounge, so I hung up and went back out there."

"What was she doing then?"

"She was sitting in the same booth screaming to Jane across the lounge to bring her another drink. Then, she called Jane a fucking loser! That was it for me, so I went to her table and told her she had enough to drink and we would be unable to serve her anymore. I offered her coffee, a soft drink, or a taxi."

"I bet that pissed her off."

"Yeah, it did. She yelled, 'What? You are cutting me off, you're kicking me out?' I told her, 'yes, that's right.' I made the mistake of saying I was sorry, because that set her off."

"What do you mean?"

"She said, 'You're sorry, are you? Yes, you should be sorry.' Then, she got out of the booth and headed toward the bar. She said, 'You should be very sorry! And, you will be.' She went behind the bar, and I said, 'Hey, what are you doing? You aren't supposed to be behind there. Please come out.'"

"Let me get this straight. She was in a booth and then went behind the bar. What did she do there?"

"She screamed 'No!' she would not come out from behind the bar. Instead, she took a liquor bottle and threw it at me. I ducked and it crashed against a wall and showered me, and nearby patrons, with shards of glass. Next, she took another bottle and threw it at some people who were sitting at a table in the corner. It shattered on the floor next to them and sprayed their table with slivers of flying glass. I was concerned someone was going to get hurt."

"Did you evacuate the bar?"

"I didn't have to, she did it for me. She screamed, 'Get the hell out of here! Everybody get out! I want to talk to Todd alone. He thinks he can treat me like shit. Well, I'll show him!' Then, she methodically threw every liquor bottle and glass she could find directly at people, but luckily, she is a lousy shot and missed hitting anyone."

"Well that, at least, was fortunate."

"Yeah, but it was weird, the sound of crashing glass seemed to excite her even more. She screamed, 'Todd is a cheating bastard! I'll kill the son of a bitch.'"

"You heard her say she was going to kill Todd?"

"That's what she said. I heard it clearly and she said it more than once."

"What were you doing during this time?"

"I was busy dodging flying glass, but eventually I managed to barricade my staff and myself in the office and call 911. Not long after that, we heard the deputies rush in, and tell her she was under arrest. She didn't like that at all. We could hear her screaming, but when I looked through the peephole, I saw her confined in handcuffs and marched out the door. Whew, were we ever glad to see her leave! I called Mike to tell him not to come in and then I called Todd to tell him what happened. As you can see, he came over."

Todd held his head in his hands. "Oh, man. I can't believe she did this. I can't believe she wants to kill me." He dropped his hands. "Detective, do you think that is a real threat? Should I be worried?"

"In my business, I take all threats seriously and in this case, so should you."

"No, shit?" Todd slumped and almost collapsed.

Dave put his arm around him. "Hang in there, buddy. It'll be okay."

"She's going to Las Colinas Detention and Reentry Facility and from what I can tell she'll be there for at least six months, maybe longer."

"That's a relief, but what about when she gets out? Will I be informed so I can be on the lookout for her?"

"Of course, we will let you know." The detective closed her notebook. "I have no more questions for you at the moment, but I will need you both to come to the station tomorrow and make a formal statement."

Todd turned away and glanced at the group of onlookers gathered in the parking lot. "There's my friend who called Dave."

"I should talk to her, too."

Detective Stanton and Todd walked over to Riki and her friends.

"Hey, Todd, what is going on?"

"Hi, guys. This is Detective Stanton."

Riki shook her hand. "Hello, Detective, we've met before."

"Yes, I remember. I understand you called the lounge because you had reason to believe Ms. Thomason was planning on coming here in an angry mood?"

"That's right. Earlier today we had an argument about Todd and I thought that she'd come here looking for him."

"I have some follow up questions I would like to ask you. Can you come by the Encinitas Sheriff's Station tomorrow?"

"Um, sure, I guess so, okay."

"Great, I'll see you then." Detective Stanton returned to the crime scene.

"Todd," Bonnie said, "tell us what happened."

"Oh, man! That woman is totally whacko!"

"We saw her taken away in the back of a squad car."

"Thank God, she's going to jail."

Bonnie said, "Why, what did she do?"

"She totally trashed the place, that's what she did. And, I mean totally. We are going to have to close for weeks to repair the damage. Fortunately, I wasn't here at the time, because it could have been much worse. As it is, she got drunk and lost it completely. Dave said she got loud and obnoxious, and then she started throwing liquor bottles at people and screaming she was going to kill me."

"She threatened to kill you?" Riki clasped her hands. "Oh, no, Todd, that's terrible."

"It's okay. She's going to jail and will be out of my life for at least six months, I hope. That's something good to come out of this." He looked up at the stars. "I had hoped something would happen so I wouldn't see her again, but I didn't really expect her to be taken away in handcuffs."

Dave joined them and took Riki's hand. "Thanks for the heads up. I just didn't figure she would destroy the place."

"Yeah, I didn't either. So, what was it like?"

"It was pretty hairy. She threw full liquor bottles at people. Booze and glass flew all over the place. We're lucky no one was seriously hurt."

Bonnie said, "She could have killed someone."

"Yeah, all in all, we're pretty lucky the way it turned out." Dave looked at Todd. "But if Todd had been here, he could be dead right now. She was violent and seemed intent on getting him. It was a good thing he wasn't here."

Todd ran to the bushes and vomited.

CHAPTER 22

EVEN THOUGH SHE was on her way to Las Colinas Detention and Reentry Facility, the County of San Diego's jail for women, Nance felt euphoric and erupted into laughter. The deputy in the front passenger seat turned around.

"What is so funny, Ms. Thomason?"

"Oh, I was just thinking about what happened tonight."

"And you think it's funny?"

"Actually, I do, I think it is very funny."

The deputy said, "You destroyed the bar and you put a lot of people in danger and you are laughing about it?"

"It is funny to me. Why, what's wrong with a having sense of humor?"

"Lady, you have a serious problem and it's not because you're drunk. You have a definite screw loose."

"Are you saying I'm mental?"

"Maybe, let's see how you answer this riddle."

The other deputy said, "A riddle? You cannot be serious."

"A shrink taught me this. It is how you can tell if someone is a psychopath."

"Go ahead ask me the riddle."

"Okay. Here it is, a woman goes to her mother's funeral and sees a man to whom she is instantly attracted, but she is too shy to talk to him. She goes home infatuated and cannot stop thinking about him. Three days later, she kills her sister. Why did she kill her sister?"

"Oh, that's easy. She did it so there would be another family funeral hoping she would see the man again."

The deputy blinked. "Hey, that's the answer. I mean that is the answer psychopaths give."

The deputy behind the wheel said, "I thought she killed her sister because she was afraid somehow her sister might attract the man."

"That's what a non-psychopath would say, but this woman is the real deal. She didn't even have to think about it."

They arrived at Las Colinas and the two deputies escorted Nance through the entrance for new inmates. The booking clerk said, "Who's this?"

The deputy who drove said, "Thomason was arrested for trashing a bar, and she is drunk and violent, not to mention, a psychopath."

"Well, in that case, she can't go through open-booking. Better put her in a holding cell."

The deputy who told her the riddle said, "Come this way, Thomason. Have a seat in here." He opened the door to the cell. "It won't be long."

"Do you think I'm a psychopath?"

The deputy paused. "It was a riddle, not a diagnosis. Don't take it too seriously."

"Oh, right. But, what if I am? How would I know?"

"Well, have you ever killed anyone?"

She coughed, "Um, no."

"Turn around so I can take the cuffs off." He unlocked the handcuffs and gave her a slight nudge into the cell. "Sit tight and they'll be with you soon."

Nance sat on a bench, crossing and uncrossing her legs until the cell door opened. "Thomason?"

"Yes."

"Come with me, please."

"Where are we going?"

"We need to take your clothes now, but you'll get them back when you leave." The corrections officer showed her a dressing room and shoved some beige clothes into her arms. "Here, put these on."

Nance complied and stood mute as they scanned her for contraband. Then, the deputy took her to the next room. "We'll take your picture and fingerprints now."

Nance said, "I guess this makes it official. I am a criminal."

"Well, you haven't been convicted yet, just arrested." The CO glanced at her. "Don't get all morose about it."

In another room, a doctor gave her a brief medical exam. "Your left ear looks red and inflamed. You may have an infection. Are you allergic to any antibiotics?"

"I don't think so. My ear was injured last night when I was on the phone."

"Your ear was injured while you were on the phone? How did that happen?"

Nance shook her head. "Just some crank call."

"And, what happened?"

"Some asshole blew a loud whistle into the phone while I was in my car. It was so loud it hurt my ear and I dropped my phone. I've taken Ibuprofen, but it still hurts a lot."

"Why would someone do that?"

"I have no idea why, she just did it, that's all."

"Oh, I see. You've had a rough couple of days, haven't you?"

"Yeah, I guess you could say that."

"Well, I can give you something for the pain and if it gets infected, we'll treat it then."

"Okay, fine."

The doctor finished the exam and a corrections officer came and took her arm. "Come with me and we will get you settled in your cell."

"When can I call my grandma to come bail me out?"

"You can make a phone call now, but at your arraignment the judge will set bail, if he or she sees fit. If you make bail, then someone can post bond and come get you."

"Okay, I'd like to call my grandmother now, if possible."

"Not a problem." The deputy took her to a bank of phones.

The phone rang four times. "This better be good, it's the middle of the night."

"Grandma, it's me. I'm in jail."

"What the hell did you do this time?"

"What do you mean 'this time'? What else have I done?"

"Oh, girl, you are always getting yourself into nasty messes."

"Well, this time I am in real trouble and I need to you to post bail. They said my arraignment is tomorrow."

"Do you need an attorney?"

"Yeah, I guess I do."

"Fine, I'll call Tom Hurd in the morning." Her grandmother sat up in bed. "Now, tell me what you did."

"Ah, well, um, nothing all that bad."

"Well, it couldn't be all that good either, now could it?"

"Oh, Grandma, please don't be mad."

"Just get on with it, girl. What did you do?"

"I had an argument with Riki today, so I went to have a drink at the bar where Todd works. Do you remember him? I ran into him the other day. Anyway, I went there to wait for him because it was before his shift started. I suppose you could say I had a little too much to drink while I waited."

"I can see where this is going. You had a temper tantrum, didn't you?"

"Ah, yes. I um, well, I lost my temper and I don't know how it happened, but I pretty much wrecked the place."

"I've warned you about drinking while angry, haven't I?"

"Yes, well I couldn't help it."

"You never can, can you? Always the same excuse, when are you going to behave?" Her grandma paused. "Well, this sounds serious and expensive. I'll tell Tom what you said when I call him, but you'll have to give him the details."

"Yeah, okay. But, no matter what, you have to bail me out."

"Good night, Nancy. Sleep tight."

****

The next morning before her arraignment, Nance met with her attorney, Tom Hurd.

"I have reviewed the police report and I have requested the video of the incident, but it has not been released yet. I'll get it during discovery."

Nance brightened. "There is a video of what I did in the lounge last night? Wow. Can I see it?"

Mr. Hurd narrowed his eyes. "I'm sure you will at some point. Why?"

"Oh, I um, just wanted to see it. I was in a strange place mentally and emotionally. My memory of what I did is rather dim."

"Hmm, that's interesting. Perhaps we can use that as a defense. I'll recommend a mental health evaluation."

"Sure, I don't care as long as I get out of here today."

"Well, that could happen, but I make no promises. Now tell me about last night from start to finish."

With a bored sigh, Nance told him about her sore ear, the fight with Riki, and her angry outburst at the bar.

"Well," Mr. Hurd said, "expect to be sentenced for six months to a year. The DA will offer a plea bargain so it may be less time. We'll just have to wait and see."

"What? Six months to a year is too long for having a little fit in a bar."

"Are you listening, Nancy? It was a full-blown meltdown. You could have seriously injured someone."

"But, I didn't. No one was hurt, right?"

"Right, and that may sway the court, but don't count on it."

CHAPTER 23

"MS. THOMASON?"

"YES Your Honor."

"I have read the district attorney's complaint; you are charged with Aggravated Assault and Battery. You caused a great deal of damage, but what is more distressing is your complete disregard for the safety of the other people in the lounge. You could have inflicted serious injuries. Fortunately, what injuries there were are minor, and although those victims decline to file a complaint, I consider those injuries. Have you had an opportunity to talk to your attorney?"

"Yes, Your Honor."

"How do you plead?"

Mr. Hurd said, "My client enters a plea of not guilty, Your Honor."

"I will set the preliminary hearing for one week from today which will be July 20 and the tentative date for the trial to begin on September 6. So counselors, are we agreed on the dates? No conflicts in your schedules?"

Mr. Hurd and the District Attorney searched through their calendars.

Mr. Hurd said, "Those dates work for me, Your Honor."

"Do you expect to go to trial, Mr. Hurd?"

"We haven't decided yet, Your Honor, but it is a possibility."

"Okay, how about you, Mr. Martin? Are you good with the dates?"

"Yes, Your Honor. I have no conflicts."

"Fine, bail is set at $40,000." Judge Randall lowered his gavel and the bailiffs came and stood behind her.

"Hey, wait. When do I get out of here? Why am I going back to the jail?"

"You have to post bond first. You said your grandmother would bail you out. Do you see her here?"

Nance turned and stared at the people sitting in the courtroom. "No, and I thought for sure she'd be here. I told her last night how important it was today. Where can she be?"

"Maybe she's late. Relax, I'll call her when I get back to the office and work out the details. I'll be in touch."

He patted her hand and she jerked it away.

"Fine, see ya."

Again, she looked for her grandmother as a bailiff cuffed her hands behind her back and led her to a holding cell.

CHAPTER 24

AT THE ENCINITAS Sheriff's Station, Riki found Todd sitting in the waiting area hunched over staring at the floor between his feet.

She sat next to him and touched his arm. "Hey, Todd, how's it going? Are you okay?"

He lifted his head. "Hi. Yeah, I'm fine."

"You don't look fine." She leaned over and looked into his face. "You look kicked."

"I guess I'm still reeling after hearing that Nancy wants to kill me."

"You don't think she is serious do you?"

"Actually, I do."

"Why do you say that?"

"I think she could kill me if she really wanted to. Just look what happened to the kid at the bookstore."

"You think she killed that little boy?" She tucked her hair behind her ears. "Why would she do that?"

"Why does she do anything? But, she acted strange that night."

"You're right, she did." Riki looked around the office. "You know, this place gives me the creeps. I haven't been inside a police station before."

"Well technically, you still haven't. This is a sheriff station."

"Oh, right. But, isn't it the same thing?"

"Probably, but I wouldn't know from experience."

"Are you going to tell the detective about your long history with Nance?"

"Yeah, I guess so, if she asks, but I think this is about last night."

"I wonder why she wants to talk to me. I don't know what I can tell her, do you?"

Todd stretched, yawned, and shook his head. He yawned again. "Sorry, I didn't get a lot of sleep last night."

"I know what you mean." Riki yawned. "I didn't, either."

Detective Stanton strode toward them. "Hello and thanks for coming in today. I have just a few questions for each of you. It won't take long." She looked first at Todd and then at Riki. "Who wants to go first?"

They looked at each other and shrugged.

"You were here first, Todd. I don't mind waiting."

"Yeah, okay. I might as well get it over with."

Todd followed the detective into an interview room, it held nothing more than a table and two chairs.

"Have a seat. I'd say make yourself comfortable, but I know that is unlikely." The detective sat across from him. "Thanks again for coming in." She switched on a tape recorder. "Do you mind if I tape this? It saves me from having to take notes as we talk."

"No problem."

"Great. I've studied this case and what strikes me as odd is that Nancy was not in the system until the incident last night, but my instinct tells me she's done things like this before, things that were not reported."

"You have good instincts."

"So, has she done similar things to you?"

"Well, nothing quite so violent, but I guess you could say she's stalked me from time to time."

"Like how has she stalked you?"

Todd lowered his head. "She did things like follow me and show up at work. She called me all the time and left messages on my machine. I got notes on my car. She would break into my apartment and leave flowers and other weird stuff. Things like that. When I got married, that stuff stopped, but she managed to get my wife to think I was cheating on her and caused her to leave me."

"Interesting, tell me from the beginning so I know what we've got here."

An hour later, Detective Stanton stood and held out her hand. "Thanks, I know it wasn't easy for you. You've been a big help, Todd."

In the waiting room, Riki scrolled through Facebook on her phone.

"Hey, it's your turn."

"How did it go?"

Todd rubbed his forehead. "Fine, I guess." He pulled his keys out of his pocket and stepped past her.

She dropped her phone into her purse. "Wait, what happened? You look like you've been beaten up or something."

"You have no idea." He headed for the door. "See ya later."

"He is taking this hard."

Detective Stanton said, "He had an unhappy past with Nancy. He helped me understand her better."

"He looks depressed."

"Well, it was painful for him to remember the things Nancy's done to him, but he'll get over it."

"I hope so. I feel sorry for him, poor guy."

"Yeah, it was rough for him."

They seated themselves at the table and Detective Stanton turned on the tape machine. "You don't mind, do you?"

"No, that's fine."

"Okay, Todd told me some disturbing things about Nancy's past, but I wonder if you've noticed anything unusual lately, other than the meltdown last night."

"Like what?"

"Like anything out of the ordinary."

"You mean, like something another person wouldn't do?"

"Right, what comes to mind?"

"What pops into my head is her strange reaction after that little boy fell off the banister and died. In fact, Todd mentioned it to me just now when we were waiting for you."

"What did you think was strange?"

"It was just her behavior."

"Be specific, please."

"Well, after she left the bookstore, she seemed happy."

"That's odd."

"Sam and I thought so, too. She breezed right past us, so we followed her to The Lavender Moon Lounge."

"And, she found out Todd worked there?"

"Yeah, he told you about that, right?"

"He said that she didn't even mention Billy's death." She drummed her finger-nails on the table. "What do you think triggered the meltdown in the lounge last night?"

"I think what set her off was the fight she and I had yesterday afternoon."

"You two had a verbal fight or a physical fight?"

"Oh, it was all verbal, but some of it was loud."

"Tell me about it."

"Well, it started Saturday night when she harassed me and Todd." Riki crossed her legs and related what happened. "Finally, I blew my college whistle in her ear."

"Oh, that couldn't have felt good."

"Yeah, I kind of think it didn't. She was mad about it yesterday and picked a fight with me which resulted in her being left behind."

"Left behind where?"

"Oh, right." Riki fluffed her hair. "Yesterday was Mary's funeral and she wanted to go with us."

"Mary Hatch? The hit and run victim?"

"Yeah, I had already invited Nance to ride with us, but after the confrontation on the phone with the whistle, I thought she'd skip it. But no, when I walked out of the gallery, she was waiting on the sidewalk. Sam and Bonnie waited for us at the bak-ery."

"She went down to the gallery instead of just walking across the street to the bakery to wait with Bonnie and Sam?"

"Yeah, that was weird, too." Riki scratched her head. "I guess she couldn't wait to pick up where we left off."

"I see." Detective Stanton looked at the wall behind Riki. "She is a troubled woman with a history of stalking and harassment. I wonder if . . ."

"What?"

She looked at Riki. "I was just thinking about your stalker. What if it was her?"

"You think it was Nance who stalked me on campus?" Riki paused. "But why, it doesn't make sense, does it?"

The detective shrugged. "To be near you, or perhaps she held a grudge against you for some reason. You two knew each other in high school, so perhaps she has unfinished business with you."

Riki tilted her head. "But, what about the body impression on my bed, did they find semen stains on the bedspread?"

"Let me find out." Detective Stanton made a quick phone call. "Your bedspread had no semen stains. They are bringing it here so you can take it home."

"So, she's the one who laid on my bed? I don't get it. Why would she do that?"

"Maybe she wanted to see if she could manipulate you into doing what she wanted. It may have been her way of controlling you through fear. Or, maybe she's a lesbian and is in love with you."

"That is too wild to even contemplate. But why did she stop stalking me after The Rolling Stones concert? I mean, wouldn't she still do stuff if she were the stalker?"

"Stalkers rarely just stop." The detective leaned back in her chair. "That is unusual."

"Well, she moved down the street, so I guess she could have still been stalking me, but I didn't notice." Riki put her head in her hands and then looked up. "Hey, I just remembered something. The day after the concert, she came into the gallery. It was the first time I had seen her in four years. My friend Bonnie was there and we all talked about going to the concert the night before and she said something strange."

"Strange? Like what?"

Riki grasped her knees. "Well, Bonnie said we had dates and asked her with whom she had gone. Now this is the weird part, she said she was supposed to meet a girlfriend there, but the woman had given her ticket to some guy she didn't know."

"That's interesting. Such as the ticket she gave to you and you gave it to Officer Fowler." The detective folded her hands. "So, is she your stalker?"

"No, because then she said she left after just a few songs and we know Officer Fowler sat between people who stayed for the whole concert."

"Officer Fowler said a woman sitting in the row behind him left early and didn't return. Every time he had tried to take her picture, she ducked her head, so we don't have a good picture. It could have been Nancy, I suppose. I'll check on it." Detective Stanton stood. "Thanks for coming in."

"Okay. See ya." She grabbed her purse and dashed out of the sheriff's station.

The detective returned to her desk, grabbed her bag, and drove to Las Colinas.

CHAPTER 25

THE DETECTIVE SMILED. "Hello, Nancy, or do you still go by Nance?"

"No, I'm back to Nancy now."

"I'm Detective Stanton. Do you remember me?"

"Sort of, I'm not sure."

"I'm the lead investigator on the case of The Lavender Moon Lounge and the case of Billy Wilson who fell off the banister at The Cubbyhole Bookstore." Detective Stanton stared at her.

Nancy said nothing.

"I am wrapping up the case of Billy's accident and would like you to tell me what you recall from that evening."

"I already told you."

"No, you didn't. You were upset so I didn't get a full statement from you, but now seems like a good time. Tell me, why were you there that evening?"

Nancy rubbed her forehead. "What does that have to do with anything?"

"Maybe nothing," the detective said. "I just want to know."

"Look, I'm tired. I have an earache. I didn't sleep well last night. Can't this wait until another time?"

"No, it cannot wait. Why were you at the bookstore that evening?"

Nancy sighed. "Bonnie needed help with the kids, so I offered to monitor the refreshments."

"Why?"

"What do you mean why? She needed help, so I offered to fill in."

"Had you helped her before?"

"No, I did this time because of Mary's accident."

"Mary Hatch the hit and run victim?"

"Right, she was dead, so Bonnie needed someone to take her place."

"How did you happen to be upstairs when Billy fell?"

Nancy coughed and looked down. She shook her head. "He snuck up the stairs, so I followed him."

"What happened when you followed him?"

Nancy pressed her lips together.

"Is there a problem, Nancy?"

"No." She cleared her throat. "He was sitting on the railing and I told him to get down, but he slipped off."

"What happened next?"

"He splattered on the floor. He was dead."

"And, then?"

"I ran downstairs."

"You helped him fall, didn't you?"

She nodded slightly, and then shook her head. "No."

"Okay. Now let's switch to yesterday and the situation at the bar. What did you do before you went there?"

"Well, I was supposed to go to a funeral with Riki, but at the last minute she ditched me, so I decided to go have a drink. My boyfriend manages The Lavender Moon Lounge, and I went there to wait for him."

"Did he know you'd be there? You got there several hours before his shift started, right?"

"Well, yeah, but so what?"

"So, did you call him?"

"Um, no I didn't."

"Why didn't you call him?"

"I don't have his number."

"What? You're telling me that he's your boyfriend and you don't have his phone number?"

She shrugged one shoulder. "I, ah, I always call him at work."

"Yeah, right," Detective Stanton said. "I don't believe you."

Nancy coughed. "Well, he calls me most of the time."

"He does? That's not what he told me."

"Why, what did he tell you?"

The detective did not answer. She stared at Nancy and waited.

"What's wrong?"

"What happened to make you start throwing things?"

"Um, let's see, I was very drunk, Todd was slow getting there, and other the manager pissed me off."

"That's all it took?"

"Yeah, that's all it took." Nancy yawned. "Look, are we done here? I want to go back to my cell."

"No, we're not quite done yet." Detective Stanton stood with her hands on her hips.

"Okay, what else do you want to know?"

"What were you doing on SDSU's campus last May?"

Nancy coughed. "I am not a student there."

"Yes, I know you're not a student at State, but you were on campus at the end of the semester, weren't you?"

She rubbed her neck. "What makes you think that?"

"You stalked Riki on the last day of finals, isn't that right?"

She closed her eyes. "You cannot be serious. Why would I do something like that?"

"You tell me."

"I, ah, I, I," she stammered and opened her eyes.

"What did you do on the evening of May 24th ?"

Nancy sighed. "That was a long time ago. I don't remember."

"Think about it. Weren't you at The Rolling Stones concert at PetCo Stadium that night?"

"Oh, yeah, I was."

"Where did you sit?"

"It was up in the cheap seats, if you can call them cheap."

"Did you keep your ticket?"

"My ticket, um, no, I lost it."

"That's okay, we can find out."

"Find out what?"

"You sent a ticket to Riki, didn't you?"

Nancy nodded. "No, I didn't."

"Did you stay for the whole concert?"

"Of course I did."

"Are you sure you didn't leave early?"

She nodded. "No."

"Riki said you told her you left early. You went to the concert to be near her, didn't you? You wanted to watch her."

"No, I didn't."

"You stalked her."

Nancy's lips pressed into a tight straight line. The detective waited. "Um no, that's not true."

"Yes, it is and I can prove it. Why don't you tell me about it?"

Nancy lifted her head. "My lawyer said not to talk to anyone without him being present." She folded her hands on the table. "I've already said enough."

Detective Stanton stood. "Okay." The detective knocked on the locked door. "Our interview is over."

CHAPTER 26

"OKAY. LET'S GO."

As the corrections officer led Nancy down the hall, Detective Stanton overheard her say, "You have an appointment with Dr. Moffett next. She's real nice, you'll like her."

"Why should I like her?"

"Well, because she's cool and she's your shrink, and you can tell her anything."

Detective Stanton followed Nancy to her psych evaluation and waited. When Nancy went back to her cell, Detective Stanton slipped into the doctor's office.

"Hi, Lisa, how's it going?"

The doctor, a little overweight with short blonde hair, turned to greet the detective with a bright smile. "Barb, nice to see you, how have you been? Still seeing that guy with the old Mustang?"

"You mean, Hal? No, we split up months ago. I'm single again."

"Oh, that's too bad. He had a cool car." The doctor sat behind her desk and gestured to the detective to sit across from her. "So, why are you here?"

"I'm investigating a case involving the woman you just saw. I hope you can tell me about her."

"Like what do you want to know?"

"Can you tell me if she has a mental disorder or what makes her tick?"

"Well, I could give you a general idea."

"Is she insane?

"No, she's not insane, but her loss of self-control at the bar last night demonstrates an absence of responsibility. That and a few other obvious traits tell me she is a sociopath, but could evolve into a psychopath."

"She's a real whacko?"

"I gave her the Hare Psychopathy Checklist test which requires a second opinion by Dr. Grady for the final analysis. You see, we combine our ratings to arrive at an average score and that hasn't been done yet."

"But, what do you think of her?"

"Well, in addition to being cunning and manipulative, she has an exaggerated opinion of herself. She has a problem with controlling her anger and is quite impulsive. She doesn't have a solid work history and her university level education is scant. She hasn't achieved any adult goals. She was a troubled kid and grew up to be a troubled adult."

"How was her childhood troubled?"

"At an early age she was abandoned by her parents and resented her grandmother who raised her. She felt unwanted at home and at school. She has never had a close friend."

"Do you think it is possible that she could become violent?"

"She lacks remorse and empathy and she has a quick and explosive temper. So yes, she could become violent."

"Do you think she could kill someone?"

"Based on her strong sociopathic and psychopathic traits, I would say yes, she is quite capable of killing someone."

"She totally denied any involvement in another case of mine, but I get the impression she's lying."

"Well, she is a pathological liar."

"She has some unusual mannerisms like she'll nod her head before answering in the negative or shake her head before answering in the positive. Know what I mean?"

"Yes, well her subconscious wants to tell the truth, but then she lies."

"She also shrugs one shoulder, instead of both. Is she lying?"

"Ah, yes, that is another mannerism of lying."

"Can you tell me how she would murder someone?"

"Her violent acts would be spontaneous and rather sloppy, like what happened in the bar, as opposed to being well planned as we would expect to see in a psychopath. But, it is possible with her combination of both traits."

"Is that bad?"

"Yes, a person with both sociopathic and psychopathic traits has the potential of becoming quite dangerous."

"Like how would she become more dangerous?"

"Well, for instance, she could create a crescendo of violence with herself directing the show."

"What do you mean?"

"She could start and not stop until she is forced to stop."

"You mean, like she could go on a murder spree?"

"Yeah, that could happen."

"You mentioned impulsive acts of violence, I have a case of a little boy who fell off a two story banister, and Ms. Thomason is the only witness. If she simply chucked the kid over the rail, would that be the act of a sociopath?"

"Yes, that fits the actions of a sociopath."

"How did she get this way, a bad childhood?"

"Perhaps, sociopathy may be a result of brain lesions, but upbringing and environment play a large role."

"What kinds of behavior do we expect from sociopaths?"

"Their behavior manifests as conniving and deceitful, despite appearing sincere and trustworthy. As you already noticed, she will shrug one shoulder when she wants to appear innocent. She also coughs or clears her throat when caught off guard. All of those signs tell me she is lying."

"But, it is treatable, right?"

"Actually, no it isn't. They found when psychopaths and sociopaths received therapy in prison they got worse instead of better. They are so intelligent they learn behaviors in therapy that they use to their advantage."

"What? There is no cure?"

"That is correct. Sociopaths and psychopaths can never change. That's why people like Charles Manson will never be let out of prison."

"He is such a sicko, why isn't he in a mental hospital?"

"He's not insane. He knows right from wrong, he just doesn't care. It is the same with Nancy."

"So, sociopaths and psychopaths go to prison and not mental health facilities?"

"That's right. Prisons are full of them."

"Are all sociopaths and psychopaths violent?"

"No, they're not. Psychopathy and sociopathy are combinations of traits, and a person could have one or more of the traits; few people have all of them, but a person with all the traits is very dangerous."

"So, you're saying that some people have a few psychopathic traits while others have more or even all of them?"

"Yes, for instance, one dominant trait of psychopathy is a lack of fear. Those who are fearless do great things like defuse bombs, fight wars, and enter burning

buildings. They don't fret or get nervous, so they make great surgeons, football players, CEO's, and even other potentially high stress and dangerous professions like
working in a prison or being a detective."

"Like you and me? Are you saying we're psychopaths?"

"Well, let's not get into my mental health, but I know you have no fear, so you
have one of the traits."

"Great, thanks a whole hell of a lot."

****

"Hello?"

"Where are you, Grandma? You were supposed to come to bail me out today."

"Now Nancy, don't be like that. I never said I'd bail you out, did I?"

"Yes, you did. When we talked last night, you said you would."

"That's what you want to think I said, but I never said it."

"So what, I want out of here and you have to come bail me out. Please come get
me."

"I don't think that would be wise, Nancy."

"Why are you playing these games with me, Grandma? I'm in jail, for shit sake!"

"Yes, I realize that, Nancy. Calm down, there is no need for you to yell at me."

"Don't tell me to calm down!"

"But, I will." A guard's hand gripped her shoulder. "Your call is over."

"No, please. I'm okay now. I'll be quiet."

"One more outburst and you're done."

"Okay, I understand." Nancy lowered her voice. "Grandma, I cannot stay in this
hell hole. You have to get me out of here soon. It's horrible in here. Please, Grandma.
I can't stand it."

"Tom Hurd told me what you did at the bar. You were quite violent and out of
control, weren't you? I just don't think now is a good time for you to come home."

"What do you mean?"

"I mean, I know how you lose your temper and have periods of continuous tantrums. I don't want you to behave that way in my home. You have done that way too
many times. You need to learn to control your anger."

She paused, but Nancy said nothing.

"You know you do. And now is as good a time as any. You just can't go around
throwing liquor bottles at people, Nancy. Tom told me there are anger management
classes, and other self-help classes you can take while you're in there. I think it would

be better if you took advantage of the free help and stay where you are. You need to work out your problems and to learn how to control your temper. It simply is not socially acceptable behavior, Nancy."

"So, you're making me stay in jail? The trial won't start until September. I can't stay here that long, Grandma. You have to get me out of here."

"No, Nancy, I don't. That just isn't going to happen. Good-bye."

CHAPTER 27

TOM HURD CALLED. "I'm sorry, but you passed your mental health exam. That leaves mental incapacity out as a defense."

"A deputy told me I was a psychopath. Doesn't that count as crazy?"

"The doctor did say she found indications of sociopathy, but that isn't considered insanity."

"I don't care. All I want is to get out of here. I have a business to run. I have clients who expect me to work for them and I've already received advance payments. I can't stay in here. I have work to do."

"I will see what I can do about your business, but it doesn't look good for you to get out any time soon. As you know, your grandmother refused to post bond. Is there anyone else you can ask?"

"Um, no there isn't."

"Well, in that case, I suggest you impress the judge by taking Anger Management and Stress Management classes. To get on his good side, I suggest you also take Healthy Relationships and Thinking for a Change."

"Seriously, you expect me to stoop to self-help classes to kiss the judge's ass?"

"It wouldn't hurt your case and the classes may help you."

"Yeah, okay." She slammed the receiver down.

****

"Hi, Riki, what's new?"

"Hey, Todd, how's it going?"

"I thought you'd like to drop by the lounge to see the damage Nancy caused before the repairs begin."

"Absolutely, I can't get my head around what she did without seeing it."

"You'll be shocked by the devastation. We have estimates, but nothing's been done yet, so you'll see it pretty much as it was that night." He looked at Riki's flip flops. "There are glass shards all over the floor, so you need to wear better shoes, hiking boots if you have them."

Riki ran up to her apartment, dug out her old boots, and carried them downstairs. "Will these be okay?"

"Yeah, they're perfect."

She laced up the boots and grabbed her bag. "Okay, I'm ready."

"Great. Let's go."

****

"Holy shit, this is unreal!"

"Those were my exact words when I saw it the first time."

"Unbelievable," she turned around, "this is wild. It looks like a horror movie in here. She must have gone totally berserk."

"Yeah, that's what Dave said, too. People were sitting at the bar, in the booths, and at the tables throughout the lounge when she started throwing bottles." He ran his fingers through his hair. "It's a wonder no one was seriously hurt."

"I never thought she'd lose it like this. I mean, this is crazy." Riki crunched her way across the glass-strewn floor. "This must be what they mean when they say someone goes off the deep end."

"Yeah, and she hit rock bottom."

"So, what happened to her? Where is she?"

"Last I heard she's sitting in Las Colinas."

"Why is she still in jail? I thought she'd be out on bail by now." She glanced at Todd. "But, I am glad she's not."

"Yeah, I know what you mean. I could happily go the rest of my life without ever seeing her again."

"Do you have to testify against her?"

"I might if it goes to trial."

"Oh, that would be toxic."

"I'm not looking forward to it."

"Well, maybe it won't go to trial. I mean, it must be on video. What could be her defense?"

"You got me there, insanity? If she has a good lawyer, she could get off with a slap on the wrist."

"No, she threw liquor bottles at people. Isn't that an assault and battery or something?"

"Yeah, she's being charged with aggravated assault and battery. Her preliminary hearing is next week."

"Well, I guess we'll find out soon enough."

* * * * * * * * *

In her first anger management class, the instructor gave her a notebook and a short pencil. "This is for you to record your thoughts. It takes out the sting when you write down what's bothering you. Try it. It will help you feel better."

"Oh, I don't know."

"Don't worry. It is completely private. I will never read your journal. But, I advise you to keep it locked in your locker if you don't want others to read it. Just remember to return the pencil before you leave the area, okay?"

Nancy sat at an empty table, opened the notebook, and began to write. 'Grandma has abandon me just like mom and dad. She hasn't visited me, or called, or even sent a letter. Todd hasn't visited me, not one time. He couldn't still be upset over what happened at the bar, could he? Riki hasn't bothered to visit me, either. I am the best friend she's ever had. I am a much better friend to her than that horrid bitch, Bonnie, but she made it clear that she doesn't want me as a friend anymore. She doesn't have to worry about that because we are officially no longer friends.'

She paused and chewed on her pencil then continued to write. 'It is obvious I matter to no one. No one comes to visit me. No one cares about me. No one cares what happens to me. Nobody loves me.' She wiped the tears off her face. She wrote, 'I am going to kill Grandma as soon as I get out of here. And after Grandma is out of the way, I will kill Riki, and Todd, and everyone else I hate in Solana Beach. They can't treat me this way and get away with it, and none of them will.'

* * * * * * * * *

"I want you to be prepared for the District Attorney to offer you a plea of a misdemeanor assault and battery which means less jail time and no trial."

"Like how much time in jail?"

"Oh, I'd say you'd get around six to eight months."

"No shit? Am I stuck here all that time?"

"Yes, you'll serve your sentence here in Las Colinas, and after you're released you'll have probation for another two years. By the way, the judge will most likely order your participation in anger management classes."

"That's just great." She slammed her fist on the table. "Everyone keeps shoving that damn anger management class down my throat."

"Hey, be cool."

"I'll have you know, I have already started that stupid anger management class. Not that it has done much good. I'm still pissed off all the time."

"Just don't get pissed off at the judge."

She gritted her teeth. "I will try not to."

                         ****

"Ms. Thomason, are you accepting the District Attorney's offer of pleading guilty to the lesser charge of misdemeanor assault and battery?"

"Yes, I am Your Honor."

Mr. Hurd said, "We request the court to waive time for sentencing, Your Honor."

"Request granted." The judge shuffled papers. "All right, I sentence you to Las Colinas Detention and Reentry Facility for a period of not less than eight months with credit for time served during which you are to successfully complete both Anger Management and Stress Management classes. And, after release from Las Colinas, I sentence you to an additional two years of probation during which time you waive your fourth amendment right to unreasonable search and seizure. Do you accept?"

"Yes, I do Your Honor."

"Ms. Thomason, you must learn to control your temper. A public temper tantrum like the one you had in The Lavender Moon Lounge is criminal behavior, especially when you put the health and safety of others at risk."

"I understand, Your Honor."

"Now about restitution, Mr. and Mrs. Johnson who own the lounge presented the court with a bill with the estimated cost of repairs in the amount of $19,527."

Nancy whispered, "I don't have that kind of money."

"Your Honor, my client would like to pay the restitution on a payment plan."

"Not a problem, you can make arrangements with the court clerk." The judge slammed the gavel down.

Mr. Hurd said, "Well, that's it. I will get back to you about the restitution."

****

For days after her preliminary hearing, Nancy succumbed to depression and didn't want to get out of bed.

"What's the matter Thomason? Feeling blue?" The Corrections Officer stood looking down at her. "Why don't you get up and move around a little, get something to eat?"

"What's the point? I lost. I give up. I might was well die. I want to die. Just let me die, okay?"

"Hmm, I think you need to see the shrink again. I am going to give her a call and then you are going to go see her."

"Why bother? What can she do for me? She can't change the mess I made of my life."

"No, but she can give you anti-depressants, which will help you feel better. Don't get me wrong, your life is still a mess and you are still stuck in here, but it will be easier to live with, and live with it you will. We don't allow wimping out through suicide in here and if we think you are at risk, you get thrown into 'suicide watch' which means you're in isolation and you'd hate it."

"Okay, whatever."

Fifteen minutes later the Corrections Officer was back at her bunk. "Get up, Thomason. You have a date with the doctor."

****

"So Nancy, they tell me you feel like killing yourself. Tell me what's going on."

"Everything and everyone is against me. I hate it in here and I can't do anything about it. No one comes to visit me, not even my grandmother."

"What about your friends? Surely someone's been to see you?"

"No, only my lawyer who was paid to see me and now my case is over and I won't even see him."

"You haven't made any friends in here?"

Nancy stared at the doctor. "You must be kidding. How could I possibly make friends with someone in here? They are all criminals."

"Nancy, I have news for you, so are you. You must accept that fact."

She lowered her head. "Yes, thanks for reminding me. I want to be dead."

"That is a rather extreme method of avoidance, isn't it? Let's try something less extreme like medication, okay?"

"Oh, I don't know. I don't like taking drugs of any kind."

"Sorry, but I must insist. I will submit a prescription for Elavil for you to begin tomorrow. I must warn you to avoid consuming beef and red wine as they can be fatal while you are taking this medication."

****

She sat alone in the recreation room. No one talked to her, or even showed any interest in her, or at least she thought. One afternoon, a woman sat next to her.

"Hi, I'm Laurel. Who are you?"

"My name is Nancy."

"What's that, your journal for Anger Management class?"

Nancy closed the notebook. "Yeah, do you have one, too?"

"Hey, we all have them."

"They say it helps writing it down." She drew the notebook toward her. "Does it work for you?"

"Nothing works for me better than booze. I love red wine."

"I'm allergic, I like margaritas best, but I was drinking Long Islands Iced Teas when I threw my fit in the bar. Wish I had one right now."

"Is that what you're in here for?"

"Yeah, it was just a little angry outburst in a bar."

"No, shit? You're in here for something so petty?"

Nancy nodded. "Yeah, I can't believe it myself."

"How can they be so stupid?"

"How about you, why are you here?"

"Oh, nothing much, I just broke into a couple of places, that's all."

"Was that hard to do? I mean, how do you actually break in?"

Laurel held up her hands and wiggled her fingers. "I have the magic touch when it comes to picking locks."

"Really, you know how to pick locks? Can you teach me how?"

"That's sort of hard to do in jail. They frown on us practicing our skills in here, can't imagine why."

She laughed and Nancy joined her. It felt good to laugh.

"There must be a way."

"I'll see what I can do."

The next morning while Nancy walked in circles in the recreation yard, Laurel walked next to her. "I have the answer to your question."

"What question?"

"Can I teach you how to pick locks, what else?"

"So? Can you?"

"I can now, I just acquired a padlock, and you can learn all you need to know with it."

"Super, that gives me something to do. Let's get started."

Nancy was a quick study and soon mastered the art of lock picking. While they practiced, they talked about themselves and their crimes, but Nancy shared only her experience with burglaries, and not stalking and killing.

"Wow, Nancy, you are lucky you didn't get busted a long time ago. I mean seriously, you are sloppy, don't you think?"

"Why, what do you mean?"

"You are going to get caught if you don't tighten your game."

"I've done okay so far."

"Yeah, right, look around. Hello Nancy, you're in jail."

"But, this was caused by just a momentary lapse in judgment."

"Yes, aren't they all?"

"Well, what do you think I'm doing wrong?"

"Just an observation, but I would say you act on impulse and have been extremely lucky to have gotten away with as much as you have."

"Gee, thanks."

"But, your luck ran out that day at your boyfriend's bar, didn't it?"

"So, what could I have done differently?"

"Oh, come on, you know the answer to that."

"Why don't you tell me since you have all the answers?"

"Well, obviously getting drunk was not a good idea. It is never a good idea to lose control."

"Okay, I get that, what else?"

"Plan things out in advance, have all the materials you need with you and use every day common materials so it is harder to trace back to you. And, always pay with cash, no credit cards. And when you do go into stores to buy the materials, wear a disguise because all stores have video surveillance now. And, make sure there are no witnesses and no evidence left behind. Always wear gloves."

"I'm impressed, you know how to do this inside and out."

"Well, I do what I have to do whatever it is."

* * * * * * * * * *

"So," Laurel said, "tonight's your last night with us. You are so lucky." She drifted over to the bunk where Nancy's meager possessions spread about. She stared at Nancy's journal.

"Yeah, I cannot believe the time has finally come for me to get out of here. It seems like I've been in here forever."

"I know what you mean." Laurel turned her big body so it blocked Nancy's view of the bed.

"You have only a week to go, no whining."

"Yeah, okay." Laurel grabbed the journal and stuffed it down the front of her pants. She moved a few magazines to fill the empty space. "I know it is only a week away, but I can't wait."

"Why, do you have something special waiting for you?"

"No, I just want out of here."

"Is there someone special waiting for you?"

"No, not really, I don't even have a place to live. All I have is my old Dodge van, but I can live in it, I guess."

"Oh, I see. That sounds like living rough. How do you survive?"

"Mostly through the kindness of others, but sometimes I have to steal to eat. I don't want to, but sometimes I have to. How about you, what are you going to do when you get out?"

"Oh, I'm going to look up a few old friends. There are a few things I need to straighten out."

"Is your grandmother picking you up tomorrow?"

"I expect she will."

"You are so lucky to have her. She sounds really nice."

"She has her moments."

Laurel reached the door. "I wish you the best of luck out there. Don't come back as they say."

"I won't if I can help it. Hey, call me when you get out and we'll meet for drinks."

Laurel was out the door, but ducked her head in. "Yeah, sure, okay. I have your number."

"Okay, till then."

CHAPTER 28

NANCY WALKED OUT of Las Colinas Detention and Reentry Facility a free woman, but freedom couldn't erase the intense, murderous hatred that had festered during her time behind bars and fueled her desire for revenge and murder.

The gate clanked shut. No one waited for her. What would she do now? Suddenly alone and desperate she felt lost and abandoned, much as she did when she was a little girl. She searched the parking lot and then saw Mrs. Williams striding toward her. Her grandma smiled big.

"Nancy, I am so glad to see you." Her grandmother hugged and kissed her. "You look marvelous."

"Odd, I don't feel marvelous. It was not what I would call a resort vacation." She narrowed her eyes at her grandmother. "I am surprised you came to pick me up since you never came to visit me. When I walked out that gate, I thought I was on my own."

"Now, don't be cross with me, Nancy." Mrs. Williams looked straight into her eyes. "I just couldn't bring myself to see you handcuffed in court or to see you locked up in jail. I'm sorry, I just couldn't. It would break my heart to see you like that."

"I thought you had forgotten me."

"Of course, I didn't forget you. I'm here, aren't I?"

"Are you ashamed of me?" Nancy looked at her feet. "Is that why you didn't visit me?"

"Oh, Nancy, of course, I am not ashamed of you."

Nancy looked up. "Then why didn't you come?"

"I started out here several times, but each time I had to turn around. I just couldn't do it. It would bring back too many horrible memories of your mother."

Her jaw dropped. "My mother was in jail? You never told me that."

"I wanted to tell you, but you were so young I thought it would be better for you not to know, and when you were older, it never seemed to be the right time, so I didn't, until now."

"But, you told me that my mom and dad dumped me with you and took off."

"Yeah, well, I made it up."

"Grandma, it's not true, none of it? You lied to me?"

"I'm sorry, Nancy. I know it sounds bad, but you were just a little girl and I didn't want to burden you, but now that you're an adult and," she swallowed, "you've been in jail, I guess you can handle the truth."

"Okay, okay, just tell me."

"Well, I'm sorry to say, your mother had mental problems. After she murdered your father, she was diagnosed as a psychopath."

"What?" Nancy stared at her. "My mother murdered my father?"

"I understand it's a shock." Mrs. Williams started walking toward the parking lot. "But yes, your mother killed your father."

Nancy walked beside her. "Oh, my God, what happened?"

"Well, they had an argument over something inconsequential, and it got out of hand. Your mother often lost her temper and did some rash and reckless things, like you." She glanced at her. "You are so much like her. You remind me of her a great deal. Anyway, this time she did something too reckless."

"She killed him?"

"Yes, that is what happened. In the heat of the moment, she took a butcher knife and stabbed him over and over until he was dead and then some." She took a deep breath and let it out in a 'swoosh.'

"It happened after I went to bed, didn't it?"

"Yes, that's right."

"I remember when that happened, I think. I woke up at your house when I had gone to bed at my house."

"Yes, when we heard what happened we brought you home to our house."

"What happened to my mom?"

"She pled guilty and was sent to the Central California Women's Facility in Chowchilla."

"Great, I'll visit her." She clasped her hands under her chin.

"Ah, no, you can't." Mrs. Williams sighed and looked straight ahead. "Three years later, she killed herself."

"What?" Nancy's jaw dropped. "She's dead?"

"Yes, somehow she managed to get drugs in prison and overdosed."

"Both my parents are dead? My mother murdered my father, went to prison, and then committed suicide. Was she crazy or what?"

"What can I say? She was a wild girl. She was defiant and willful. She didn't like to follow rules and she often had tantrums and got into trouble." Mrs. Williams rubbed her forehead. "Your grandfather rather encouraged her when she was young, but then he was sorry when she landed in prison for murder."

"My grandfather, you hardly ever talk about him. How did he die? I remember Grandpa, but not too well."

"No, you wouldn't. He died soon after that."

"I remember he did a lot of yelling."

"He had trouble accepting that his daughter was a murderer. He didn't want you to live with us. He wanted to put you up for adoption."

"He didn't want me? Didn't he love me? Was I bad?" Tears flooded her eyes.

"No, you were not bad. You were a traumatized little girl, and he was a stubborn old jerk. He needed a long sleep. He died of an accidental overdose."

"He overdosed, too?"

"Yes, one night he was desperate to sleep and took a few too many sleeping pills. It was sort of like what happened to Michael Jackson."

"When was that?"

"That was about a year after you came to live with me, I think. You must have been around four, weren't you?"

They reached the car. "So, then he died?"

They got in and Mrs. Williams started the engine. "So, then he died, and it was just you and me. We had a better life without him."

"Grandma, you sound as if you wanted him out of the way. Did you help him die?"

"Well, I may have helped make sure he had plenty of pills to do the job."

"You mean you killed him?"

"You have to understand that he wanted to put you in Foster Care. I would not allow that to happen. I had to protect you, so I took care of him."

"I come from a family of killers. You killed my grandfather and my mother killed my father and herself."

"Yes, I guess that sums it up." Mrs. Williams paused while she changed lanes. "Speaking about killing people, tell me, did they question you about any other crimes while you were incarcerated?"

Nancy cringed when she heard the word incarcerated. "What are you talking about?"

"I won't turn you in, Nancy, it is okay. You can tell me."

"Tell you what?"

"I was wondering if they suspected you of those fatal accidents in Solana Beach." She looked out her side window. "What fatal accidents?"

"Oh, you know what I'm talking about."

Nancy continued to look out her side window. "No, I don't."

"Don't be coy with me, dear."

"I am not being coy, Grandma." She rummaged in her purse. "I have no idea what you're talking about."

"Listen, I read the papers and watch the news, so I know what's going on and I couldn't help but notice that after you moved to North County there were at least three deaths, and maybe more that appeared to be accidents, but we know better, don't we?"

"Oh, I get it." She found her sunglasses and put them on. "You think I am responsible for the accidental deaths of some insignificant unfortunates in Solana Beach. Is that what you are talking about?"

"Well, it was obvious because the accidental deaths stopped when you went to jail."

Nancy shrugged one shoulder. "Grandma, I had nothing to do with those accidents."

"Oh, come on. You don't expect me to believe that, do you? You are too much like your mother." She glanced at Nancy. "I know you caused those deaths and they were not accidents, and I sure as hell hope, for your sake, there are no more fatal accidents."

Nancy raised her eyebrows. "I don't know what you're talking about."

"This is a warning Nancy, no more fatal accidents, none. It has to stop." Her grandma looked at her. "You forget that I know you better than anyone, better than you know yourself."

Nancy seethed, and took Laurel's advice; she planned.

CHAPTER 29

"I HOPE YOU'LL be comfortable, dear."

Nancy cleared her throat. "I will try."

Mrs. Williams hugged her. "Good, that's all we can expect." She gave Nancy another affectionate squeeze. Nancy stiffened. "What's on your agenda for tomorrow?"

She pulled away. "Not much, maybe I'll just stay in my pajamas all day and watch TV."

"That sounds great. Tomorrow morning I have an early doctor's appointment, but I'll be home in time for our soaps. We'll have such fun watching our stories together, just like old times."

"Yeah, just like old times. I can't wait."

"Were you able to keep up to date with our stories while you were away?"

"I think so. There wasn't much else to do in jail, but watch TV."

She went into her old room and was surprised to find The Swirling Red Mist hanging opposite her bed and the desk, the credenza, and computer from her office arranged in one corner.

"Grandma, how did you get these things?"

"Your landlady called me. I believe her name is Kathy. She wanted to know what to do about your office. I told her you were not able to continue working and I would pay another month's rent. I didn't tell her why, but I think she knew."

She stood in front of The Swirling Red Mist and studied it. "Some of your things are in storage, but you had such a cute office and living area, I couldn't bear putting everything into storage. I found this painting very interesting, and I fell in love with it. I don't know why, but this painting reminds me of you in some way. While you were away, I often came in here to look at it and think about you. And, I can't explain why, but when I am close to the painting I feel close to you."

She turned and looked at the rest of the room. "Anyway, since there was plenty of room in here, I brought a few things home hoping they would help you feel more comfortable."

"So, I lost my office? What about my business?"

"Tom told me I might as well dissolve your business, so I went through your calendar and cancelled all the events you had listed and refunded the advances you received. Essentially, your business is gone."

Nancy flopped onto the bed. "So, I lost everything. That's just super." She rested her head on her crossed arms. "I have nothing now."

"I'm sorry Nancy, but what did you expect, everything to be the same? You didn't think you could just pick up where you left off, did you?" Mrs. Williams put her hands on her hips. "I did the best I could for you, didn't I?"

"Yeah, sure you did." She rolled onto her side and stretched out on the bed. "I need time to decompress, so if you don't mind, I think I'll just rest until dinner, okay?"

"Of course, I understand. Take your time. We'll order a pizza when you're ready."

Her grandma closed the door and Nancy bolted off the bed. She went to the wall and pulled an extension cord from the socket. She stared at The Swirling Red Mist while she pulled it through her hands over, and over.

Mrs. Williams found a long, boring movie for them to watch while they ate dinner and Nancy contemplated her grandmother's impending fatal accident. Midway through the movie, she stretched her arms over her head and yawned.

"I am tired, Grandma, I think I'll go to bed now."

"Okay. I may not see you in the morning. I have to leave early for the doctor's appointment, but I'll make us a nice brunch when I get back."

"Sounds like a plan." She closed her bedroom door, got into bed, and waited.

Her grandmother had been snoring for an hour when she got out of bed, grabbed the extension cord, and slipped outside. At the top of the long flight of concrete steps, she stretched the cord across the top step at a height of about four inches. Satisfied, she slipped back into bed and slept better than she had since she killed Billy.

A few hours later, Mrs. Williams rapped on Nancy's door. "I'm leaving now, dear. I'll be back as soon as I can."

"Okay, Grandma. I hope everything goes well. Bye-bye."

Nancy listened as Mrs. Williams opened the front door and hurried out. She tripped with a surprised shriek, and plummeted headfirst to the concrete slab. Her skull cracked, and her head twisted at an unnatural angle, her neck broken.

When Nancy heard the last satisfying thump, she got of bed and sauntered outside where her grandmother lay motionless at the foot of the stairs. She untied the extension cord, went back inside, and with the cord still in her hand, she called 911. Then, she plugged the extension cord back into the wall and connected a lamp.

She started a pot coffee before she went out and took a position near Mrs. Williams' head. She held her grandma's lifeless hand in hers, composed a sad expression, and waited.

****

One of the paramedics took her elbow. "Here, let me help you up. The ME needs to look at her."

"Yes, okay."

"Tell me what happened. Did you see her fall?"

"No. I was still in bed, but I heard her fall. She screamed and then there was a horrible thumpa, thumpa, tumbling sound, and then it was quiet." She shrugged one shoulder. "I ran out here as fast as I could. She wasn't breathing, so I ran back inside to call for help."

"You did the best you could," the paramedic said.

Yes, Nancy nodded, and it worked too.

The medical examiner found no bruising or any marks on Mrs. Williams' ankles. Nancy overheard him say to the detective from the San Diego Police Department, "It appears to be an accident. There is nothing to suggest a crime has been committed, but I'll know more after I conduct an autopsy."

The detective introduced himself. "Hello, Ms. Thomason. I'm Detective Randy Nichols with the SDPD. I'm the lead investigator on this case. Tell me what happened to your grandmother this morning."

"Well, I was in bed when I heard her fall. I ran out and found her at the bottom of the stairs." She watched her grandmother's body lifted to a gurney. "Then, I called 911."

"I understand that you were released from Las Colinas yesterday."

"Yeah, so what does that have to do with anything?"

"Why are you so defensive?"

"I'm not, but you make it sound like it had something to do with this."

"Did it?"

"No, why would you think that?"

"Hey, you get out of jail and the next morning your grandmother dies falling down her stairs. In my line of work, we call that a coincidence."

He paused to give her time to respond, but she watched her grandmother's body pushed into the medical examiner's vehicle. She covered her mouth and said nothing.

"And, I don't believe in coincidences."

"I don't get it. What does my release from jail have to do with her falling down the stairs?"

"That's what I would like to know." He stared at her a long minute. "When people get out of jail and the next day their closest relative ends up dead, I have to wonder what the hell happened."

She cleared her throat. "Sorry, I can't help you there. All I know is that she had a doctor's appointment this morning. She said good bye, rushed out, and fell down the stairs."

"I will need you to come to the station to give a statement."

"Sorry, I just can't face that right now."

"Okay." The detective pulled his business card out of his pocket and handed it to her. "Call me tomorrow and we'll set up a time for you to come in."

Nancy took his card. "Okay, thanks."

Finally, the ambulance left followed by the cops. Alone in the house, now her house, she danced around her inheritance. Coffee was ready. Life promised her a happy future.

****

"Hello, Nancy. Remember me?"

"Laurel?"

"Yes, surprised to hear from me?"

"Um, well, yeah. How are you?"

"Not so good, but I hear you are doing quite well."

"What do you mean?"

"I mean you offed your grandma, so you scratched one name off your list."

"What are you talking about, what list?"

"The list of everyone you were going to kill when you got out of jail. And, damn it, Girlfriend, you started the night you got out, didn't you?"

"I never told you about any list."

"You're right, you didn't. I stole your journal and read it and I still have it, for sale or for evidence."

"What, you stole my journal? You are blackmailing me?"

"You got that right, I am."

"But why, I thought we were friends?"

"Jailhouse friendships are just that. Get real, why don't you?"

"Okay, I guess you want something for the notebook, what is it?"

"I think $10,000 would cover it."

"You expect me to give you $10,000?" She laughed. "You cannot be serious."

"Oh, but I am. You see, I can turn this notebook of yours over to the SDPD and when they read about how you planned to kill your grandma as soon as you got out, well I don't have to tell you what would happen next."

"But, $10,000 is a lot of money and I don't have that much available."

"You must, the old lady was loaded wasn't she?"

"But it is all tied up in bonds and securities. It will take me some time to get it together."

"Like how much time? I need the money NOW."

"I understand. Um, can we talk about it? Can I meet you someplace where we can talk?"

"What is there to talk about? I want the money or I go to the cops."

"Yes, but I may have to arrange a payment plan with you. I don't think I can get that much cash all at once."

"Okay, well get what you can. We can meet in an hour."

"Ah, no I need more time. Why don't I buy you a steak tonight? We can meet at The Chart House in Solana Beach at 8:00. I will do what I can about the money."

****

Nancy drove to Corner Liquor and bought a medium size bottle of red wine. She went back to her house, crushed her entire thirty-day supply of Elavil, poured it into the bottle, and shook it until all trace of the drug had dissolved.

She taped a bow on the neck of the bottle, wiped it clean of fingerprints. Then, without touching it she placed the bottle in a gift bag.

Inside The Chart House, she saw Laurel right away; she stood out even in the packed restaurant. With long blonde hair and a huge body, she looked like a pale whale. In fact, her nickname in jail was The Pale Whale, although no one had the nerve to say it to her face.

"Hi, Laurel." Nancy slid into the booth across from her. She handed the gift bag across the table. "This is for you, a get out of jail and welcome to freedom present."

Laurel took the bottle and beamed. "This is my favorite! I haven't had good California red wine in years and now I have a whole bottle all to myself." She glared at Nancy. "Don't try to horn in on any."

"No, of course not, it is all for you. I did open it and poured myself a small sample, just to make sure it was good enough for you. But you can't drink it in here. It's for later. Are you hungry for a big steak? The porterhouse is great, but so is the filet mignon."

"Sounds great, thanks, but dinner with you isn't why I'm here."

"I understand, but can we at least eat as we once did as friends?"

The server took their order and Laurel brought out a handful of photocopies and pushed them across the table.

"You've already started, haven't you? I heard about how your grandma fell to her death the day you after you got out."

Nancy looked at the copies of her written declaration of murder. She swallowed hard.

"How did you hear about it in there?"

"Jailhouse news travels fast, you ought to know that."

Nancy sighed as she stared at the photocopies. "Yes, I guess I do."

"You haven't killed Todd yet, though. I could save his life and the other three if I turn it in to the cops."

"Where is the original?"

"Wouldn't you like to know?"

"It will take me some time to get $10,000, but when I pay it I want the notebook back, intact."

"When I get the money, you will get the journal."

Their orders came and they were quiet. When Laurel finished her steak, Nancy said, "Would you like to finish mine? I hardly touched it."

Laurel's head snapped up and looked at Nancy and then her eyes landed on the huge steak. "You sure? Thanks. I haven't eaten meat like this ever. I am lovin' it."

Nancy slid her steak onto Laurel's plate. "Enjoy."

Laurel scarfed down the second steak and sat back.

Nancy tapped her fingers on the table. "How do I know you actually have the journal? You could have taken these copies last month for all I know."

Laurel smiled, wiped her mouth, and grabbed her purse.

"Please tell me where you have the notebook. I need it back."

"Sorry, I have to leave now. Thanks for dinner and the wine. Call me when you have the money. And I want all of it, don't try to short me."

"No, I wouldn't think of doing something like that."

Nancy paid the bill and followed her into the parking lot, started her car and managed to follow behind Laurel's beat up Dodge van as she drove south to Mission Bay Park. Laurel parked next to the grass and Nancy circled around so she parked facing Laurel from across the parking lot.

Nancy watched Laurel unfold a lawn chair, bring out a plastic cup and the bottle of wine, and collapse in the chair.

Laurel opened the wine and filled her cup. She drank and enjoyed her last day as the shadows darkened around her. The bottle was almost empty when she took a long drink, swallowed, and gasped. She clutched her throat, stopped breathing, and drooped in her chair, dead.

Nancy got out of her car and approached her.

Nancy touched her hand. "Laurel, can you hear me? Are you okay?" She laughed. "It worked."

Nancy straightened and looked around. Families were busy packing up and going home. No one noticed them. Off the grass and in the sand a group of teenagers stood next to a bonfire. They talked and laughed. Off to Nancy's right, a party revved up to high speed. No one noticed this big dead woman holding an empty wine bottle. And no one noticed Nancy as she opened the door to the van and entered.

The place was a mess; clothes and food wrappers littered the space. Nancy searched under all the debris but could not find the notebook. She looked under the seats to no avail. Where could it be? She opened the glove box and out popped the notebook. Next, she found Laurel's purse and pulled out the photocopies.

In her car, Nancy laughed as she flipped through her jail journal. Nothing seemed to be ripped out or missing. That silly woman thought she could dictate to her. And, now she was dead, the greedy thief.

Nancy got out of her car, pulled her hoodie over her hair, and carried the notebook, with the photocopies folded within, to where the teens stood next to the bonfire.

"Hi, my name is Lynn."

A boy said, "Hey Lynn, join us, have a beer."

"Oh, that is so nice of you, but I was really just wondering if I could stand by your fire for a few minutes. I am a bit chilled."

"Sure, take all the time you need."

When the boy went back to drinking with his friends, Nancy threw the notebook onto the fire. She watched until all the pages burn to ashes, then she left. In her car, she burst out singing Maxwell's Silver Hammer as she drove home.

CHAPTER 30

THE HAIRCUTTER ASKED, "What would you like done today?"

"I'm ready for a new look, I want a big change. Cut it to about to my chin and give me curls." Two hours later, she walked out with short, curly hair.

The day before she left for Solana Beach, she darkened her hair and bought a new wardrobe all in black. With short, curly, dark brown hair and black clothes, Nancy looked like a different person. She felt different, too. She felt stronger, invincible, empowered.

She drove to Solana Beach and checked into a room at the Holiday Inn Express located down the street from The Lavender Moon Lounge. She slipped into all black beach clothes, grabbed a floppy hat and her towel, and left for the beach.

At Fletcher's Cove, she strolled down the concrete slope to the beach, crossed the sand, splashed her feet in the shore break, and ambled south where Solana Beach merged into Del Mar. Sunbathers dotted the sand and beach volleyball players attracted a small crowd of cheering fans. Her gaze drifted east to the train trestle that stretched across the lagoon and watched The Coaster zoom north to Solana Beach Amtrak Station. She took a deep breath of the fresh ocean air and headed back toward the cove. Half way there, she passed a staircase leading to a condominium complex on the bluff and heard voices above her. She glanced up as a man and a woman descended the steep stairs. The man looked a lot like Todd, but the chubby woman with dull brown hair was someone she had never seen before.

When they reached the sand, the man led the way. "Let's sit over here where high tide won't reach us."

"Yeah, like last time." His chubby girlfriend giggled. "But, that was sort of fun, wasn't it?" She giggled again.

The man chuckled. "Yes, it was like an impromptu wet tee shirt contest with only two contestants." The man leaned over and gave the woman a long kiss.

The woman giggled. "Oh, Todd, you knew that was going to happen, didn't you? You set that up on purpose." They kissed again.

Nancy looked up the steep staircase to the top of the bluff where a locked gate blocked beach access to the Pacifica Condos. She ignored the affectionate couple and returned to the Holiday Inn Express. She dumped her things on the bed and called the Pacifica Condos management office.

"Do you have any condominiums for rent?"

"Yes, we have two condos available at the moment."

"Great, can I meet you tomorrow morning?"

"How's 9:00 suit you?"

"That's perfect."

****

The next morning, Nancy was at the rental office ten minutes early. "Hello, I'm Lynn Thomason. I called yesterday about a condo to rent."

"Yes, of course. I remember, Lynn. I am Scott Noon the manager. As I told you yesterday, there are only two condos for rent. One is near the pool and the other near the street. I'll show you both and you can take your choice."

"Okay, let's see them.

Both condominiums were small, but adequate and pretty much the same.

"I'll take the one near the pool."

"That was fast."

"I don't believe in wasting time."

"Alright then, the paperwork is in the office."

****

She spent the day moving in and looked forward to relaxing in the Jacuzzi. She put on her suit, grabbed a towel, and headed for the pool area. Determined to be friendly, she stifled a groan when she saw another woman already soaking.

"Ah, this feels so good." She waded to an air jet opposite the woman and positioned herself so the jet of hot water shot right at the sore spot on her back. "Ah." She sank lower and rested her head on the rim of the tub. "This is fabulous."

Nancy looked at the other woman and recognized her latest replacement. "Hello, I'm Lynn. I just moved in today."

"Hi, I'm Ellen Taft. I live here with my boyfriend Todd. I moved in last month."

"Well, I guess that makes both of us newbies." Nancy looked around the pool area. "It seems nice so far. This hot tub does it for me."

"Yeah, it's great, isn't it?" Ellen adjusted her position. "I soak just about every night when I get home from work."

"What do you do?"

"I'm a nurse at Tri-City Hospital. It's stressful being a nurse and sometimes it is so physically strenuous my body positively aches when I get home. Soaking here helps me relax."

"I bet it does."

"So, Lynn, do you work or go to school?"

"I'm trying to decide." She looked up at the stars. "I just received a sizable inheritance, so I am taking time to think about what I want to do next." She shrugged her left shoulder. "I'm leaning toward either a year touring Europe or going back to school for my PhD, but then again, I might just stay here and cruise."

"What a great choice. You are so lucky you don't have to work."

"Yes, it is nice having the time to relax and enjoy myself while I think about what I want to do with the rest of my life." Nancy looked around the pool area again. "Where's your boyfriend?"

"He works nights across the street at The Lavender Moon Lounge. I'm going over there later. Hey, I have an idea. Why don't you come with me? He's a great guy, I'm sure you'd like him."

Nancy coughed. "No doubt I would, but no thanks, maybe another time, I spent all day moving in, and I'm tired."

"Okay." Ellen stood. "Well, I have been in here long enough." She waded through the water, grabbed the railing, and climbed out. "It was nice meeting you, Lynn." She wrapped her towel around her waist, and picked up her bag. "I hope you will be as happy here as I am. Bye."

"Thanks. I expect great things to happen here. See you later. Bye-bye."

"Maybe I'll see you in here again sometime."

"You can count on it. You will see me here tomorrow night and every night."

CHAPTER 31

"HI, ELLEN, I beat you to it tonight."

"So I see. How are you, Lynn?"

"I'm fine. How's it going with you?"

"Great! I was hoping you'd be here tonight because I brought margaritas for us to share. We can sip while we soak and get to know each other."

"But aren't there rules about drinking in the Jacuzzi?"

"Who knows? Who cares? Who's to see? It's deserted this time of night so no one will even notice."

"Wicked," Nancy said, "okay, let's party."

Out of Ellen's tote bag came a jug of margaritas and two plastic cups. "Sorry, no salt."

"That's okay. I'm not a big fan of salt."

"Neither am I." Ellen giggled, and then she gulped her drink and refilled her cup.

"I am getting a little too hot." Nancy lifted herself onto the edge and finished her drink. "Well, I have go now. Are you going to your boyfriend's bar tonight?"

"No, I don't think so, I'm a little drunk. I think I'll just watch TV until he comes home."

"Enjoy." Nancy stood. "I guess I'll see you tomorrow."

Ellen tried to pour herself another margarita, but the jug was empty. "Wait Lynn, I'm leaving, too." She stood, lost her balance, and fell back into the hot tub with a big splash. She giggled. "Oops, I guess I am more than a little drunk." She gripped the railing, and pulled herself up the first step.

"You look as if you could use some help." Nancy grabbed her hand and helped her climb the last two steps and onto the deck.

"Yeah, I am woozy, must be the Xanax kicking in." Ellen giggled. "Would you mind walking me home, Lynn?"

"Not at all, I'd be happy to."

Ellen linked arms with Nancy. "Thanks for your help, Lynn. I think I would fall without your support."

"No worries."

They reached Todd's apartment and Ellen unlocked the door, staggered inside, and tossed her things onto a chair while Nancy stood at the door and glanced around the apartment.

Ellen braced herself against the wall and giggled. "Thanks, Lynn. You're the best."

"You'll be okay now, won't you?"

"Yeah, I will be fine." She gestured toward the living room. "Would you like to come in for a while? I'm going to make another batch of margaritas." She giggled.

"Um no, I don't think so."

"Oh, okay. See you tomorrow?"

"Sure, and it'll be my turn to bring the margaritas."

* * * * * * * * * *

After a week of meeting Ellen in the Jacuzzi every night, and always sharing jug of margaritas, Nancy asked her burning question.

"So, tell me about your boyfriend. Have you known him long?"

"Oh, no, we met just a few months ago. It was right after Todd's ex-girlfriend went to Las Colinas."

"That's interesting."

"Let me tell you, Lynn, she was a real piece of work, from what Todd told me." Nancy gritted her teeth. "What do you mean?"

Ellen giggled. "Well to get herself thrown into the slammer, she went berserk in the lounge where he works and totally trashed it to the tune of $20,000! Todd wasn't even there at the time, but it totally freaked him."

"Yeah, that must have been traumatic for him." Nancy slipped lower in the water. "What happened to her?"

"Well, since she tried to kill people by throwing liquor bottles at them, they locked her up in county jail." Ellen giggled. "I wish they would keep her there forever. She is such a freak, that's where she belongs."

Nancy changed air jets. "When does she get out?"

"Let's see," Ellen found her cup empty, "she should be getting out around now, I guess. They're supposed to tell Todd when she gets out, but he hasn't heard anything yet, so I guess she's still in there."

"She's that bad, huh?"

Ellen refilled her cup. "She is the absolute worst. It would be nice if she never got out. Todd doesn't want to ever see her again." Ellen giggled. "Those were his exact words, too."

"So, what do you suppose she'll do when she gets out?"

"I have no clue, why?"

"Well, she could come back here."

"Here? Why would she come back here?" Ellen gulped her margarita. "I don't see why she'd want to do that. There is nothing for her here."

"No?"

Ellen downed the last of her drink, giggled, and poured herself another. "Apparently, she had a little event planning business here in Solana Beach, but lost it when she went to jail. Besides, Todd didn't love her then and he sure as hell doesn't love her now."

"Oh, of course he wouldn't. He has you now."

"Yes, that's right." She took a long drink. "From what he told me, she has no friends here. She has nothing to come back to. She'll probably go somewhere new where no one knows her and start over."

"Does she have somewhere else to go?"

"Who cares? All I know is Todd said she was bad news and he never wanted to see her again. And, that goes for everyone who knew her, too." Ellen gulped her drink.

"So, you've met her friends?"

"What friends? She has no friends, believe me. She knew a couple of women who I've met, but they are not her friends. They live on South Cedros Avenue just down the street from where she used to live. Todd's known them since high school and he is good friends with them. Riki owns The Erika Hollis Gallery, and Bonnie owns The Cubbyhole Bookstore. You'll have to check out their shops. Riki's cool. I like her. You will, too. With Nancy in jail, Todd and Riki became closer friends. They get together every morning for a walk on the beach."

"You don't worry she's after your boyfriend?"

"No, Riki has a boyfriend. She and Todd are just good friends."

"So Riki was good friends with Nancy, too?"

"No way, are you nuts? Before Nancy went to the bar that day and threw a fit, she first had a big fight with Riki. It was so bad Riki told her she would never speak to her again, and she hasn't." Ellen tossed down her drink. "I wouldn't either, if I were her."

"I see." She gritted her teeth and stood. "Well, I have to go now." She sloshed out of the hot water, tied a towel around her waist, and tossed the jug and plastic cups into the white plastic shopping bag.

She unclenched her jaw. "See you later. Oh, and I'll bring the margaritas again tomorrow."

"Wow, thanks Lynn, but you don't have to do that."

"No worries, I want to."

"But, it's my turn."

"You work and I don't. It's the least I can do."

"Thanks, that is very nice of you. Okay, till tomorrow."

"Yes, until then."

****

"Dr. Mills, I can't get to sleep and when I do manage to fall asleep I can't stay asleep." She rubbed her forehead.

"Is something bothering you?"

"My grandmother recently died in a tragic accident and I am so distraught and upset I can't sleep. I can't turn off the constant chatter in my head. I need something to help me sleep."

"Insomnia is difficult to treat. I think you need an anti-anxiety medication that will help you relax when you go to bed. I'll give you a prescription of Xanax. Take one before bed, no more, okay?"

"Yes, thank you, Doctor."

She left the doctor's office humming her favorite song as she drove straight to CVS and filled the prescription. She also bought a package of plastic gloves and a box of plastic baggies.

In her car, she put on the gloves, opened the bottle of Xanax, and put all thirty pills inside a baggie. She zip locked it and shook it a few times. She dropped the plastic gloves and the baggie of Xanax tablets into her purse and threw the empty prescription bottle into a trashcan in the parking lot.

When she got home, she blended margaritas with ice, and poured a little of the mixture into the unwashed jug from the previous evening. She sloshed the liquid around, poured the excess into the unwashed plastic cups (one cup with her own DNA and the other with Ellen's), swirled it around, and poured the excess into the sink. She put the unwashed jug and cups into the white plastic shopping bag and set them aside on the kitchen counter.

Next, she put on plastic gloves, poured the Xanax tablets into a coffee grinder, ground them to a fine powder, and blended the powdered Xanax into the fresh jug of margaritas until it dissolved. She tossed the coffee grinder into the trash along with the plastic gloves, and tied the trash bag tight. On her way to the hot tub, she threw it into the dumpster.

Nancy had unpacked the Xanax spiked margaritas just as Ellen rushed in. "Give me a drink quick, Lynn. I need one tonight!"

"You got it, Girlfriend."

Ellen didn't notice the bitter taste of Xanax in her margarita as she knocked back the entire contents of her cup.

"Whoa, what's the hurry tonight?"

"Oh, Todd and I had a terrible fight this morning." Ellen slipped low into the water. "I'm still pissed off about it."

"Well, drink up and soon it will seem like it never happened."

Nancy kept Ellen's cup refilled. Ellen got drunker and groggier until she couldn't talk coherently or even keep her eyes open. Her head fell back onto the rim of the tub, clunk.

"Ellen, are you okay?"

Ellen did not respond. Nancy drifted over next to her.

"Ellen, are you awake?" Still there was no response.

Nancy glided over to Ellen's floating feet, reached under the water, and tugged until Ellen's head slipped under the bubbling water. She never awoke, or even sputtered, as she succumbed to drowning.

"Bye-bye, Ellen, I am happy to say I will never hear you giggle again."

Nancy sang Maxwell's Silver Hammer as she got out of the water and wrapped her towel around her waist. She turned her back to the tub, and with her towel gloving her hand, she tucked the Xanax coated baggie into Ellen's tote bag. She walked away without looking back.

When she got to her place, she washed and dried the jug and cups she used that night and put them away. All trace of Xanax was gone. There was nothing in her condo to link her to Ellen's not-so-accidental drowning. The white shopping bag holding last night's Xanax free jug and cups waited on the counter.

Confident she had everything under control she got into a hot shower, and laughed. When she stepped out, she heard excited voices coming from the pool, and threw on a bathrobe and waited.

A few minutes later, there was a knock on her door. "Good evening, I'm Deputy Carson and I'm investigating the drowning death of one of the residents here. May I have your name, please?"

"I'm Lynn Thomason. Why, who drowned?"

"Did you know Ellen Taft?"

"Yes, I know her. What's happened? I just saw her in the Jacuzzi a little while ago."

"You were with her in the Jacuzzi?"

"Yes, that's right. Wait." She put her hand to her throat. "Did you just say she drowned?"

"Yes, unfortunately, Ms. Taft was found dead in the Jacuzzi."

"No, that can't be. I was with her less than a half hour ago." She cleared her throat. "She was fine."

"When you last saw her, she was okay?"

"Yes." Nancy shook her head. "Well, she was upset about a fight she had this morning with her boyfriend, but after we shared a jug of margaritas, she felt a lot better."

"We didn't see any evidence of drinking."

"No, you wouldn't. I brought the margaritas tonight and I packed up the cups and the jug when I came home."

"Would you mind if I see them, please?"

"You want to see the cups and the jug? I haven't had a chance to wash them yet."

"That's perfect. I will take them to the station so they can check the contents."

"Why? I told you we had margaritas."

"It's procedure, that's all."

"Oh, okay. But, Ellen and I were both drinking and only she got sick." Nancy went into the kitchen and came back with the white plastic shopping bag. "But then, I didn't drink as much as she did." She handed the bag over. "Here you go, Deputy."

"Thanks."

She closed the door and stood in the glow of The Swirling Red Mist as a wave of euphoria swept over her. She laughed and laughed and laughed.

CHAPTER 32

"HELLO. I'M TODD Cummings, the manager. Is there something I can help you with, Deputies?"

"Mr. Cummings? I am Deputy Hoffman and this is Deputy Jones. We're from the San Diego County Sheriff's North Coastal Station. Can we speak with you privately, please?"

"Is there something wrong?"

"Well, we'd rather talk to you somewhere private," said Deputy Hoffman. "Do you have an office where we can talk?"

"Of course, my office is over here." Inside the office, Todd asked, "What is this about?"

"I think you'd better sit down."

Todd sat. "What's wrong?"

"Do you know a woman named Ellen Taft?"

"Yes, she's my girlfriend. Why, what's happened? Is she okay?"

"No, I'm sorry, she isn't." Deputy Jones put his hand on Todd's shoulder. "Unfortunately, Ms. Taft had an accident this evening in the Jacuzzi."

"What kind of accident? Is she all right?"

"No, I regret to tell you she drowned. She seems to have fallen asleep and slipped underwater. We suspect she may have consumed alcohol while she was in the Jacuzzi."

"She's dead?"

The deputies nodded.

"No!" He looked from one deputy to the other. "Are you sure?"

"I'm sorry, but we are very sure."

"I can't believe it. We had a fight this morning and I yelled at her as she went out the door." Todd covered his face with his hands. "And, now I can't even apologize."

"We're very sorry for your loss, Mr. Cummings," said Deputy Jones.

"She's dead and it's my fault."

"I know how you feel, Mr. Cummings, but you were not responsible for her drowning. It appears to be an unfortunate accident."

"You're sure it was an accident?"

"I beg your pardon?" Deputy Huffman said.

He shook his head. "It's nothing."

"Was she in the habit of drinking when she got home from work?"

Todd nodded. "Sometimes, yeah, well, usually. If she was still upset, she most likely took pills, too." Todd wiped tears from his cheeks.

Deputy Jones asked, "You say she was in the habit of taking pills, as well?"

"I'm afraid so. She's a nurse in a hospital and is often stressed out when she gets home and takes Xanax to help her unwind."

"Does she have a prescription for Xanax?"

"I'm not sure. I think she gets it from work."

"I know this is hard for you, but we'd like you to come with us to identify the body, if you wouldn't mind."

"Me, identify her body? Oh, shit." He rubbed his fists into his eyes. "Have you told her parents yet?"

"Other deputies are on the way to their residence."

Deputy Jones said, "Is there someone you can call to come in and finish your shift, Mr. Cummings?"

Todd nodded and reached for the phone. "I'll call Dave, the other manager."

"Okay, we will wait outside for you."

Todd put his head on his desk and sobbed. Drained, he blew his nose and made the call.

"Hi, Dave," his voice cracked, "this is Todd."

"Is something wrong, Bro? You sound weird."

"Yes, something terrible happened to Ellen. She, ah, drowned in the hot tub tonight."

"Oh man, I'm sorry. Do you want me to come in?"

"Yes, please. The deputies are here and want me to go identify her body."

"Oh, man. That sucks. Okay, I'll be there as soon as I can."

"Thanks, Dave." Todd hung up the phone and lowered his head in his hands.

When Dave arrived, he introduced himself to the deputies, and then he went inside.

"Hey, there," Dave gave Todd a quick hug. "Sorry, man."

"Thanks, Dave." He slowly left the office and joined the deputies. "Okay, I'm ready."

****

"Good morning, Todd. How are you?"

"Bad, Riki, real bad." He lowered his head.

"Why? What's going on?"

"Ellen drowned in the Jacuzzi last night."

"What?" Her jaw dropped.

Todd nodded.

"Oh, my God," she gasped, "how awful. I am so sorry, Todd." She put her arms around him and stroked his back. "What happened?"

"She got wasted in the Jacuzzi and drowned." Todd took a deep breath and sighed. "Apparently, she passed out and slipped underwater."

"Oh, no, that is so tragic."

"They haven't gotten the results of the toxicology tests yet, but I think she took pills in addition to drinking."

"She accidentally overdosed in the hot tub?"

"Yeah, it was her usual pattern after work to take a few pills to relax. Then, she'd make a jug of margaritas to drink in the Jacuzzi."

"No one was with her?"

"Lately, she had been meeting a new neighbor in the hot tub, but this time she was alone. She just passed out, slid underwater, and drowned."

"This is like déjà vu all over again. You know, we haven't had an accidental death here since Nancy went to jail. What if she's out?"

"I thought the same thing when they told me about it. I thought this cannot be happening."

"You said Ellen had been meeting a new neighbor in the Jacuzzi, have you met the neighbor?"

He brushed tears out of his eyes. "No, I haven't."

"Do you know her name?"

"I think Ellen said her name was Lynn."

"Lynn? You're not kidding are you, Lynn as in Nancy Lynn Thomason?"

"It can't be Nancy. She's still in jail."

"How do you know?"

"Detective Stanton said she'd let me know when Nancy was released, but I haven't heard anything yet."

Riki counted on her fingers. "Isn't it about time for her to get out?"

"I guess so, but if she's out why haven't I been told?"

"Who knows? Maybe they forgot. I mean, they must be pretty busy, so maybe they just screwed up."

"Yeah, I guess that could have happened."

Riki took his hand and looked into his eyes. "What if it wasn't an accident at all? What if Nancy murdered Ellen?"

"I think that's a stretch, don't you?" He shook his head. "Nancy doesn't even know about Ellen. How could she possibly manage to be in the Jacuzzi with her?"

"The same way she knew about your wedding and got on the same assembly line with your wife. We both know she's capable of doing anything she wants."

Todd rubbed his chin. "Ellen did point her out to me once. I saw her from behind, but she didn't look anything like Nancy. She had short dark hair and it was sort of curly, I think."

"So, she has a new hair style, big deal. That's not so hard to do."

"Stop, Riki. You're scaring me."

Nancy watched from her usual spot on the sand and laughed.

****

One morning, not long after Ellen's death, Todd climbed the cliff stairs after his walk on the beach, and just as he opened the gate, she rushed toward him with outstretched arms.

"Todd, it's me, Nancy! Remember me?"

Todd gasped, stared at her, and stepped backwards. His foot dangled in the air searching for the next step down. When his foot didn't find the step, he leaned backwards.

"Todd, watch out. You're going to fall. Let me help you."

He tipped further back and lost his balance. "Ahhhhhh!" His legs flew up and he was airborne. His hands flailed desperate to grab something, anything to stop his backward plunge, but there was nothing to save him. He crashed against the concrete steps and steel railings, dead when he hit the sand.

Riki heard the commotion, turned around, and saw the body of a man crumpled at the bottom of the staircase with a group of agitated people gathered around him, and ran back.

A man said into his phone, "Come quick, a man just fell down the cliff stairs south of Fletcher's Cove. I think the poor guy is dead."

She inched closer to the body on the sand. "No, Todd!" She knelt beside him and felt for a pulse, then a heartbeat, but there was nothing.

Lifeguards arrived, so Riki stood and backed away. She asked the woman standing next to her, "Did you see what happened?"

"Yeah, I saw him fall. He bounced against the railings and steps all the way down. It was horrible."

The man with the cell phone said, "I didn't see him fall, but someone said a woman at the top of the stairs surprised him, and then he fell backwards all the way to the sand." He looked up the staircase. "That must be her."

Riki followed his gaze up the staircase and found herself staring at Nancy.

CHAPTER 33

WHEN RIKI GOT home, she opened her laptop and brought up the website for Las Colinas Detention and Reentry Facility. She clicked on 'Who's in Jail' and searched for Nancy Thomason. The screen popped up, 'The person you are searching for is not in our custody!'

She felt sick and closed the lid. Why didn't she do this after Ellen died? Now it was too late. Todd was dead.

Riki called Mrs. Williams, but the phone rang and rang, and switched to voicemail. Riki jumped into her jeep and drove to the Encinitas Sheriff's Station. She called Mrs. Williams at every stoplight on the way and again as she entered the sheriff's station.

She stood at the front desk shifting her weight from foot to foot.

The desk clerk said, "Hello, can I help you?"

"I hope so. My name is Erika Hollis and I need to speak with Detective Stanton."

"The detective is out of the office right now. Is there something I can help you with?"

"Um, no, I need to talk to her."

"She could be a long time."

"That's okay, I'll wait."

"Not a problem. Have a seat. I'll tell her you're here when she gets back."

She sat close to the desk and took out her phone. Her anxiety intensified when she called Mrs. Williams every five minutes during the next hour. Lost in her thoughts, she unconsciously chewed her inner cheek while she waited.

"Erika?"

Riki looked up and blinked. "Oh, Detective Stanton, I am so glad to see you."

"Why? What's wrong?"

"Everything is wrong."

"Let's go into an interview room so we can talk."

Riki sat on the edge of her chair and Detective Stanton turned on her tape recorder.

"Okay, what's bothering you?"

"I'm here about Nancy Thomason. Do you remember her?"

"Yes, of course. She trashed The Lavender Moon Lounge in Solana Beach, right?"

"Right, she's the one."

"What about her?"

"Well, I don't know how to explain it, but I think she killed Todd Cummings at Fletcher's Cove today."

"But, she's incarcerated in Las Colinas."

"No, she's not." Riki crossed her legs. "I searched her online and she's out."

"No one informed me. There must have been a glitch in the system, it happens sometimes." She clicked her pen. "You say she killed Todd Cummings today at the beach? I haven't heard about any murders at the beach today."

"No, you wouldn't, because it looked like an accident, but I saw her there so I know she did it. When I got home, I Googled the Sheriff's site to see if she was still in jail and she's not."

"Todd Cummings? He worked at The Lavender Moon Lounge, right?"

"Yeah, that's him."

"And, he was her old boyfriend and the reason she threw the fit in the lounge?"

"Yes, and that same night she threatened to kill him and now she has."

"I see." Detective Stanton folded her hands. "Tell me what happened today."

"Todd was at the top of the cliff stairs and fell backwards all the way to the sand."

"Were you there?"

"I didn't see it happen, but I was there." Riki uncrossed her legs and leaned toward the detective. "He and I had gone on our usual morning walk and I left him at the bottom of the cliff stairs and kept walking to Fletcher's Cove. I hadn't gone very far when I heard screaming and shouting, and when I turned around, I saw someone lying on the sand and a bunch of people standing around. I didn't know it was Todd until I ran back and saw him lying there." She slumped back in her chair and covered her face with her hands. "He was dead."

"Where did you see Nancy Thomason?"

"She was at the top of the stairs looking down."

"How do you know she was involved?"

"Some people who were standing around his body told me that Todd had been at the top when a woman startled him, and caused him to fall backwards. One of the men pointed up the stairs and said, 'there she is' and I looked up and there was Nancy looking down at me. I know it was her even though she had different hair."

"Like how was her hair different?"

"It was short, curly, and dark brown, but I got a good look at her face and it was definitely her."

"Did she react when she saw you looking at her?"

"Yeah, she looked kind of surprised and then took off in a hurry."

"I see."

"And, I think she killed Todd's girlfriend, too."

"She killed his girlfriend, too? When did she kill her?"

"It happened last week. Her name was Ellen Taft and she drowned in a Jacuzzi."

"I'm familiar with that case. The drowning happened at a condo complex in Solana Beach, didn't it?"

"Yes, they lived there together."

"The medical examiner determined she had taken pills and booze in the hot tub. He concluded it was an accident."

Riki ruffled her hair. "Of course, he did."

"What do you mean?"

"There are fatal accidents wherever Nancy goes. Somehow she drugged Ellen and got her drunk so she would pass out in the Jacuzzi and drown." Riki shifted in her chair. "Todd told me Ellen had been meeting a new neighbor in the Jacuzzi named Lynn who had short curly brown hair. Lynn is Nancy's middle name."

"Hmm, it is possible she's responsible."

"How can two people who live together die a few days apart in unrelated accidents? It seems unlikely to me. I mean, does that ever happen?"

Detective Stanton shrugged. "It could happen."

"I know she's responsible. And, she's done it before." Riki tucked a strand of hair behind her ear. "She's murdered many times."

"You mean she's killed other people besides Todd and Ellen?"

"Yes, but they are her most recent victims." Riki's toes bounced in her sandals. "Can you tell me when she got out of Las Colinas?"

"Sure, I'll call right now and find out."

"You see," Riki said, "I'm worried about Mrs. Williams, Nancy's grandmother. I have been trying to reach her since I found out Nancy was no longer in jail, but she's not answering her phone. It could mean nothing, but I'm concerned. Would you mind if I try calling her again?"

"Of course not, please do."

Riki speed dialed Mrs. Williams's number. "There's still no answer. If she went out for something, I think she'd be home by now. I hate to suggest it, but something may have happened to her. Is there a way for you to check to see if she's okay?"

"Not a problem, what's her name?"

"Her name is Maureen Williams and she lives in San Diego. She must be around sixty-five, I guess."

Detective Stanton made a call. "Okay, thanks." Her expression was grim. "A little over three weeks ago, Mrs. Williams fell down her front steps and broke her neck and died. The medical examiner decided it was an accident."

"Another accidental death and more stairs, when did this happen?"

"She died on March 4th and coincidentally, or perhaps not so coincidentally, Nancy was released from custody the day before."

"That's it, she did it. I know she did." Riki's knees bounced. "She killed her grandmother the day after she got out of jail and now she's on a murder spree."

"Well, we don't know that for sure."

Riki was suddenly still. "But, isn't it too coincidental?"

"I see your point. Coincidental fatal accidents are rarely coincidences or accidents."

"Yeah, and she must have a thing about stairs. When she's around, stairs turn into death traps. First there was the little boy at the bookstore, then Mrs. Williams, and now Todd."

"Yes, I remember your telling me about the little boy when we talked after the incident at the bar. I interviewed Nancy in jail about Billy's fall, but she flat out denied it. I have no evidence to prove otherwise."

"She is such a fake and a master at lying and manipulating. What I think happened was she went upstairs to snoop in Bonnie's apartment again. I say again, because shortly after Bonnie moved in, someone broke into her apartment and trashed it. Hey, now that I think of it, my apartment had a break in when I first moved in, too. I assumed it was my stalker, but was it really Nancy?"

"We considered her as a person of interest at the time, but we came up empty. We had no evidence against her." The detective rubbed her chin. "But, it is possible and maybe even likely, Nancy stalked you and broke into your apartment and Bonnie's." The detective tapped her fingers on the table. "The night Billy died, what happened?"

"I wasn't there, but my best guess is that Nancy went up the stairs first and Billy followed her. Of course, she didn't want any witnesses, so when Billy caught her in the act, she tossed him over the side of the banister to shut him up." Riki shuddered. "Then afterwards, she was so happy he was dead, she bounced over to The Lavender Moon Lounge. Sam and I followed her and we heard her singing Maxwell's Silver Hammer just like the witness at Fletcher's Cove had."

"What witness at Fletcher's Cove?"

"Oh, well that happened last summer. A man fell off the bluff above Fletcher's Cove and the day after I heard some guys talking about it and one of them had seen a woman the night before leave the scene and she sang Maxwell's Silver Hammer."

"Can you remember the details?"

"Let's see, we hadn't lived there long when Bonnie had the break in. She called the Sheriff's department and while the deputies were inside investigating, Sam and I waited outside and Nancy came up to us and asked what had happened. I inadvertently told her there was a witness who had been out walking his dog on Highway 101 and she had a weird reaction to it as if she had assumed there could be no witnesses."

"You wouldn't by any chance be able to remember the date?"

"You mean when the man fell off of the cliff?"

"Yes, can you narrow it down a bit?"

"As a matter of fact, I can. It happened the same evening as the grand opening of my art gallery, which Nancy planned, by the way. On the night of June 20th, a man walking his dog fell off the bluff above Fletcher's Cove. Presto deluxe-o the witness was gone, except he wasn't the real witness. He was just some guy walking his dog."

"I remember that case and it was ruled an accident."

"Yeah, aren't they all?" Riki sighed. "Let me tell you, the day after it happened I was at Fletcher's Cove when they recovered the dog walker's body and I overheard some men talking behind me. One of them was the real witness, but after what happened to this other guy, he decided not to talk to the authorities out of fear he'd end up dead, too."

"How do you know he was the real witness?"

"Because I heard him say he saw a woman leave the parking lot at Fletcher's Cove about the same time the man slipped off the cliff and she resembled the same woman he saw leave Bonnie's backdoor after the break in. He said he heard her singing Maxwell's Silver Hammer after the break in and after the man fell off the cliff.

He also said that he saw something glittery in the woman's hair and that night at the grand opening, Nancy had worn a sparkly clasp in her hair."

"Why didn't you tell me this before?"

"I don't know. I thought that you would figure it out. You're the professional, not I." She rubbed her neck. "Actually, it is just little bits and pieces of things that I didn't want to think about, you know what I mean, and now they fit together. I have no proof, of course, just ideas."

"Yes, I see."

"Besides I didn't want to be on her hit list, but I think I am."

"What makes you think that?"

"Hey, I knew her in high school, and she did a lot shit to people in retaliation."

"Hmm." Detective Stanton leaned back. "So what you're saying is that Nancy killed the dog walker, little Billy, her grandmother, Ellen Taft, and Todd Cummings?"

"Yeah, but there are more," Riki clasped her hands under her chin. "A woman who ran a dog grooming place down the street from me fell in front of a car the first day Nancy came into my gallery. In fact, it happened about fifteen minutes after she left my place."

"Where did that happen?"

"It was at the corner of Lomas Santa Fe and South Cedros Avenue."

"Can you recall when this happened by any chance?"

Riki paused. "Yes, it was the day after The Rolling Stones concert, so it was the 25th of May."

"Why do you think she's responsible for the accident?"

"I'm not sure, but it just seems to be the beginning. Ophelia died before I knew her, but my neighbors told me she was a cantankerous and confrontational old busy body. Maybe she and Nancy had a run-in when she left my place so Nancy literally bumped her off."

"Hmm, that's interesting. I'll look into it. Do you have any other suspicions?"

"Well, there was Mary Hatch who was the victim of a hit and run."

"She worked at the bakery, right?"

"Right, she worked the counter at Bread Temptations."

"Why would Nancy kill her?"

"Well, it seems that Nancy had a crush on Sam, because not long after she moved in across the street from the bakery he started getting flowers and candy delivered anonymously."

"He had no idea who sent them?"

"No, but it was sort of like the things I had received."

"How were they similar?"

"Well, he got a bouquet of flowers and a box of candy like I did, and like mine, Sam's came with weird notes. His were from someone who said she was his number one fan."

"Were Nancy and Sam seeing each other?"

"No, Sam is a very nice guy so he was friendly to her, but he was dating Bonnie and wasn't interested in her."

"But, there must be more to it than a crush."

"Yeah, about that, I think I may know what set her off." She leaned forward. "You see, the day before Mary was killed, she and I were in the bakery talking about Nancy when who should pull up and park right across the street from us, but Nancy. Mary was telling me she found out a woman named Lynn ordered the candy and asked me if I knew anyone by that name. I nodded at Nancy and said, 'her.' Mary was astonished and stared at Nancy. Then, she said, 'her name is Lynn?' real distinctly so Nancy could have read her lips." Riki looked down. "I kind of think she did, because Mary was killed the next day."

"And, Nancy's middle name is Lynn."

"Right, and she uses it when she doesn't want to be Nancy."

"Okay, let me get this straight. You're saying Nancy pushed the man off the cliff, pushed a woman in front of a car, ran over the woman in Leucadia, tossed Billy over the banister, somehow caused her grandmother to fall down a flight of stairs, drowned Ellen at the condos, and today, she caused Todd to fall down the cliff stairs?"

"Yes, that's right. I know it sounds unbelievable." Riki rubbed her forehead. "I have trouble believing it myself."

"So before Nancy Thomason was arrested for what happened at the lounge she had killed four people, and since she's been out, she's killed three more?"

Riki nodded. "Yeah, I think so."

"That makes her a serial killer in the extreme." Detective Stanton tapped her fingers on the table. "You could be right. It certainly fits together."

"Really, you think so, too?" Riki leaned forward. "I am so relieved. I wasn't sure you'd believe me without any evidence." Riki placed her hands flat on the table. "Look, Nancy needs to be stopped before she kills the rest of us."

"I'll send deputies out to bring her in for questioning. If I get corroborating evidence, we will arrest her."

"I must be on her hit list along with my friends Bonnie and Sam. What should we do?"

"Well for starters, avoid using stairs."

Riki pulled her hands off the table. "Gee, thanks."

"Sorry. I'm kidding. Bad cop joke. Joking helps us deal with the horror we see in this job." She leaned toward Riki. "Don't worry. We'll find her. If she's targeting the three of you, she is still in the area. Until we pick her up, I'll have patrol cars cruise South Cedros Avenue more frequently. And, once she's arrested, she'll no longer be a danger to you and your friends."

Riki sighed. "Why doesn't that make me feel safer?"

"Sorry, but it's about all I can do at the moment."

"So, she started out stalking and progressed to killing? Does that usually happen?"

"Well, it is less common for women to become serial killers, but it does happen."

"Is she a psychopath?"

"Maybe, but her shrink says she's a sociopath although she seems to possess traits of both."

"She's a sociopath?" Riki paused. "What's the difference?"

"Well, for one thing, sociopaths are impulsive so their crimes are a bit sloppy compared to psychopaths who plan their crimes. And, sociopaths tend to have explosive tempers while psychopaths keep their emotions under control."

"So the argument we had that afternoon contributed to her blow up later at The Lavender Moon Lounge?"

"Don't blame yourself for how she behaved at the bar. It went deeper than anything you could have said."

"Good, I don't want to be responsible."

"You're not. Don't worry. We'll pick her up as soon as possible."

"Will you call me when you have her in custody so I can relax?"

"Sure, thing."

CHAPTER 34

HE GREETED RIKI with a hug. "Hi, how are you?"

"Oh, Mark."

"What's wrong?"

"I just left the Sheriff's Station."

"Why? What's happened now?"

"You haven't heard?"

"No, heard what?"

"Todd Cummings died today."

"No!"

"Or rather, he was killed today."

"Killed, what do you mean he was killed? What happened?"

"Someone at the top of the cliff stairs startled him and he fell backwards." Riki looked at the floor. "It happened after our walk together."

Mark put his arms around her. "That's terrible!" He hugged her tight. "How weird this happened so soon after Ellen died."

"I know." She nodded her head against his chest. "I thought so, too. I think Nancy made him fall. Do you remember when she tore apart his bar? She screamed she was going to kill him."

"Yeah, I remember she screamed that at the time, but she was drunk and hysterical. No one took her seriously, did they?"

"Yeah, well I took her seriously today. I wish I had after Ellen drowned. Todd would still be alive if I had. That's why I went to the Sheriff's Station to talk to Detective Stanton."

"Tell me about it."

Riki leaned back and looked into his face. "Well, Detective Stanton already knew a great deal about Nancy and surmised she was my stalker last year and now she's turned into a serial killer. She said that Nancy is a sociopath, and I told her I thought she was out to kill Bonnie, Sam, and me."

"Oh, come on. You didn't tell her that did you?"

"Yes, I did, because she is. I mean, look how many people have died since she first came here. If she killed all those other people with no problem, do you think she'd have any trouble murdering us? She's a serial killer."

"Well, she is rather odd, isn't she? I guess it wouldn't be too hard to believe she's a stalker and a serial killer." He hugged her close to his chest. "Do you think she wants to kill me, too?"

"Probably not, because you never pissed her off the way we have, but I am most definitely sure she is out to get us. The three of us are her only irritants left. I know we're next."

"Have you told Bonnie and Sam yet?"

"No, not yet, I'm going to when I leave here."

"Wait a minute," Mark said, "isn't she still locked up in Las Colinas?"

"No, she's been out since the 3rd of this month and Detective Stanton didn't even know about it until I told her."

"No shit? How did you find out?"

"I looked it up online, and get this, I found out that the day after she was released from Las Colinas, her grandmother fell down her front steps, broke her neck, and died."

"What? That's incredible."

"That makes three deaths that supposedly were accidents since she's been out of jail and it's been less than a month. That's what makes me think she's on a murder spree."

"It's possible, I suppose."

"I know it's weird, but think about the other fatal accidents: what if Billy caught her going up to Bonnie's apartment so she tossed him over the banister. And, what if she pushed the dog walker off the bluff because she thought he witnessed her leaving Bonnie's building? And the horrific part is that he wasn't even the real witness, she killed the wrong guy."

"Those are just speculations. What proof is there?"

"I have no proof, only supposition, but it all fits and makes sense to me and to Detective Stanton, as well. And, I think Nancy drove the car that killed Mary, because Mary figured out Nancy sent the candy and flowers to Sam and Nancy knew she knew. And, Ophelia was killed by a car fifteen minutes after she left my place the first day she came into the gallery."

"Wow, put that way it does point at Nancy, doesn't it? It adds up, but you don't have any proof."

"It is the detective's job to prove it."

"So, the detective agreed with your take on things?"

"Yes, she did. She said that Nancy was, in her words, a serial killer in the extreme."

Mark rubbed his chin. "So, she was your stalker, too, is that right?"

"Yeah, but wait," Riki put her head down and scratched her head, "when I was moving in, a friend of mine from school helped me and he kept seeing a woman spying on us. I never saw her, but he saw her everywhere. Even when we went to Carl's Jr., she sat right behind me and eavesdropped, but he scared her off before I could get a good look at her."

"Did he think she looked like Nancy?"

"No, but she could have been Nancy had she worn a disguise. Changing her appearance is something at which Nancy is quite adept." Riki pulled her hair into a knot on top of her head. "In high school, she would sometimes come to school dressed in what I thought were costumes, you know?"

"No, like what do you mean?"

"Oh, she would wear hats or wigs and totally different clothes like a nice dress or grungy jeans. Once she wore a prom gown and another time she wore pajamas. For a while, she was into gothic and wore long black dresses with clunky black boots and white makeup with black eye liner. She liked getting attention because no one noticed her much."

"She sounds like she was a weird kid. Was she mentally ill?"

"Now that you mention it, yeah, she was. She was always doing strange things like snooping in other kid's lockers and leaving creepy notes. Sometimes at lunch, she'd stare at people to unnerve them. Some people couldn't take it and would have to get up and leave just to get away from her. Some girls would even burst into tears. That was sort of like stalking, I suppose."

Mark took her hand. "You think she's killed all those people and they didn't just have really bad accidents?"

She looked in his eyes and squeezed his hand. "I know it sounds unbelievable, but how else can you explain it? The detective thinks she's a sociopath, and so do I. We both think she's capable of doing all those things."

"You say the detective said she's a sociopath and not a psychopath. What's the difference?"

"I asked the detective the same thing. Actually, they share many of the same traits, so Nancy could be both, I suppose." Riki looked out the window. "Basically from what Detective Stanton told me, sociopaths are impulsive and cannot control their tempers while psychopaths are deliberate and maintain self-control."

Mark counted on his fingers. "So according to your theory, Nancy killed four people before she was incarcerated, and since she's been out she's killed three more? You think she's killed seven people?"

"Yeah, pretty scary, isn't it?"

"Are they going to arrest her?"

"Well, Detective Stanton said she'd have Nancy brought in for questioning and arrested if she has corroborating evidence."

"Don't worry." Mark embraced her. "She'll be stopped before she kills anyone else."

"I hope you're right, but please be careful, just in case."

"Me? I'm not worried about her, I'm not on her list, remember? Besides, what can she do to me?"

"I hope nothing, but please don't take any chances, okay?"

"Okay, I'll be careful." He kissed her. "You be careful, too."

Riki parked in front of the gallery and walked down to Bonnie's, but found the bookstore closed, so she continued to Bread Temptations where Bonnie was having coffee with Sam in the kitchen's cozy corner. Riki sank onto the sofa next to her and accepted a cup of coffee from Sam. Then, she told them about Todd's death and her discussion with the detective.

"How weird, we know a serial killer. I always knew Nancy was evil-crazy, and now she hates us and we are all targets, right?"

Sam said, "Hmm, what did the detective say for us to do?"

"She said to not take the stairs."

"That helps a whole hell of a lot."

"I know. It was a stupid cop joke." Riki sipped her coffee. "Detective Stanton said Nancy would be arrested soon and once she's in custody, we'll be out of danger."

Bonnie put her cup down. "But, Nancy is very skillful at changing her appearance. She may be right here in Solana Beach living among us and we wouldn't even see her."

"Yeah, you're right. She could walk by us right now and we wouldn't know it was her."

Together they stood silent and looked out the bakery's front window.

CHAPTER 35

"I WOULD LIKE to go to the Lexus dealer in Kearny Mesa, please."

The cab driver said, "Certainly, but the traffic is heavy today. It will take about forty-five minutes."

"Not a problem. I am in no hurry." Nancy hummed her favorite post-murder song on her way south.

At the Lexus dealership, she wandered around the showroom until she found the car she wanted, red, sleek, and sexy. She bought it with her debit card, drove off in ecstasy, and soon found herself cruising through La Jolla. On impulse, she pulled into a strip mall with a walk-in hair salon.

The hair cutter asked, "What would you like done today?"

"I want bright red hair and cut off as much of the perm as you can. And, I want spikes on top and no curls."

"Wow. That is quite a change. Are you sure?"

"Yes. Today I bought a sexy new red Lexus, and I want my hair as sexy as my car."

"Okay, sexy it is."

Two hours later, Nancy looked at her new candied apple red hair in the mirror and dared to touch the short spikes on top. "I like it. I like it a lot."

"You look sexy and you look wicked and devilish, too."

"You think so? Wicked and devilish suits me even better than sexy any day."

She drove up the coast on Highway 101 all the way to Carlsbad before she turned around and cruised back to Solana Beach. There at the condos, she exchanged her new red Lexus for her old black Honda, and drove the Honda to her apartment on Summit Ridge. She set her alarm for 5:00 a.m.

****

Mark began the challenging gradient up Torrey Pines Road as he did every morning. He pumped the pedals hard and fast reaching the top in fifty minutes. When he turned around to breeze down the grade, he failed to notice the black Honda parked facing downhill, and he didn't notice the woman with the spiky bright red hair sitting behind the wheel. He also didn't notice when she started her car and snuck up behind him.

As Mark's speed increased, the car pulled up beside him. It kept pace and drifted closer. He glared at the driver, but the redhead did not acknowledge him. When she edged even closer, he slammed his fist hard on the hood. "Hey, watch it!"

She eased away a few feet, but drifted back closer.

"Back off!" Mark yelled.

Instead, when they banked for a curve, the car swerved into his leg and propelled him into the canyon with such force all he could do was hold onto the handlebars. A huge boulder loomed in front of him and he crashed into it, the bike wrenched out of his grasp and bolted away. He continued hurtling down the canyon bouncing off boulders until he stopped tangled in a Manzanita bush. He pulled out his phone, called 911, and passed out.

* * * * * * * * * *

Riki called Mark, but he didn't answer, so she walked down to the bike shop. There she found The Bike Guy's front door locked. She looked in the windows, went around to the back, and knocked on the backdoor.

Frustrated, she went to Bread Temptations where Sam worked the counter. "Have you seen Mark today?"

"Now that you mention it, I haven't." He looked at his watch. "And he should have been here a half hour ago for his usual pastry."

"I just went to The Bike Guy, and he's not there."

"That's not like him. I wonder what's going on."

"Yeah, me, too."

She left the bakery and went to The Cubbyhole Bookstore.

"Hey, how's it going? You look kicked."

"I'm worried about Mark. His shop is closed, and he's not there. Even Sam doesn't know where he is."

"Do you think something's happened to him?"

"I don't know."

"Well, let me know when he turns up, okay?"

"Yeah, okay. I don't know what to do."

"What can you do, but wait?"

She went back to the gallery and just as she unlocked the front door, she got a call from Scripps Memorial Hospital. "Do you know a man named Mark McDonald?"

"Yes, I do. Is he all right?"

"He's in the emergency room."

"What happened? Is he okay?"

"He was in a bike accident this morning and is about to go into surgery."

"I'll be right there."

Riki sped down the freeway to the hospital, and rushed into the emergency room. "I'm here about Mark McDonald."

"Are you related to Mr. McDonald?" the receptionist asked.

"No, I'm his girlfriend."

"Do you know his family? Is there anyone we should call?"

"His parents are deceased, and he has no brothers or sisters. I don't know about aunts or uncles. I'm his closest friend."

"Okay, I'll let Dr. Lawrence know you're waiting. He'll talk to you when he's out of surgery."

"How is he? Can you tell me how badly he's injured?"

"I'm sorry, I can't tell you anything. You'll have to speak with Dr. Lawrence."

"Well, do you know what happened?"

"He was brought in by paramedics. They said he was going down the Torrey Pines grade and went over the edge and fell quite a distance. They said it wasn't easy bringing him up."

"He fell into the canyon?"

"Yes, but that's all I know. You'll have to ask the doctor for more details."

Riki took a seat in the waiting room and called Bonnie. "I'm at the hospital. Mark's been in an accident."

"What happened? Is he okay?"

"He's in surgery right now and they won't tell me anything. All I found out was he was riding his bike and went off Torrey Pines Road into the canyon."

"Nancy."

"Yeah, I think so, too."

"How do you think she did it? Pushed him off with her car?"

"Yeah, most likely, because she'd want to make it look like an accident like all the others."

"Yeah, accidentally on purpose, you mean. The serial killer is on a killing spree."

"You know, I didn't think she'd go after him, but she did." Riki's voice cracked. "I thought it was just the three of us she wanted to kill."

"She must have gone after him to get to you. To hurt you before she kills you, or perhaps she wants to make sure he can't protect you when she goes after you."

"Who knows? She is such a sicko. I think you and Sam are her next targets. Promise me you will be extra careful. You know how she goes on rampages and she's in the midst of one right now."

"You're in danger too, you know."

"I'll be safe in the hospital, but you guys are vulnerable. Please don't take any chances."

"Okay, you be careful, too."

"Don't worry, I will."

****

"Excuse me, are you Erika Hollis?"

Riki looked up. "Yes, I am."

"I'm Dr. Lawrence. I understand that Mark McDonald is your boyfriend?"

"Yes, that's right."

"He has no family that you know of?"

"His parents are dead and he is an only child."

"Well, you will be happy to know he'll be okay. He has a broken left femur and collarbone, but he should heal nicely. He also has severe bruising on his left leg and other assorted scrapes and bruises, but nothing life threatening. It is a good thing he was wearing a helmet because it could have been much worse. He is a fortunate man."

"Is it possible he was pushed off the road by a car?"

"I would say that's very possible, maybe even probable, judging by the bruising on his left leg."

"Do the police know?"

"I called the San Diego Police Department before I came out to speak to you. They should be here soon."

"I can't believe this happened to him."

"What do you mean?"

"I thought he was exempt."

"Exempt from what?"

"I know who did this to him." Riki put her head in her hands. "She's already killed seven people, but I didn't think she'd go after Mark."

"You know the woman who tried to kill him and she has killed seven other people? That's incredible."

"I know." Riki lifted her head. "It is horrific. She's a psycho and makes every murder look like an accident. That's how she keeps getting away with it." She shuddered. "I'm afraid my other friends are the next ones to have fatal accidents."

"What about you?"

"Yes, I'm afraid I am in line for a fatal accident, too."

"Have you gone to the police?"

"Yes, I spoke to Detective Stanton at the Encinitas Sheriff's Station. She tried to find Nancy, but hasn't yet."

"I'll have the police talk to you when they get here."

"Mark will be okay, though?"

"Yes, in time I expect him to make a full recovery."

"Thank, God. That is good news. Can I see him?"

"He's sleeping right now, but you can sit with him for a few minutes."

"Okay. I'd like that." Riki brushed tears out of her eyes.

Dr. Lawrence pulled his ringing phone out of his pocket and glanced at it. "Sorry, but I have to take this." He talked into his phone as he walked down the hall.

Riki went to Mark's bedside. All she could see was bandages and bruises. She whispered, "Oh, Mark. I am so sorry." Tears filled her eyes and she returned to the waiting room.

Twenty minutes later, two men in tired suits approached her. "Ms. Erika Hollis? I am Detective Vargas and this is Detective Anderson. Can we speak with you for a moment?"

"Yes, of course. I am so glad you're here."

Detective Anderson gestured to a corner. "Let's sit over there so we can talk privately."

Riki dropped into a chair that had a view of Mark's room and told them what she had told the doctor. "Could you call Detective Barb Stanton at the Encinitas Sheriff's Station, please? I think she'll want to know about this."

CHAPTER 36

THE BELLY UP was dark and South Cedros Avenue was hushed when Nancy turned the corner at Bread Temptations. She parked at the end of the cul-de-sac and snuck down the alley to The Cubbyhole Bookstore, picked the lock, and crept upstairs to Bonnie's apartment.

She put her tote bag on the living room couch and listened to Bonnie snore in the next room. She began to assemble Bonnie's fatal accident when a phone rang. She stood motionless. Bonnie awakened and fumbled for the phone.

"Hello?" Pause. "Will he be okay?"

Nancy wanted to hear better, so she slipped into the bathroom.

"That's good news. Wait, a minute, I have to pee." She got out of bed. "I'll be right back." She tossed the phone on the bed.

Damn. Nancy looked around the bathroom for something, anything, she could use as a weapon. On the counter was an assortment of cosmetics and toiletries. Nothing to help her there, not even a pair of scissors. Next, she looked at the toilet and her eyes landed on the heavy porcelain lid on top of the toilet tank.

She lifted the lid and held it firmly in both hands as if it were a baseball bat ready to strike. She held the pose and waited.

When Bonnie stumbled into the bathroom, Nancy swung the hefty porcelain lid smack into her face. The immense force broke her jaw and nose on impact. Blood gushed as she crumpled to the floor at Nancy's feet. Still gripping the heavy lid, Nancy looked down at Bonnie bloody, broken, and defenseless on the floor weakened, battered, defeated, but not dead, yet.

"You bitch!"

Bonnie stared at her. "Why are you doing this?"

"All I wanted was to be friends with Riki, but you were always in the way." Nancy raised the lid. "Weren't you?"

"No! Don't do it. Please!"

"Begging won't help."

Bonnie covered her head with her arms as Nancy adjusted her grip and lifted the lid over her shoulder.

"I hate you." Then, with a sharp wallop, she brought the heavy lid down onto Bonnie's arms. Broken, her arms fell away allowing Nancy to smash the lid onto her head. Blood spurted onto her long blonde hair soaking it to a dark wine-red, her beautiful face crushed beyond recognition.

Anger escalated into madness. "You deserve to die!" A volcanic eruption of rage exploded within Nancy as she bludgeoned Bonnie, breaking her skull into pieces until her brain oozed out onto the bathroom floor in a bloody pulp. When the toilet tank lid broke, Nancy dropped the chunks onto Bonnie's body.

Her breathing slowed. She looked at the mess in the bathroom. Blood and gore dripped down the walls and the floor was wet and slippery. She tiptoed around what was left of Bonnie, and grabbed a bath towel off the rack on her way out. In the hall, she wiped blood from her face, blotted as much blood as she could off her clothes, and wiped her sneakers on the carpet. She threw the blood soaked towel on top of Bonnie's head.

She grabbed her bag from the couch and let herself out. She wanted to shout, "Yay, I finally killed Bonnie! I hated her all through school and now I finally got rid of her forever!" but didn't. She strode back to South Cedros Avenue, Bread Temptations, and Sam while she hummed Maxwell's Silver Hammer.

She picked the lock and tiptoed through the kitchen and up the staircase to Sam's apartment. At the landing, she took a can of charcoal lighter fluid from her bag, and skulked through the apartment to Sam's bedroom. She paused and stood over him while he slept.

She whispered, "Sorry Sam, but you chose the wrong one."

She squirted lighter fluid over his blanket and all around the bedroom and throughout the rest of his apartment. As she descended the stairs, she left a trail of flammable liquid on each step. With the remainder, she saturated the dining room and kitchen and emptied the last of the can on the kitchen floor. She lit a box of matches and threw it onto the incendiary puddle, closed the door and walked away.

The fire roared into an inferno racing through the bakery as it followed the accelerant. It set the stairs ablaze as it progressed to the apartment and devoured everything in its path. It sped into the bedroom, flames reached Sam's blanket, licked his face, and awakened him.

Engulfed by flames and smoke, he jumped out of the burning bed into the growing blaze. He opened his mouth and inhaled the super-heated smoke, his lungs seared. He bowed and fell into the flames dead.

In the shadows across the street from Bread Temptations, Nancy pulled her hoodie over her hair while she watched flames destroy the bakery and the man who didn't want her, the son-of-a-bitch.

She shrunk back when a Sheriff's deputy approached the onlookers. "Does anyone know if someone is in the building?"

Kathy said, "The baker lives upstairs. I don't see him out here so he could be inside."

"I hate to tell you this, but the blaze is too hot and too intense for us to search the building."

"Oh, my God, this cannot be happening." Kathy buried her face in her hands.

CHAPTER 37

"MARK'S ASKING FOR you."

Riki clicked off her phone and slid it into her pocket, sprang to her feet and followed the nurse to Mark's room. She bent over his bruised and swollen face and searched for an uninjured place to plant a kiss, and chose a small, unbruised spot on his forehead.

He opened his eyes, and she held his one uninjured hand in both of hers. "How are you feeling?"

"Like hell. How do I look?"

"Like hell."

Mark tried to smile, but winced instead. "So, what happened to me?"

"You don't remember?"

"Well, I remember starting down the grade and then waking up here."

"Someone in a car pushed you off Torrey Pines Road."

"No shit? I don't remember a thing."

"That's probably for the best. It must have been horrific at the time."

"The doctor said I wasn't injured all that bad."

"Well, you have a broken collarbone and left femur, but other than that, you're in pretty good shape."

"That's a relief." He shifted his weight. "Everything hurts."

"Don't worry. You are expected to make a full recovery."

His eyelids fluttered. "Yeah, that's good." His eyes closed.

Detective Stanton came to the door. "How is he?"

"He'll be fine." Riki kissed his forehead. "Good night, Mark."

The detective said, "I have something to tell you."

"Okay, let's go to the waiting room so we can talk."

"Good idea. You should be sitting when you hear what I have to say."

Riki stopped and looked at the detective. "This sounds bad."

"Yes, something else has happened, and it is not good."

"What?"

Detective Stanton touched Riki's back. "Let's sit first and then I'll tell you."

Riki led the way to the corner where she had spent several hours. She and the detective sat facing each other.

"Well," she said, "what's happened?"

"There was a fire at the bakery tonight. They still haven't gotten it under control."

"The bakery's on fire?" Her hand flew to her throat. "Oh, no, is Sam okay?"

"There is no information about Sam as yet. Do you happen to know if he was with Bonnie tonight?"

"Um, I don't think so, at least, not when I last spoke to her." She pulled out her phone. "I talked to her just a while ago. She didn't say anything about Sam or the fire. All she said was that she had to go to the bathroom, but while I waited for her to come back to the phone, Mark asked for me so I hung up."

"I see. Can you call her now to see if Sam is with her?"

"Yes, of course." Riki clicked on Bonnie's number, but it went to voicemail. "There's no answer. Maybe she saw the fire and ran down the street and forgot to take her phone."

"So, Sam could be with her."

"Yes, I hope so. I need to know they're safe." She stood. "I'm scared. I need to go home. I need to find her, I mean, them. They must be outside together."

"I understand how you feel. I need to talk to the SDPD detectives before I leave, so I'll be here a while longer, I'm afraid. Will you call me to let me know whether or not you find them?"

"Why, do you think Sam is still inside the bakery? You think he's burned to death?"

"Let's not think that way, okay? He may be fine, we just don't know yet. But, if you see him, please let me know."

"Nancy started the fire, I know she did." Riki put the phone back into her pocket. "We are all on her hit list. I didn't think Mark was on it, but it turned out that he was. And, now the bakery is on fire. Bonnie's place must be next." She looked at her clenched hands. "I warned Bonnie about Nancy tonight. And, now . . . anything could have happened to her. I have to find her."

"There is a crowd outside the bakery and it is possible you will find both Sam and Bonnie out front."

"Okay, I'll check there first." She started down the hall.

"Hey, wait. You can't go now. I want you escorted by deputies."

Riki stopped and turned. "The deputies can come along, but I'm leaving now."

"I can't get them here sooner than fifteen or twenty minutes. You will have to wait."

"No way am I waiting fifteen or twenty minutes. You cannot be serious." Riki started for the elevator again. "She's my best friend. I have to find her."

"Riki please, I can't protect you if you go alone."

"I'll take my chances."

"Well, at least let me walk you to your car."

"Okay, let's go."

The parking lot was well lit and empty except for a few cars that dotted the expanse.

When they got to the jeep, Detective Stanton checked it over. "All clear, it looks safe to me."

"Great, see ya later." Riki got in and waved through her closed window.

"Okay, but be sure to call me in a half hour. The deputies will meet you at the bakery so stay there."

She fastened her seatbelt. "Okay, I will talk to you then."

The detective nodded and crossed her fingers.

****

Detective Stanton watched Riki's taillights until they disappeared. She scanned the parking lot as she moved toward the hospital entrance and saw no sign of movement. Once she was inside the building, she pulled out her phone and called dispatch.

"This is Detective Stanton. I need an APB on a woman named Nancy Lynn Thomason. She goes by both names. She's around twenty-three, 5'7", short curly brown hair, and drives a black Honda sedan."

"Do you have any idea where we should concentrate our efforts?"

"Yeah, along Highway 101 from Del Mar to Oceanside, and check all side streets as well."

"You got it."

The detective got on the elevator and returned to Mark's room. The detectives from the SDPD were questioning him.

"Excuse me, mind if I join you?"

"No, of course not, Detective, we would have waited for you, but when we heard Mr. McDonald was awake we wanted to take advantage of it before he passed out again."

"I understand. It is not a problem." She waved her hand. "Please continue."

Detective Anderson said, "Did you see who hit you?"

"No, not really, at least I don't remember."

"You didn't see the car?"

"Well, I think it was black." Mark closed his eyes. "I don't remember much else."

"So, you didn't see the driver?"

He shook his head. A flash of red was there and then gone. "If I did, I don't remember."

Detective Vargas put his notebook in his pocket. "Thanks, that helps. If you remember anything else, please call me or Detective Anderson at this number." He placed a business card on the table next to the bed.

"Sure, I want to help if I can."

"We'll be in touch. Hope you feel better soon. Bye."

"Okay, thanks, see ya."

The men back away and the detective approached the bed. "Mr. McDonald, I am Detective Stanton from the Encinitas Sheriff's Station. I have been working with your girlfriend."

"Yes, she told me she contacted you after Todd died."

"That's right, she did. She suspected Nancy Thomason was responsible. What are your thoughts?"

"I don't know." Mark's eyelids drooped close.

"Do you think she drove the car that pushed you off the road?"

"It is possible, I guess." He opened his eyes. "Hey, where's Riki?"

"Oh, she meant to stay, but she was called away momentarily. She'll be back soon, I'm sure."

"Is she okay? Is something wrong?"

"Why do you say that?"

"Because that crazy woman is involved, isn't she? She is dangerous. Riki thinks she's a killer. She told me you said Nancy was a serial killer in the extreme."

"Yes, I believe she is."

"So, is Riki in danger of being attacked by her?"

"No, I have deputies on their way to escort her as we speak."

Mark relaxed, his eyes closed again. He mumbled, "That's good. Thanks."

"Well, I guess that is all we can expect at the moment," said Detective Vargas.

The three detectives went back to their corner in the waiting room. Detective Anderson pulled out his notebook, sat, and crossed his legs.

"So, who is this suspect of yours, a Nancy Thomason?"

"Yeah, she is sort of a fringe friend of Mark and Riki's."

"What do you mean she's a fringe friend?"

"You know, she's a friend-wanna-be. She is the kind of person who turns other people off so she never has any real friends."

"Oh, I see, she is on the outside looking in."

"Exactly, and, Riki thinks she's killing off her friends with fatal accidents."

"Accidents, oh, you mean like running this guy on his bicycle off the road?"

"Right, and so far she's gotten away with it." Detective Stanton scratched her head. "Hey, she may be good for a fatal accident in San Diego."

"Yeah, what fatal accident would that be?" Detective Anderson yawned. "I thought she focused in North County."

"Her grandmother lives, oops sorry, I mean her grandmother lived in San Diego. The day after Nancy was released from Las Colinas, her grandmother took a tumble down her front steps and broke her neck and died."

"I'll check on it. Do you remember grandma's name by any chance."

"Let me find it in my notes." Detective Stanton flipped through pages. "Ah, here it is, her name was Maureen Williams. Her accident happened March 4th."

Detective Vargas said, "What put her in Las Colinas?"

"She went crazy in a bar in Solana Beach and wrecked the place."

"So, she wrecks a bar and when she gets out she murders her grandma?"

"Yeah, and we're looking at her for two other fatal accidents in Solana Beach."

"No shit?" Detective Vargas rubbed his chin. "She's been busy."

"Who else did she kill?"

"Well, after her grandmother, she apparently found her ex-boyfriend living with another woman so she managed to drown the new girlfriend in a Jacuzzi and then she helped the ex-boyfriend fall backwards down cliff stairs at a condo complex down the street from Fletcher's Cove."

"Wow, she is a real serious murderer."

"And, Mr. McDonald's girlfriend went where?"

"Her friends might be in danger so she went back to Solana Beach to make sure they are okay."

"You're not worried this crazy woman will find her and kill her, too?"

"She won't be alone long. I have deputies on their way to guard her." The detective looked at the last page in her notebook. "Oh, shit. I haven't called that in yet. You'll have to excuse me."

Detective Vargas hid a smile with his hand. "Certainly Detective, take your time. We'll check on this lead you gave us."

****

From Via de la Valle, Riki turned onto South Cedros Avenue and immediately saw ferocious flames and thick smoke coming from the bakery. She screeched to a stop across the street from the gallery and ran to the fire.

A hand touched her arm. "Riki, isn't this awful?"

She pulled her eyes away from the flames. "Oh, Kathy," she hugged her friend, "I just can't believe this is happening. It is devastating. Have you seen Bonnie and Sam?" Riki surveyed the people standing around them.

"No, I knocked on Bonnie's front door about ten minutes ago, but there was no answer. I haven't seen Sam. You don't think they're inside the bakery, do you?"

"No, I called Bonnie about a half hour ago and she was at home." She ran her fingers through her hair. "I called her again before I left the hospital, but it went to voicemail. I thought maybe she forgot to take her phone when she dashed down here."

"No, I don't think so. I haven't seen her."

"What if something's happened to her, too?"

"What do you mean? Like this fire?"

"Yeah, sort of, you see, Nancy is back. And, it turns out she's a serial killer on a killing spree."

"You cannot be serious." Kathy stared at her. "Nancy Thomason is a murderer? And, she's out of jail?"

"Yes, she killed at least four people before she went to jail and since she's been out she's killed her grandmother and Todd and his girlfriend."

"Oh, my God, she is a serial killer. That is horrific." Kathy shuddered as she looked at the crowd.

"And, today, or I guess it would be yesterday now, she pushed Mark off Torrey Pines Road with her car, and he's in the hospital with a broken collar bone and a broken femur."

"Oh, no, she tried to kill Mark? I can't believe it, how awful." Kathy put her head in her hands. "I wondered why he hadn't opened this morning, but I never imagined anything like this."

"I know it is hard to digest, isn't it?"

"Yeah, it really is. He'll be okay?"

"The doctor said he'll be fine."

"So, they think Nancy pushed him off the road?"

"Yeah, the cops are at the hospital right now."

"Wow, I am shocked. But, you know, she always was sort of strange, if you know what I mean?"

"Yes," Riki said, "I know exactly what you mean."

"I never imagined she was a murderer though. Did you?"

"Well, there were times when I thought maybe she was responsible for some accidental deaths, but I wasn't sure. Now I am."

"What accidental deaths?"

"Well," she swallowed, "remember the kid who went over the banister at the bookstore? Nancy was the only one who saw it happen."

"You think she killed that little boy?"

"And, I think she killed Mary, too."

"You're not kidding are you?"

"No, I'm serious."

"How do you know?"

"Well, I have no proof, only suspicions, but I think I'm right. After Todd died, I told the sheriff detective what I suspected, and she said she was going to arrest Nancy, but that never happen, and now Nancy's tried to kill Mark and she's killed Sam." Riki wiped tears from her cheeks. "And, who knows what she's done to Bonnie. I can't find her."

"Oh, my God," Kathy put her head in her hands, "I can't believe it. How could I have let her live here?"

"It's not your fault. She was my friend, and I vouched for her, didn't I? I knew she was a weirdo, but I didn't know she was evil."

"It isn't your fault, either."

"Thank you for saying that because I feel sort of responsible for all this."

"Don't, she did this, Riki, not you."

"I know, you're right, but it seems like it started with me. I mean, she wouldn't have ever moved here if it weren't for me."

Kathy hugged her. "You were just trying to help."

"I'm worried about Bonnie and Sam."

"I hope nothing's happened to them."

"Me too," Riki sighed. She took out her phone. "Look, I have to call Detective Stanton. She wanted me to call her whether I found them or not. We hoped they would be standing out here together."

"I'm so sorry, Riki." Kathy hugged her again. "It doesn't look good for Sam."

"Poor Sam, I'm afraid the same may be true for Bonnie."

****

Everyone fixated on the fire while Nancy slithered through the shadows back to her car. As soon as she closed the door, she burst out laughing and couldn't stop as she drove back to Summit Ridge. The evening had been a success so far, how impressed would Sam be now?

In her bathroom, she took off her bloody smoke laden clothes and stuffed them into a trash bag, and caught a glimpse of herself in the mirror. Her bright red hair glowed as if it, too, were on fire. Again, she burst out laughing, but when she stepped into the shower and saw the red water swirling down the drain, she became hysterical.

She sang Maxwell's Silver Hammer as she dried herself and slipped into fresh black sweats. She settled on the sofa in front of the panoramic window and sipped a margarita while she enjoyed watching the drama unfold around the fire below. But then she had to leave, the bakery was still in flames when she left for her final assault.

****

"Good news, Detective."

"Great, I could use some good news, what is it?"

"Deputies Simon and McAllister just reported they have the suspect detained in Del Mar."

"Where exactly in Del Mar?"

"They are on Camino del Mar at 15th. They are holding her in their squad car until they hear from you."

"They are sure she's Nancy Thomason?"

"Well, the woman has no identification on her person, but she fits the description. The deputies say she has a bad attitude problem so they are pretty sure she is the right woman."

"Thanks. Tell them to take her to the station and I'll meet them there. It shouldn't take me more than twenty minutes.

"Will do, Detective, I will let them know."

* * * * * * * * *

"Hello, Detective. This is Riki. I can't find Bonnie. I have looked everywhere. I have called her over and over, but she doesn't answer."

"Could she be milling around outside the bakery?"

"That's where I am right now, but she isn't here." Riki rubbed her neck. "I don't know where she is. I don't know what to think. What could have happened to her?" Her voice caught. "I don't know where she could be."

"Well, don't worry, she'll turn up. The good news is, we found Nancy and have her detained. I am on my way there right now."

"What a relief. Where did they find her?"

"She was stopped in Del Mar. She was just jogging along Camino del Mar when the patrol deputies spotted her. She matched Nancy's description."

"That's strange that she's out jogging this time of night in Del Mar. In fact, I never knew Nancy to jog at all, let alone in the middle of the night. Are you sure it's her?"

"Well, the woman has no identification on her so I am going to verify her identity at the station, but from what I've been told, we have Nancy in custody."

"Whew, I am so relieved." Riki scanned the crowd for the hundredth time. "I guess there is no need for you to send deputies, right? I think I'll go home now."

CHAPTER 38

"BONNIE! OPEN UP. Are you there? Bonnie! Can you hear me? Are you okay?" She slumped against the door. "Bonnie, please be alive."

She pushed away from the door and dragged herself to the gallery. Before going upstairs, she checked the backdoor and found it open. She stopped. Muffled sounds came from upstairs in her apartment. Nancy! She flew into the alley with her keys in her hand, but no jeep. "Shit!"

Nancy heard her and ran downstairs. She turned on the light in the studio while outside Riki pressed her back against the wall.

"Riki, where are you? You know, I'll find you so you might as well give up now." Nancy moved into the gallery.

Terror ripped through Riki. She inched down the wall to her neighbor's truck, squeezed behind it, and duck-walked between the parked cars and the wall. At the fourth car, she took out her phone, punched in 911, and risked a peek around the fender.

Nancy stood in the alley with her hands on her hips and scanned the area. Riki snapped back behind the fender, fumbled the phone, and bit her lip as she watched it clatter out of reach. She ducked behind the tire.

"I know you're out here, Riki. And now I know where you're hiding and I'm coming to get you." Nancy walked toward her. "Don't even think you'll get out of this alive, because when I find you I will kill you." She looked under the car next to Riki's hiding place. "I will strangle you with my bare hands and enjoy every minute it takes for you to die. And, you know I will do it, too, don't you? No one survives when I decide to kill them, not even you." She laughed. "Have you seen Mark today? He's sort of lost in action." She laughed again. "Or tonight, what do you think happened to your dear friend Bonnie and her boyfriend?"

Mark? Bonnie? Sam? Riki wanted to scream, but clamped her mouth shut and crouched in her hiding space. When she no longer heard Nancy walking toward her, she looked under the car and saw Nancy's silhouetted head facing her.

She froze.

Nancy said nothing.

****

The detective picked up her bag. "Well, good night guys. I have to go."

"You're leaving us so early?"

"Yeah, my team has the suspect in custody. She is in transport to Encinitas as we speak. I am on my way to identify her."

"Wow! Your men on the street are really on the job tonight, congratulations Detective."

"Thanks. See you later."

****

"Hey, Barb, your suspect is in room three and she is in a nasty mood." The man at the desk shook his head. "Better take back up with you when you interview her."

"Thanks, but first I'll check to make sure she is who I hope she is."

She entered the dark room next to interview room three and the arresting deputies followed her in. She glanced through the two-way mirror at a distraught woman who was not Nancy.

"What the fuck?" The detective turned to the deputies. "This isn't her. You said this was Nancy Thomason."

"She matches the description we were given."

The detective looked at the woman again. "Yes, you're right she does, sort of. But this is not Nancy Thomason."

"Are you sure this isn't the woman you're looking for?"

"Positive. Please apologize to whomever you have and let her go."

"But, Detective . . ."

"And, call it in that Nancy Thomason is still at large."

"Yeah, okay."

She turned and stomped back to her car. She pounded her fists on the steering wheel. "Oh, shit, Riki!" She called Riki, but there was no answer. She put her car in gear, and sped down Old Highway 101 back to Solana Beach.

****

Riki held her breath, closed her eyes, and squeezed her hands. It was then she realized that she still held her keys. She dared to look under the car once more; Nancy now stood facing the opposite direction.

"They are all dead now! I killed them." She laughed. "That is what happened to them and the same thing is about to happen to you. What do you think of that, Riki?"

Riki threw her keys as hard as she could.

Nancy ran toward the clanking keys while Riki duck-walked past the last five cars. When the last car's alarm blared, she stood and ran across Lomas Santa Fe in front of a truck that swerved to miss her. It honked loudly.

Nancy turned and ran toward Lomas Santa Fe.

Riki kept running until she reached the depot building. She pounded on the locked doors. "Help, someone! Please open! I need help! Please help me!" No one did.

She took deep breaths and looked for a way to escape, and then she saw it.

To her left, a long zigzag ramp led to the passenger's platform below. A fence separated the northbound track from the southbound track and extended the length of the depot. If she ran down the ramp and along the fence, crossed both sets of tracks, she would reach the old coast highway and safety, but it would take time and energy she didn't have. To Riki's right, stretched the footbridge, and Highway 101 was just a short distance beyond.

She chose to take the footbridge. Midway across she heard traffic zip past on the highway. Safety was within reach, she was so close, she was almost there, almost safe.

Suddenly, she jerked to a stop; her hair yanked from behind. Riki screamed.

"All I wanted was to be your friend, but you are nothing but a stuck up bitch." Nancy gave Riki's hair a violent tug. "Well, it doesn't matter now, because I am going to kill you."

"Let go of me!" Riki twisted around.

Nancy lost her grip and her face contorted into an evil sneer. "I hate you! I always have. And tonight, just like Bonnie and Sam, you are going to die."

"You killed them? Are you crazy?"

"Yes, I suppose I am." She lowered her head like a bull and charged.

Riki jumped out of the way seconds before Nancy rammed her head smack into the guardrail, bounced off, and collapsed blocking Riki's route of escape.

Riki sped back the way she came and headed down the path to the zigzag ramps. She looked back at the footbridge expecting Nancy, still incapacitated, but she stood next to the depot building.

Riki ran down the zigzag ramp and made it to track level.

"Go ahead and run Riki. You won't get away from me." She found a couple of rocks at her feet and threw them. "I'm going to kill you!"

****

Detective Stanton squealed to a stop behind Riki's gallery and jumped out of her car. She saw no one. The alley was empty. As the detective visually searched the area, she saw something glitter on the pavement. She walked over to the object and recognized Riki's phone. She held it in her hand and absently started walking towards Lomas Santa Fe. Raised women's voices came from the direction of the train depot. She called for back up and ran. She was the first deputy on the scene.

****

A rock whizzed past Riki's head followed by another. She stumbled, but regained her stride and ran past the "Authorized Personnel Only" sign and along the safety fence that divided the tracks.

A hurtling southbound freight train blasted its air horn and entered the depot. She stopped. Should she risk death by Nancy or by freight train? She glanced back to see Nancy jump over the railing. The distance between them shortened to yards, then feet. Then she saw another woman jump over the rail behind Nancy, closing the gap. The train quickly gained on them.

Riki turned and ran as fast as she could. Now she raced Nancy, the speeding freight train, and someone else too. Nancy panted close enough to grab her, but the freight train with the air horn blaring was within seconds of cutting off her escape route as it sped towards her at full speed.

Riki mustered her remaining strength and surged along the fence reaching the end seconds before Nancy, Detective Stanton, and the freight train. Without stopping, she made a wild leap across the tracks and rolled to a stop in the dirt unscathed on the other side.

Detective Stanton yelled, "Nancy, stop. Stop now!" The train blasted its air horn and the detective reached out for Nancy. "Nancy! Stop!"

Nancy was just about to dash in front of the train when Detective Stanton grabbed her shoulder and pulled her backwards out of the path of the train. Nancy flew backward landing hard in the bushes. The detective fell forward in front of the train. She screamed, and then was silent.

Brakes screeched. Metal scraped. The air horn blared.

The chaotic cacophony frightened Riki. She closed her eyes, hid her face in her knees, and wrapped her arms around her legs. The train screeched to a halt, the thunderous sounds silenced. In the distance Riki heard faint police sirens getting louder heading her direction.

Nancy lifted her head and surveyed the scene. A swirling red mist floated over the train directly toward her. It drifted closer until it swirled over her head. It descended upon her, blanketing her in the swirling red mist. Nancy crawled into the bushes laughing.

-end-

Special thanks to:

James McDermott, Constance Freed,

Joan LeslieWoodruff, Ed Pollock, George Simmons,

Ellen Garthofner Ruane, Barbara Ashworth Kessinger,

Nancy Turpin, Christina Smith-Valenzuela,

and Sara Miller.

.

Also by

Geree McDermott

"Colorific Abstracts"

(an art book of Geree's abstract drawings)

And (coming soon)

Coloring Books for Artists of all Ages!

About the Author

In 2011, Geree McDermott lost a breast to cancer.
She endured a year of chemotherapy and survived.
For therapy, she began writing.
The result is this book.

Made in the USA
San Bernardino, CA
07 June 2019